LAST STOP IN BROOKLYN

LAST STOP IN BROOKLYN

A Mary Handley Mystery

Lawrence H. Levy

B\D\W\Y
Broadway Books
New York

This is a work of fiction. All incidents and dialogue, and all characters with the exception of some well-known historical and public figures, are products of the author's imagination and are not to be construed as real. Where real-life historical figures and public figures appear, the situations, incidents, and dialogues concerning those persons are entirely fictional and are not intended to depict actual events or to change the entirely fictional nature of the work. In all other respects, any resemblance to persons living or dead is entirely coincidental.

Published in the United States by Broadway Books,
an imprint of the Crown Publishing Group,
a division of Penguin Random House LLC, New York.
crownpublishing.com

BROADWAY BOOKS and its logo, B \ D \ W \ Y, are trademarks of Penguin Random House LLC.

Library of Congress Cataloging-in-Publication Data has been applied for.

ISBN 978-0-451-49844-1
Ebook ISBN 978-0-451-49845-8

PRINTED IN THE UNITED STATES OF AMERICA

Cover design by Alane Gianetti
Cover photograph by Mark Summers

10 9 8 7 6 5 4 3 2 1

First Edition

To David Campagna, my great friend
for over forty years and a man of many talents.

PROLOGUE

On December 4, 1891, Russell Sage had a hunch. That was nothing new. Hunches were a big part of his business life. What usually followed was exhaustive research, then weeks of stock manipulations until he had seized control of a targeted company. There were few regulations on the stock market, but even so, his methods were considered to be at the very least unethical and most probably illegal. And the result was almost always the same: he would invariably make a lot of money while others took financial baths. But this hunch was different. It bore no fruit for him: no money, no prized company. The result of this hunch was that he was hiding in his office.

The Wall Street magnate and railroad titan rarely shied away from anyone. Even at the ripe old age of seventy-five, he was a tireless worker and a fearless risk-taker who had no qualms about making suspect stock transactions and buying politicians to ensure his success. The "almighty dollar" was his religion, and God have mercy on anyone who tried to separate him from it. His devotion had paid off, and he was currently one of the richest men in the United States.

Sage and his partner, Jay Gould, had been cohorts of Boss Tweed, the infamous head of New York's Tammany Hall, and Sage had no qualms about showing his support when Tweed was arrested. When cartoonist Bernhard Gillam depicted him along with Gould and Cornelius Vanderbilt in a scathing rendering where they comfortably rested on millions of dollars as many poor workers carried them, he wasn't concerned. Sage didn't care what people thought. He considered himself untouchable.

Yet on that day, something had changed. This man with his closely cropped hair, conservative suit, and signature bow tie was experiencing a new emotion. He was scared.

This is insane, Sage thought, watching his hand shake as if it weren't part of his body. He didn't recognize the name of the man who was in his outer office demanding to see him, and if Sage didn't know who he was, he was not worth knowing.

"I'm sorry, Mr. . . . ," said Peter Ramsey, Sage's secretary, who had already forgotten this innocuous man's name and had hoped he would repeat it.

"Norcross. Henry L. Norcross," he responded, exasperated at Ramsey's lack of attentiveness. "Please write it down, so I don't have to keep repeating myself."

"Not necessary. It is now indelibly implanted on my brain. But no matter how disappointing the news might be, it's not going to change. Mr. Sage is presently out of town."

"Stop lying to me!" Norcross shouted as he rearranged the strap of a bulky satchel he was carrying on his shoulder.

"Mr. Norcross, could you please lower your voice?"

"Mr. Sage has a board of directors meeting for Western

Union this afternoon and a stockholders meeting for his railroad properties tomorrow. Don't try to tell me that he'd miss those. He never misses them."

"You seem to know so much about his activities. You tell me where Mr. Sage is." Ramsey raised his voice almost to Norcross's level. It was a signal to Sage. Essentially, Ramsey was telling Sage that if he had any desire at all to see this man, now was the time to show himself or he would dismiss him posthaste.

Sage didn't know what to do. Like the man had said, he did have a board of directors meeting later that day. Even if he slipped out the back door, where was he to go? Trekking all the way home and returning in a few hours seemed like a waste of time. He was a man who firmly believed in rational thought, and he could not find any justification for his completely irrational desire to flee. Suddenly, he got angry. If this fellow thought he could come into his office and intimidate him, he was dead wrong. *I don't get intimidated. I'm the one who does the intimidating.*

Sage straightened up and marched into his outer office. "What's all the commotion about out here?" he asked, sporting his best stern Russell Sage visage.

Upon seeing him, Ramsey felt the need to cover and acted surprised. "Oh, Mr. Sage, you've returned. I didn't see you come in, sir."

"How unexpected, and from out of town, too," Norcross said facetiously. "I wonder if he still has his luggage in his office."

Sage would have none of this and responded sternly. "Look here, Mr.—"

"Norcross," Ramsey offered, trying to be helpful.

"I'm a busy man, and you're disrupting my office. Quickly state your business and then leave."

"I appreciate your directness, Mr. Sage," said Norcross, then he reached into the inside pocket of his suit jacket and handed Sage a piece of paper. "This is my letter of introduction from John D. Rockefeller."

"Oh," said Sage, softening a bit, "from John." He quickly glanced at the letter, then exclaimed, "What kind of charlatan are you? This isn't from John!"

"True, but it got you to take the letter, and I strongly advise you to read it. It's in your best interests."

As Sage read the letter his face became tense and somewhat contorted. "One million two hundred thousand dollars! This is preposterous!"

The other employees in the room looked up. It was a tremendous amount of money, but they had heard Sage negotiate sums of that nature before, or had at least seen it in the paperwork.

"I know you have significantly more than that," said a calm Norcross, completely undaunted by Sage's outrage. "It's a mere drop in the bucket to you."

"In cash? You're crazy if you think I have that kind of money lying around my office!" After looking into Norcross's eyes, Sage immediately regretted his outburst. He concluded that this man not worth knowing, this nobody, just might be crazy. He tried to rid his voice of any hint of anger, attempting to sound reasonable until he could come up with some solution, one that would not involve costing him one million two hundred thousand dollars. "You understand, of course, that it is a large amount of money and even for a man of my means, it will take a while to accumulate?"

"Well, I don't really have a while, so, in that case—" Norcross slid the satchel he was carrying into his left hand as if he was about to throw it to the floor.

Sage instantly reacted, waving his hands wildly. "No, no, no, no! Put the dynamite back. We'll figure something out. I promise."

The mention of dynamite caused all eyes in the room to click toward Norcross. Up until this point they'd had no idea their lives were in danger. The question was, should they run for the door or would that just cause him to set off his bomb? At the moment, no one was moving.

The door to the office opened and in stepped a thirty-five-year-old man dressed in business attire. Sage had never seen him before, but he welcomed any diversion that might distract Norcross until they could find a solution.

"Hello, sir. May I help you?"

"I come from John Bloodworth and Company, Mr. Sage. I have some papers for you to sign."

"Ah, perfect!" Sage said, then turned toward Norcross. "My banker. I couldn't ask for better timing." He motioned for the man to approach.

~

Jay Gould was annoyed. He was sitting in the coffee shop across from the Arcade Building at 71 Broadway, where Sage's office was located. Gould and Sage had regular strategy meetings the day the Western Union board of directors met. Gould had misread his pocket watch and had arrived twenty minutes early. There wasn't enough time to return to his office and get anything accomplished. He could have gone straight to Sage's office, sure Sage would drop anything he was doing for him. Instead, something unusual happened. He decided to stop, have a cup of coffee, and relax. A driven man, if Gould wasn't the king of the robber barons he was at the very least a prince. Relaxing wasn't part of his nature, but this day his inner voice told him it was a good idea, and for some reason, inexplicable to him, he listened.

As he sipped his hot brew, he felt the tension slowly drain from his body. It felt odd but also good, and he decided that maybe he'd do this more often, fully knowing that he probably wouldn't. Gould checked his pocket watch. He had been there eighteen minutes, and it was time to stroll across the street for his meeting.

That was when he heard it: a loud explosion that rocked the ground under him and rattled the entire establishment. Paintings fell off the wall, a mirror shattered, and a tray of dishes crashed to the floor. Gould quickly jumped back in his chair as his coffee cup tipped over onto the table, spilling its contents. Loud screams permeated the air, shortly followed by people rushing out of buildings onto the street with an odd mix of panic and a desire to see what had happened.

Staying curiously detached, Gould slowly rose and made his way outside. It wasn't exactly what he had expected pandemonium to be. Some people *were* running wildly with no direction in mind, fueled only by a desire to escape, but the majority had stayed put and gathered in large groups, primarily out of a morbid curiosity to view whatever disaster had taken place. Scared whispers ran through the crowd, occasionally punctuated by ear-piercing shrieks.

Gould's view was blocked, and he bulled his way through

to the front, where he saw a man sprawled out on his back in the middle of the street. A typewriter had landed on his face, the impact of which made him unrecognizable. Gould couldn't help noting the irony of a businessman and his type-writer being merged in death. Then he glanced upward and saw smoke billowing from the blasted-out windows on the second floor of the Arcade Building, the obvious origin of the unfortunate man and the typewriter before a bomb blew them out of their office. Gould's indifference vanished, and a cold chill shot through his body. He recognized the offices immediately as those of his friend Russell Sage.

A profound numbness soon replaced the chill. Gould wasn't used to strong emotions, and it was as if his nervous system had decided that he wouldn't be able to withstand feeling that much. And it wasn't because he was paralyzed with concern that the man under the typewriter might be his friend Russell Sage, or because Sage was even on his mind.

It was because he knew, at that exact moment, that his life would never be the same.

~

Inspector Thomas F. Byrnes was only five feet eight inches tall, yet he was hailed as a "giant in his time." His meteoric rise to the head of the Detective Bureau of the New York City Police Department was filled with acts from which legends were made. In his rookie year, he saved a superior police officer's life during the Draft Riots of 1863 and re-ceived a promotion. By 1870 he was already a captain, and sensational cases seemed to find him. He was the first to use photographs of criminals for identification purposes, thus popularizing the term "rogues' gallery." He also invented an interrogation process that he labeled "the third degree," a phrase that had become part of the country's vocabulary. While still on the police force, Byrnes published a book in 1886 about crime fighting entitled *Professional Criminals of America*. Policemen looked up to him, criminals feared him, and many tried to curry his favor.

On this particular night of December 4, 1891, Byrnes, now forty-nine, held a wooden box under his left arm as he knocked on the door of Russell Sage's Fifth Avenue mansion. Byrnes had known Sage for years, as he had most of New York's elite. Being the darling of New York law enforcement came with certain benefits but also involved extra duties. The power brokers liked to keep the police close in case they needed them, and that night Byrnes was needed.

The butler answered the door.

"Please inform Mrs. Sage that Inspector Byrnes is here," Byrnes instructed the butler, his Irish origin evident as he spoke. The butler momentarily stared inadvertently at Byrnes's extremely bushy mustache, which seemed to engulf his mouth, and before he could respond, a distraught Olivia Slocum Sage was at the door. Byrnes had telephoned to inform her of his impending arrival, and considering the events of the day, she was naturally anxious.

"Thomas, so good of you to come."

"It woulda been sooner, but it took a while 'til Jay Gould left my office."

"Jay?"

"He's very much shaken by what happened. Arrived dressed in a bizarre disguise, claimin' he's next on the list."

"List, what list?"

"He's convinced there's a list of wealthy industrialists who have been marked for attack. I informed him I know of no such list, and he wouldn't accept it."

"That's so unlike Jay. He's always been so bold and unafraid."

"No tellin' how people'll react when somethin' like this happens. I've also gotten concerned calls from Andrew Carnegie, John Rockefeller, and others."

"I suppose it's typical of our class. When tragedy occurs, it's about them and not who it actually struck." She sighed and shook her head. "So, what news do you have?"

"We're well on our way to gettin' to the bottom of this."

"Thank the Lord. What kind of sick mind would do such a thing?"

"It's best ya don't know about some of the animals I have ta face. How is he?" With that, Byrnes gestured with his head toward the stairs that led to the second floor.

"Some glass shards were embedded in his skin and had to be removed, but he'll be up and around in no time. All in all, he's a very lucky man."

"I'll say. May I see him?"

"Yes, of course. Go right up." As Byrnes started to climb the stairs, Olivia called to him. "Don't tell him I said that . . . about his luck. He's in a foul mood."

"I suppose I would be, too, if someone just tried to blow me ta kingdom come."

Olivia nodded in agreement, then Byrnes continued his ascent. Though her first name was Margaret, she preferred being called Olivia, which was her middle name. She and Russell Sage were an odd match. After his first wife died,

Sage married Olivia, who was forty-one and had never been married. Olivia was a champion of many charitable causes, and Sage was a renowned skinflint who refused to contribute. What made it an even more unusual pairing was that Sage had financially ruined Olivia's father. Rumors abounded that it was a marriage of convenience that had never been consummated and thus left Sage free to participate in his many dalliances with younger females. Whatever their relationship was, it seemed to work for both of them. At this point, they had been married for twenty-two years without a hint of a weak link in their bond.

Wearing a long linen nightshirt with lace around the collar and propped up by numerous pillows, Sage was sitting in his large canopy bed, from which he had removed the curtains. No matter what the time of day, he preferred being able to see all around him. It was a habit he had acquired at an early age. He was the youngest of seven children and had to be on constant guard against a prank or a random swat. At the moment, he was trying to read but his wounds distracted him. He was a man who wasn't used to any form of discomfort and didn't wear it well.

He responded to a knock at his door with an annoyed "Come in."

Byrnes entered. "Is this a bad time?"

"How could it be? You're a policeman, and I was attacked by a maniac. The only better time would have been if you had prevented it in the first place."

"You surely don't think I could have—"

"No, no, no. Please excuse me, Tom. I've never been face-to-face with a bomb before."

"Havin' faced a few bombs in my day, I know how they rattle yer nerves. Sent me runnin' for a whiskey more than once."

"Don't tempt me. I might turn into a drunk."

"Now, we both know that's one thing Russell Sage will never be. Yer too fond of yer business ta disrespect it."

Sage mulled over Byrnes's words. They were hard to refute. "Speaking of my business, should I assume my office is a total loss?"

"It'll take a good bit of rebuildin' and then some."

"Of course! What did I expect? A damn bomb exploded!"

"Do ya want ta hear about the others?"

Byrnes was referring to Sage's employees, and Sage couldn't have cared less. All of them were easily replaceable, but he knew society dictated that he be concerned.

"Yes, please. I hope they're all right."

"Most of them have minor wounds, like yours."

Sage gave Byrnes an indignant look, suggesting that his discomfort could hardly be called minor. Byrnes soon corrected himself.

"Minor, that is, in comparison ta what happened to your stenographer, Mr. Norton."

"What happened to Bentley?"

"Benjamin," Byrnes corrected him. "He was blown out of the window, along with his typewriter, which landed on his face."

"Oh, my lord!" he exclaimed, more appalled at the event than the state of poor Benjamin Norton.

"Needless ta say, he is no longer with us. Then there is William Laidlaw."

"Laidlaw? I don't know a man named Laidlaw."

"Really? He was found on top of ya."

"Oh, him. That was some bank clerk. Never met the man before."

"I'm sure he wishes ya still hadn't. He'll be in the hospital for some time."

"This whole thing is awful, incomprehensible! What about that demented anarchist who blew us all up? I suppose that lunatic got away scot-free!"

"I was just gettin' ta that." Byrnes walked to a mahogany dressing table and set down the wooden box he had been carrying the whole time he had been at Sage's residence. He opened it and casually pulled out a severed head. "Is this the man who bombed yer office?"

Not the least bit fazed, Sage stared at the head, analyzing it, then responded in a completely calm, unemotional tone. "Yes, that's him."

"Are ya certain?"

Sage nodded. "Remarkable. He had his head blown clear off and not a mark on his face."

"It's the one bit of luck we've had in this case. Now we can find out who he is."

"What difference does it make? You can't put a head on trial."

"No," said Byrnes as he put the head back in the box and closed the top. "But we can find out if he has any friends with similar inclinations. Good night, Russell. Get some sleep. They say it's the best cure." And with that, Byrnes picked up his box and left.

It had never occurred to Sage that someone might come after him again and he'd be forced to relive the horror of that day with possibly less fortunate results. The calmness and indifference he'd exhibited when hearing about the demise of Norton and the crippling of Laidlaw suddenly disappeared. This was different. It was him, and he saw no good night's sleep in his future until Byrnes got to the bottom of this.

1

Mary Handley was being followed. She didn't know why or who the person was, but she had no doubt about it. The first time she had realized it was ten days earlier. A passing carriage had splashed street water in her direction, and as Mary jumped to avoid getting doused, she inadvertently turned and caught a glimpse of him. Taken by surprise, her tail, as they refer to such a person in detective parlance, immediately struck up a conversation with a complete stranger, acting as if they were old friends. Later, when she glanced his way, he would duck into a store, stop to roll a cigarette, or pretend to window-shop. It wasn't that he was terrible at following people but rather that Mary had been acutely aware of such things ever since a few years back, when she had let a particularly heinous criminal named Shorty catch her off-guard with disastrous results.

On this particular day, August 30, 1894, the Thursday before the first federally sanctioned Labor Day holiday, Mary was walking on the sidewalk next to the beach at Coney Island. No one there seemed to mind that this holiday was merely President Grover Cleveland's attempt to appease labor after the troops he sent to squash the Pullman Strike in Chicago killed thirty strikers. It was a day off from the drudgery of their jobs, and they were going to do their best to enjoy it.

Mary didn't like Coney Island, though she had been there quite a few times with her good friend Sarah Cooper, formerly McNish, whom she had known since childhood and who had been married for a dozen or so years to a successful lawyer. Sarah had four children ranging in age from four to eleven, the oldest being Virginia (Ginny); then Harold (Harry), who was nine; then seven-year-old James; and finally four-year-old Lucy. Mary loved playing with the children on the beach, riding the carousel with them, and watching them marvel at the arcade games and sideshows. She had even taken Ginny and Harry with her on the Gravity Pleasure Switchback Railway, a roller coaster that reached the death-defying speed of six miles per hour.

Sarah and her children were the only reason she would go to Coney Island. To her, it represented a microcosm of the nasty bigotry and inequities that existed in the world. Black bathers were forced to use separate bathhouses from white bathers, as if their ethnicity were a transmittable disease. The arcade had games like "Kill the Coon," where white people would line up to throw balls at a black man who would stick his head out of a hole in a curtain that was painted to represent an African jungle or some other such locale meant to be demeaning. Jews were banned from several establishments that had been built there.

Most people either agreed with these practices or didn't question them, making them acceptable. Mary and Sarah's repulsion placed them firmly in the minority, and they did their best to educate Sarah's children about the equality of all people, hoping it would stick in spite of what they witnessed. Sarah's dilemma was that she had no desire to deprive her children of the fun of the beach. So, call it hypocritical, call it love, the result was that they all went. But Mary wasn't with Sarah and her family that day. She was on a case.

It was the type of case that Mary would have normally refused: a domestic one involving infidelity. Matters of that kind were rife with emotional turmoil and usually the messiest. If Mary found evidence of adultery, the client would often fly into a rage. If she concluded that the spouse was being true, the client usually didn't believe it and chastised her for doing shoddy work. In other words, it was impossible to please, and even if all these reasons hadn't existed, there was something unsavory about spying on the love lives of others. At the end of each day, Mary felt the need to take a long, cleansing bath.

Mary's private investigator career had blossomed over the past four years, so much so that she could afford to turn down cases she considered undesirable. She had taken this one under protest and under much duress for a very specific reason: her mother, Elizabeth.

"What good is having an unmarried daughter who is a private investigator if she won't help out a friend?" Elizabeth had asked while standing in the family kitchen stirring a stew she was cooking. Naturally, the word "unmarried" was emphasized. Elizabeth hoped that returning to the same sore subject time and time again, no matter what they were discussing, would spur Mary into doing what Elizabeth wanted her to do: give up her career, find a man, get married, and have children, as if family and working were mutually exclusive. Nothing, certainly not consideration for Mary's feelings, could stop Elizabeth.

"One matter has absolutely nothing to do with the other," Mary answered. "So don't try to goad me into doing something I despise."

"Are you referring to marriage or to this perfectly fine offer from a very reliable man who needs your help and is willing to pay your fee?"

"Mother—"

"Even though you really shouldn't charge him," Elizabeth jumped in. "His mother has known you and your brother, Sean, since you were born and has been one of my closest friends here in Brooklyn ever since the day I first set foot on these shores from good ol' Ireland."

"Tell me, Mother. What was so good about ol' Ireland? You were starving there."

"It has to do with respect for where you came from and for family, something that you obviously don't understand since you're still unmarried."

"Okay, you win."

"Win what? This isn't a contest."

"Yes it is. I will take the case if you will stop pestering me about marriage."

"Well, that doesn't seem fair. Because I've asked you to do a charitable deed and help out a friend, I can never mention—"

"Not never, right now, today, while I'm with you."

Elizabeth stiffened and reluctantly acquiesced. "I suppose I can do that . . . though I should point out to you that a few months back you had a big birthday. Most women, by your age . . ."

Mary winced, thrusting her crystal-blue eyes skyward while shaking her head and thus tousling her blond hair. "Yes, Mother, I'm very well aware that I'm thirty and firmly entrenched in society's old maid column. If I weren't, I'm sure I could count on you to remind me of it as often as possible. Good-bye, Mother."

Leaving her parents' house at a slow but deliberate pace, Mary realized that it had been a while since she last stormed out in a fit of anger. *In a way, we have made some progress.* But her optimism soon faded. The fact that she had resigned herself to her mother's behavior did not mean it had changed or that she felt any less miserable when she saw her. It was merely a coping device to avoid shouting matches.

Brian Murphy was the name of her client and the son of her mother's friend Lauren Murphy. He was concerned that his wife, Colleen, was having an affair.

"I don't know who the bastard is, Mary," Brian said, then stopped. "I'm sorry for my salty language. I guess it comes from being away at sea for too long." Brian was in the merchant marine and would often be away for months at a time.

"I've heard and said much worse, Brian," Mary responded. "Your language should be your least concern at this point."

"I suppose a good deal of the blame should be placed on me. I am away a lot. . . . But Colleen knew that when she married me. We've got three children, for God's sake!" Brian stopped again, trying to get control of his anger.

Brian had insisted on meeting Mary at his home in Carroll Gardens, an Irish working-class neighborhood in Brooklyn. She wanted to get to the point and get out of there, lest Colleen and the children return. Should that happen, matters could escalate and get very ugly quickly. "The question is, really, why do you think she's having an affair?"

"Her behavior has changed tremendously since I've been home from my last voyage. In the past, she'd greet me enthusiastically and get her mother to watch the kids for a few days while we got reacquainted, so to speak." He looked at Mary.

"I know what you mean. Go on."

"This time it was a peck on the cheek and that was it. She disappears for hours at a time, and, well, she seems distant, indifferent. It's very unlike her."

"And you've been married for how many years?"

"Eight years."

"Sorry to bring this up, but eight years and three children? She may not love you any less, but isn't it possible the bloom may be off the rose by now?"

"I know Colleen. If the bloom is off the rose, then it's bloomin' someplace else."

Mary agreed to find out what she could, and that was why on this Thursday before Labor Day, she was at Coney Island, keeping an eye on Colleen. It was Mary's seventh day on this case, and Colleen hadn't exhibited any behavior that would indicate she was having an affair. Mary had observed her shopping at the market, dropping her children off at the house of a friend who watched them while she was at work, and doing many other activities that weren't close to being those of an unfaithful wife. Even walking along the beach that day seemed perfectly innocent. It was totally understandable that a woman who had full responsibility for the house, the children, and the bills while her husband was away might want to sneak out for a few hours in order to clear her head and discover whether she still had any thoughts worth thinking.

As Mary followed Colleen, strolling east, away from the honky-tonk amusement park, she glanced back occasionally to view what her own tail was doing. At that moment, he was buying an ice-cream cone from a vendor. It was several scoops of strawberry stacked high and could have doubled as a cover for his face if Mary wasn't already well acquainted with his looks. He was a black man, about forty years old, of African or Arab descent, possibly both. He had a narrow, neatly groomed beard, running from both sideburns, outlining his jaw, and meeting at his chin, covering most of it. Above his mouth was a closely cropped mustache. The man wasn't bad at his job, whatever that was. The sudden splash by a passing carriage that had revealed him to Mary ten days earlier would have been difficult to anticipate, even for the most seasoned detectives.

The further they walked east, the nicer the surroundings got, and they started passing hotels that catered to a much wealthier crowd. The Brighton Beach Hotel was first. It was a resort opened by William Engelman, who had made his fortune selling horses to the army during the Civil War. The rich would stay at the ocean's edge and splash water on themselves, but that was usually as far as anyone would go. They considered swimming to be unseemly. Besides a place to cool off during a hot summer's day, the beach was a place for them to show off their bathing suits, which, regardless of whether they were male or female, covered most of their bodies. Then they would leisurely dine at one of the posh restaurants that had opened up at one of the beachfront hotels.

Past the Brighton Beach Hotel were the Manhattan Beach and Oriental Hotels. Newer, they were developed by Austin Corbin, a railroad titan who owned the Long Island Rail Road. Corbin had colluded with John Y. McKane, the corrupt political boss of the Coney Island area, to acquire the land on which his hotels now stood. McKane filled the local council meeting with his cronies and Corbin was able to buy the land from Brooklyn for fifteen hundred dollars instead of the fair market price of one hundred thousand. McKane was presently in jail for his many illegal activities while Corbin roamed free, enjoying the fruits of his. A rabid anti-Semite, Corbin was a founding member of the American Society for the Suppression of Jews and generally intolerant of anyone who was "different." No Jews or people of color were allowed in any of his establishments.

Colleen passed the Manhattan Beach Hotel but turned in on the path to the Oriental Hotel and entered. Mary followed her inside. The Oriental Hotel was Corbin's newest hotel and built in a Moorish style. Though Mary preferred not to patronize establishments owned by men like Corbin, she took solace in the fact that she wasn't purchasing anything. Besides, she had learned long ago that if she refused to enter all businesses run by prejudiced white men, she'd have trouble buying anything or traveling anywhere. In this instance, there was a plus side. The man who was following her would not be allowed inside, and she could concentrate completely on Colleen.

Mary took a seat next to a tall floor lamp that would give her some semblance of cover. She momentarily turned to look around the lobby and spotted Austin Corbin strolling by in deep conversation with another man whom Mary didn't recognize. The man was in his late thirties and had blond hair and a mustache. He was dressed in what was obviously a very expensive suit, expertly tailored and imported no doubt. As they chatted away, laughing intermittently, she concluded they were of like thought. She realized her speedy assessment might be a result of her own form of prejudice, but he *was* chumming it up with Austin Corbin.

Mary turned back toward Colleen, who seemed perfectly happy to wander through the lobby, peek into the various shops, and do what any busy mother might do given a few hours of freedom. At this point, she was prepared to go back to Brian Murphy and tell him not to worry about his wife. The poor woman just needed some time to herself.

Mary was about to leave when, from a distance, she saw a man approach Colleen. He was about five foot ten, possessed what appeared to be a fairly slim, athletic body, and was appropriately dressed for the summer, wearing a white linen suit and a straw boater hat. She only saw him from behind, the hat making it even more difficult to get a good look at him, but there was something familiar about his walk. She wasn't able to place it, and it momentarily bugged her. Colleen's face lit up when she saw the man. Their greeting wasn't particularly passionate, but they were in a public place. Mary's sympathy for Colleen quickly started to ebb. She didn't necessarily think her husband was right, but it was unusual. Colleen was from a working-class family. The odds were against her bumping into a man she knew at the Oriental Hotel, a man who by his dress clearly had money.

Laughing and enjoying each other's company, Colleen and her gentleman friend headed down a corridor with their backs to Mary. Mary rose and followed. When they got into an elevator together, Mary knew she was in trouble. She had learned long ago that when on a case she needed to wear sensible dress and shoes even if she defied fashion. Fortunately, one of the results of the bicycle's soaring popularity was that styles for women had changed in order to allow them the freedom to ride. Corsets, petticoats, and billowing skirts, all of which hampered movement, were giving way to bloomers and even baggy pants. Mary didn't have a bicycle, but the changing style gave her the ability to wear more amenable dress when on a case without attracting attention. She scolded herself for thinking she wouldn't need the mobility that day, then took off her shoes and held up her dress as she ran up the stairs. She got to the second floor in time to stick her head into the hallway and see the elevator stop. A couple got out, but it wasn't her couple. She continued to the third floor, but the elevator didn't stop there, so she had to rush up to the fourth floor.

Colleen and the man had already exited the elevator and were walking down the fourth-floor corridor with their backs to Mary when she arrived. Still staying a good distance away, Mary slowly followed them and watched them enter a room at the end of the hall. She then walked to their door, noted the room number, and left.

Knocking on the door seemed too risky. Mary had only met Colleen a few times, and the last was years ago, but there was a very good chance she would recognize Mary. Besides, even if she didn't, she'd have to make up some story in order to get the man to identify himself, so she could report who Colleen was seeing to Brian. There was an easier way.

Mary went to the front desk and approached the clerk. "I was just up on the fourth floor and I was aghast at what I saw. A man was quite irate. Apparently, he had ordered champagne on the teleseme a full hour ago, and nothing had arrived."

"Oh my goodness," exclaimed the clerk, who immediately checked the teleseme. If a guest turned on the teleseme in his room and pointed to the item he desired, the information at the desk would be received by two different devices. Discolored water in one would reveal which room was requesting service, and the second device, identical to the one in the guest's room, would point to what the guest wanted. "Are you sure?" said the clerk, a bit puzzled. "No champagne has been ordered from the fourth floor in the last hour."

"Sure?" responded Mary. "You should have heard him. Not very pleasant. I believe the expression is 'fit to be tied.'" Mary stared at the clerk for emphasis. "Maybe you know him. He was wearing a white linen suit and a straw boater hat. He told me his name, but unfortunately I don't remember. The shouting startled me."

"Do you know what room he was in?"

"Ah yes, very smart. What room? I should have mentioned that right away. I saw him enter room four twenty-four."

"Room four twenty-four," the clerk repeated while scouring the guest list. "Yes, four twenty-four. He's been with us several times before. Always takes the same room. Mr. Walter Cooper. I better take care of that right away. Thank you so much." And the clerk left to make sure his guest got the champagne with the hotel's compliments.

The clerk was so immersed in his desire to do his job that he didn't notice the blood drain from Mary's face when he mentioned the guest's name. She knew the man's walk had looked familiar. Walter Cooper was her friend Sarah's husband!

Mary staggered toward the exit in a daze. It was true that she had only seen the man from behind and from a distance, and he *was* wearing a hat, but she chastised herself for not recognizing Walter. Was it that she didn't want it to be him or that she genuinely didn't recognize him? Both prospects were disturbing, but it didn't matter. She was now faced with an even bigger dilemma, involving a host of questions. Should she tell Sarah, how should she tell her, what would it do to her, what about the children, what would happen if she didn't tell Sarah, how would it affect their relationship if she told her or didn't tell her?

These thoughts were swimming through her head as she stepped outside. Suddenly, she got angry, very angry. *How dare Walter do that to Sarah and their children! Sarah is a beautiful, vibrant woman, and he—* Mary didn't want to think about it anymore. Wild-eyed, she looked around and spotted the man who was tailing her, his ice cream now melting. She marched up to the man and swatted the cone out of his hand.

"What do you want from me? Either tell me or I'll thump you right here!" she demanded.

Needless to say, the man was taken aback. He'd had no idea Mary knew he was following her. He paused, then stammered for a few moments until he finally got his words out. He had a French accent. "I am Basem Ben Ali. My brother has been convicted of murder. He didn't do it, and I want you to prove his innocence."

Surprisingly, this news calmed Mary. She much preferred dealing with murder than with her best friend's errant husband.

2

Mary told Basem Ben Ali to meet her back at her office in a couple of hours, and he obliged. Besides preferring her client discussions to be in a private setting, she had had her fill of Coney Island and did not want to spend one more minute there than was absolutely necessary. The momentary wave of calmness that overtook her when Basem Ben Ali asked for her help was indeed fleeting. The anger she felt at Walter's betrayal of her close friend surged through her body once more. She caught the train, taking the Sea Beach Line away from Coney Island toward downtown Brooklyn. Mary calmed somewhat during the train ride. One's body, or rather one's mind, seems to sense that living at that level of emotional distress for extended periods of time is unhealthy and it finds a way to momentarily quiet the storm. But her outrage was bound to surface again.

Mary's office was in Lazlo's Books, a fairly well-known bookstore in Brooklyn owned by her good friend Lazlo. His name was emblazoned on the store because he fancied himself an expert on all things literary. He had also deemed himself an expert in many other areas, but he felt it all could be traced back to his love of books.

"Anything worthwhile in this world has at one point or another been put down on paper. Everything else is inconsequential," Lazlo had once told Mary, the twinkle in his eye making him seem younger than his fifty-eight years.

"Are you trying to tell me," Mary had shot back, "that your many witticisms are inconsequential? I am shocked."

"Don't be. I do write them down, so the world will benefit from them when I am but a mere memory."

"I believe there's a word for that. Ah, yes: 'narcissism.' "

"Actually, a little bit of narcissism is healthy. It only turns ugly when one exaggerates one's abilities, and that can hardly apply to me." Lazlo's wily smile had somehow been enhanced by his flock of bushy gray hair with an accompanying mustache.

Mary enjoyed their repartee, and she was hoping Lazlo would cheer her up. About a block before getting to Lazlo's she saw a sign in a grocery store window that read, HIRING. DOGS AND IRISH NEED NOT APPLY. She had seen similar signs in other parts of Brooklyn and New York. It was a sour reminder that the ugliness on display at Coney Island wasn't limited to the end of Brooklyn.

As she entered the bookstore, passing the small sign in the right corner of the window that read, OFFICE OF MARY HANDLEY, CONSULTING DETECTIVE, she perked up. It had been four years, but that sign still gave her a lift each time she saw it.

The store was quiet with only one potential customer, an older woman, currently perusing the biography section. There was one salesclerk and a very bored Lazlo, who brightened when he saw Mary, a woman he had dubbed, in his mind but not aloud, his surrogate daughter.

"Ah, Mary, so good to see you. You must tell me all about your adventures today."

"Is business that slow?"

"I'm contemplating christening it Snail Thursdays," he whispered, then gestured toward the one customer. "A professional browser."

"She never buys?"

"Never."

"Then my arrival should cheer you up. I have your rent." Mary started to dig through her pocketbook.

"Please, Mary, how many times do I have to tell you? I don't want your money."

The discussion of rent was a constant bone of contention between the two. Lazlo had originally given Mary an office in the back of his store for free when her detective career was floundering and she was doubling as a salesclerk in his store. When business started to flourish and she no longer could work for Lazlo, she insisted on paying rent. They were both bullheaded, and the argument went on for a while, Lazlo refusing money and Mary demanding he take it. Finally, Lazlo acquiesced. He asked for one dollar a month, but Mary insisted on it being much more. They finally settled on seven dollars. Mary took out the money and handed it to him.

"Once again, I am uncomfortable and feel more like I'm collecting a tithe rather than accepting remuneration for services rendered."

"Duly noted."

"Now that we've dispensed with the unpleasantries, tell me about your day."

Lazlo was a very good friend and completely discreet, but Mary still didn't mention Walter, as if saying it out loud would make it too real. She told him about the woman she was following, the man who was following her, and how much she detested Coney Island.

"Coney Island," Lazlo remarked. "It's where intelligence and human decency go to die."

At that point they were interrupted by the female browser, who was sporting a very pleasant smile. "Excuse me, Mr. Lazlo, but I was wondering whether you carry *La revue blanche*. I understand it has some marvelous articles by a young writer named Marcel Proust."

"I'll be with you momentarily. If you can't wait, I'm sure Martha will be happy to help you." And Lazlo pointed to the sole salesclerk in the store.

"Oh, I'm in no rush. I'll wait," she said, then smiled again and walked off.

This time Mary spoke in a whisper. "Well, it looks like the tide has turned."

"She won't buy it. Believe me. She's done this an infinite amount of times."

"Lazlo, you need to reassess the situation."

"Why reassess something that is so clearly—"

"You're missing a key element. Her browsing is not limited to or even involves books."

It finally dawned on Lazlo what Mary was implying. "Well, should that be true, she is most definitely barking up the wrong tree. I view 'relationship' as synonymous with 'abhorrent.' "

"That's impossible. 'Relationship' is a noun and 'abhorrent' is an adjective. It looks like she already has you off your game." And Mary left for her office, her conversation with Lazlo having lifted her out of the doldrums.

Approximately forty-five minutes later, Basem Ben Ali appeared at her office door, and Mary ushered him to a seat facing her desk. Basem was from Algeria. Mary knew that meant he was most probably fluent in both French and Arabic. Since he spoke English in a thick French accent, Mary surmised there might be a communication problem. Luckily, she knew a reasonable amount of French. Lazlo had chastised her a few years back for not reading the French version of *Madame Bovary* by Gustave Flaubert.

"In order to get the true sense of Flaubert's genius," Lazlo had said, "you must read his original words. Anything else pales in comparison."

Mary resisted and argued for a while, but he eventually wore her down and she did study French. After reading it in Flaubert's native language, she had to admit that Lazlo was right, and at this time, she was especially pleased because it allowed her to make her new client feel comfortable by speaking in one of his native languages.

"*Je l'espère votre voyage à mon bureau a été facil,*" she said, expressing her hope that he'd had an easy trip to her office.

"It was simple. No problem," he replied in English.

"*Cela est trés bon à entendre,*" Mary responded, indicating that it was good to hear.

Ali took out a tobacco pouch and brown papers, began rolling a cigarette, and again spoke in English. "They're mass-producing these now, but I still prefer to roll them myself. I hope you don't mind, Miss Handley."

Mary always kept up on the latest scientific advancements. "*Si vous ne craignez pas les risques pour votre santé, je ne me dérange pas,*" she replied, informing him that if he didn't mind the health risks, she didn't mind either.

"The reports are conflicting, and besides, I enjoy it too much to discard it. By the way, Miss Handley, could you please speak English? Your French accent is difficult to understand."

Mary emitted a short chuckle at the irony that she was the one having trouble communicating. "Certainly, Mr. Ali. I would be happy to. Please tell me about yourself."

He explained that he was born in Algeria, had served four years in the French Foreign Legion, then had come to America. "I lived in Pennsylvania for a number of years, returned to Algeria, and now I'm back. Because of my accent, people always assume I know very little English."

"I guess I am guilty of it, too. I apologize, and thank you for alerting me to my pronunciation problems in French. I obviously need to work on that."

"It's understandable. People in America only need to speak one language. I grew up having to speak two, so learning a third wasn't much of a burden."

"I suppose the other language you grew up speaking is Algerian Arabic."

"Very good, Miss Handley, and quite refreshing. Most Americans lump all Arabic languages into one when there are many dialects and differences. I have learned never to speak my native tongue here. The few times I did the reactions I received were . . . off-putting."

"The Statue of Liberty has been sitting in New York Harbor for eight years, and I'm still hoping that one day we will finally live up to its welcoming inscription. We're a nation of immigrants, and yet a person who is different is often shunned. It defies explanation."

"I applaud your candor, Miss Handley, and I now see it is not just an investigative technique." He lit his cigarette and the strong aroma of Turkish tobacco was immediately evident. Mary found it unpleasant, but she had already given him permission to smoke.

She crinkled her nose and continued. "I can use candor or be devious. I do what the situation requires. And though I appreciate your caution, you didn't have to follow me for ten days to ascertain that. If you had approached me, I gladly would have told you much sooner."

"It's a strange land with strange customs. I wanted to be certain. Mea culpa."

"Ah, Latin. Do you speak yet a fourth language?"

"Only those two words, I'm afraid."

"I know at least four," she said with mock conceit. "Now, tell me about your brother."

"He was convicted three years ago of murdering a prostitute in Manhattan. My brother is not a saint. He was jailed briefly for vagrancy, but, I assure you, he is not a killer."

"Why have you waited three years to investigate?"

"It took time to save up enough money to return to America."

"Of course. Can you give me some information about the murder?"

"He was renting a room in a—I believe the best word to describe it is 'fleabag.' No?"

"Probably right. Go ahead."

"I've been down to see it. The East River Hotel. He was—"

"Is your brother's name Ameer Ben Ali?"

"Yes. Most people here call him Frenchy. It's ironic because his French isn't much better than his English, which is less than marginal. He contends his lack of fluency in French is evidence of his patriotism for a free Algeria. I personally think it's just his way of hiding that he's not very good at language."

Mary was already familiar with the crime. In fact, most of New York and Brooklyn were. A prostitute around sixty years old by the name of Carrie Brown, who was nicknamed "Old Shakespeare" for her tendency to break into Shakespearean verse when drunk, had been brutally murdered in Manhattan at the East River Hotel. A man they called Frenchy had been arrested and convicted. Normally, a prostitute's murder would not get so much press, but the style in which she was murdered resembled the infamous Whitechapel murders that had both terrorized and fascinated London. That killer had been dubbed "Jack the Ripper" from the signature on a letter that someone had written to a newspaper claiming to be the culprit. More importantly, he had never been caught.

"You realize, Mr. Ali, that all of New York was in a panic over that murder, and that dredging it up again could intensify anti-immigrant, anti-Arab, and anti-black sentiment."

"I have no choice. My brother is innocent."

His belief in his brother's innocence was so resolute that Mary felt Basem Ben Ali deserved a full investigation. It was not that long ago that her brother, Sean, had been arrested on murder charges, and her belief in him had been the only thing he had on his side.

"I will take your case, Mr. Ali. I hope you won't be disappointed with what I uncover."

Delighted, he hastily agreed to her fee, then gave her an address where he had rented an apartment. "If you need me during the day, I work at Leo's Meats. It's a butcher shop on Montague Street."

"Are you sure it's all right? My father works in a butcher shop, and I know how busy it can be."

"It's not a problem. My boss is very understanding."

"He must be in order to give you the time off to follow me."

"He is, but this is just a job to—what's the word—to defray costs. If I lose it, I'll get another one."

" 'Defray' is the word, and once again I'm impressed by your command of the English language." They shook hands, and he left.

Mary had something else on her mind that she hadn't mentioned to him. Shortly before the Carrie Brown murder, Thomas Byrnes had made a bold claim that if Jack the Ripper ever came to New York from London he would have him in custody within thirty-six hours. Byrnes had arrested and secured a confession from Ameer Ben Ali within that time frame, a feat that added to his already legendary reputation. In order to free him, she would have to prove that the most respected policeman in New York had, at the very least, made a mistake, and Thomas Byrnes would be the first to tell you: he didn't make mistakes, and he especially didn't like people who said he did.

3

It was late afternoon when Mary arrived at Superintendent Campbell's office. They had been friends since he had hired her for the Goodrich case years before, and he had remained a valuable source of information. His secretary, a Miss Carroll, ushered her into his office and left.

"You didn't have to call ahead to see if I was available. Nothing I do here is of enough import to take precedence over you," Superintendent Campbell said as he rose to greet her. "Actually, nothing I do here is of enough import to take precedence over anything. No offense."

"None taken, Chief. I know how much you adore your job." Superintendent Campbell longed for the days when he was Chief Detective Campbell. He had loved being in the field and loathed the mounds of paperwork he had to do in the superintendent's job. But he was getting older, it was good money, and chief detective was no longer an option. That was one of the reasons Mary still called him Chief. She knew how much he liked it.

As they both sat facing each other, a quick glance was

enough for her to comment, "You're keeping off the weight, Chief. I'm impressed." He wasn't svelte but he also wasn't what one would call heavy. It had been his constant battle since he took a desk job.

He grimaced. "Everything that's good for you tastes like straw."

Mary smiled. "Think of it as building character."

"I see it as God's way of depriving me of heaven on earth so I can really appreciate his place when it's time."

"So, God's insecure?"

"It's just a theory. I haven't worked out all the kinks yet." He put his gastronomic issues aside, and sat back in his big desk chair. "To what do I owe the pleasure of this visit?"

"What do you know about the Ameer Ben Ali case?"

"The Arab who killed Carrie Brown?"

"Allegedly."

"Not allegedly. He was tried, convicted, and guilty as all—" Superintendent Campbell realized he was about to curse and switched gears. "Sin."

"Please fill me in on the facts as you know them."

"You wouldn't be talking this way unless you've taken on his case, which is a huge mistake. He's an unrepentant killer, and the man who staked his reputation on that case is—"

"Thomas Byrnes."

"That should be enough of a deterrent."

"Chief, this is Mary."

"I'm well aware of your fearless nature, but this time you've chosen the losing side. Ameer Ben Ali rented the room across from Carrie Brown; there was a trail of blood from her room to his, including his doorknob; and contents from her stomach were found on his shirt. It defines 'open-and-shut case.'"

"Didn't she have a customer that night?"

"Yes, but he wasn't a factor. Read the trial transcript. It has everything."

"I fully intend to, but I had hoped you might have some information that's not in there."

"I don't. Like I said, the man's guilty as sin. Stay away from this case, Mary."

"Thanks for the warning, Chief." She stood and started to leave, both of them fully aware that she would not heed his monition.

"I knew her," he said. It caused Mary to turn and look at him quizzically. "Carrie Brown. . . . Old Shakespeare," he explained with an expression on his face that she could only interpret as sentimental, at least as sentimental as a man like Superintendent Campbell could get. "Years ago, I arrested her for assaulting a client. Turned out to be self-defense. She had a family, you know. Lost them because of her drinking. I was young, and I still thought I could make a difference. I gave her the speech about it not being too late to change her ways and do something positive with her life."

"Chief, you've ruined my whole image of you."

"Images are for people who care."

"Then you should have no objection when I, at my whim, tease you mercilessly about it."

Superintendent Campbell responded with a slight crinkle in the corner of his mouth, his version of a smile, then continued. "She burst into laughter and asked me to be her boyfriend. All the way back to the station she recited the balcony scene from *Romeo and Juliet*—over and over. *O Romeo,*

Romeo! Wherefore art thou Romeo? Deny thy father and refuse thy name. Or, if thou wilt not, be but sworn my love, and I'll no longer be a Capulet."

"You'd make a wonderful Juliet, Chief."

He cleared his throat. "The point is, that woman may have been a prostitute, but she was also full of life and deserved to live out her days as much as anyone. Not have it snuffed out by some animal."

"I wholeheartedly agree. All I'm trying to determine is if we have the right animal."

With that, Mary left.

~

The celebrating started early on this first federally sanctioned Labor Day weekend. In the Gut section of Coney Island on the West End, where honky-tonks papered the streets and gambling and drinking were the norm, they partied way into the night in the name of the workingman. The fact that many of these people were jobless reprobates and Labor Day was like any other day didn't matter. It was an excuse to raise all kinds of hell, and they were experts at that.

Meg Parker had enjoyed a very profitable evening. The four johns she had entertained were the most she had corralled in one evening since a rowdy Fourth of July a decade earlier. Her usual dark disposition turned upbeat. She even allowed one of them to call her Margie, a name she hated because it was what her father used to whisper in her ear when he snuck into her room at night. Now in her midforties, Meg knew only too well that most johns wanted a younger woman. Of course, she had the extra handicap of being black. In her heyday, white men would come around looking for the experience. "A taste of the forbidden fruit," she'd call it. Now she needed the assistance of dim lights and lots of drink. "Give me a cracker who's been hittin' the gin," she used to boast, "and I'll close the deal faster than any of those silly white girls out there."

It was two A.M. that Friday morning and it was time to pack it in. She could go home, pay her bitch of a landlady the back rent she owed, and still have some left over. All in all a darn good haul. As she stumbled along, tipsier than she'd have admitted, a man stepped out of the shadows of a doorway, spooking her. She jumped back, staggering a step or two more than a sober person.

"Sorry," he said, seeming genuinely concerned. "I didn't mean to startle you."

"What the hell did ya think would happen when you jump out at a girl like that? This place is full of crazy fuckers."

"Well, rest assured I am not." The man stepped further into the light and Meg got a good look at him: a blond white man with a mustache, about five feet eight inches tall, with an overall genteel appearance. He was wearing a fashionable cutaway black coat with black trousers, a black vest, and a gray silk puff tie. A small leather bag was in his right hand, but far more important to Meg was that he smelled of money, lots of it. She instantly switched gears and tried to present the most proper appearance her inebriated state would allow.

"I can see now that you are a proper gentleman. Please excuse my language. It was unbefitting a lady like me." She then stumbled backward a step before regaining her balance.

"That's unfortunate," he said as he edged closer. "I was

hoping you weren't a lady at all." She stared at him for a moment, trying to process his words. "I sincerely apologize for any misunderstanding." He started walking away.

"You lookin' for some dark meat, sweetie?"

He turned back toward her and smiled. "I want to see the Elephant."

"Sure, darlin', as long as you're payin'."

The Elephant Hotel, originally called the Elephantine Colossus, was a thirty-one-room hotel that was literally built in the shape of a huge elephant with a trunk, large ears, and of course, tusks. It was constructed with wood and covered with tin to give it the gray elephant color. A gold crescent seat on its back added more authenticity. At first it was a tourist attraction with telescopes in its eyes for viewing the ocean and a museum in the elephant's left lung. At this point, the neighborhood had deteriorated and it had turned into a prostitute hotel. *I want to see the Elephant* had become synonymous with *Let's go fuck there.*

Hoping to get five dollars, Meg asked for twenty. He agreed. She was delighted, but she didn't show it. She had learned long ago never to let a sucker know he was one. As they entered the Elephant Hotel and ascended the long winding staircase, Meg was thinking she could take off a night or two. Hell, a whole week.

The room was on the top floor with a sizable window that had a picturesque view of the ocean. He unlocked the door, and Meg strutted inside as he closed it.

"Well, here we are," she said.

"Yes." He held up a twenty-dollar bill. She snatched it, stuffed it into her pocketbook with methodic efficiency, and then grinned.

"I guess it's time for me to get naked, or does the gentleman prefer to disrobe?"

"Neither is necessary," he replied as he set his leather bag on the floor. "Stand by the wall next to the window. I like to look at the ocean."

"I pegged you right off as a man who knows what he likes." She smiled at him. "Okay, darlin', come and get it." She leaned back against the wall and reached down to pull up her skirt. With her hands occupied, he made his move.

In an instant, he was choking her. Meg had fought off many a male attacker before, but his technique was so efficient she could only get in a slap or two before she was unconscious and stretched out on the floor.

The man retrieved the twenty-dollar bill from her pocketbook. Then he opened his leather bag, removed a small black velvet pouch containing his tools, and went to work.

4

It was Friday morning and Captain Alexander "Clubber" Williams strode through New York police headquarters at 300 Mulberry Street like he owned it. In a way, he did. Williams was one of the most respected and feared policemen in New York. He had gone into many districts where policemen were routinely carried out on stretchers and quickly exerted his authority, acquiring the nickname "Clubber" because of the tough justice he doled out with his police club. He had almost single-handedly broken up the Gas House Gang and when he moved to Thirteenth Street Station, he dubbed their community the "Tenderloin District" in reference to the fine dining he'd enjoy after taking bribes from their gambling houses, brothels, and nightclubs. Do-gooders had brought him up on charges numerous times. Nothing ever stuck.

Williams walked into Thomas Byrnes's office and closed the door. Byrnes looked up from his desk. "Damn it, Alex. I hate it when ya do that. The men'll think we're conspiring."

"We are."

Byrnes sighed. "What now?"

"He hit again."

"Ya sure?"

"Same technique. It's him all right."

"Damn it! I thought we had scared him off. . . . Where?"

"Coney Island, in the Gut."

"At least that gives us some time. It's far away, and so much human garbage passes through there it'll be a while 'fore it gets back ta us."

"It already has. How do you think I know?"

"Then ya know what we have ta do."

"The usual. You're predictable as all hell, Tommy."

"I don't see it hurtin' you."

"I'm not complaining. Just observing."

"Observin', huh? You accidentally hit yerself on the head with yer club and now yer Schopenhauer?"

"Who the fuck is Schopenhauer?"

"Exactly. Next time ya think about gettin' up on yer high horse with me, remember I know who the fuck he is and ya don't."

Williams's infamous temper flared up momentarily. The two of them locked eyes, then it all dissipated and they began to laugh. "You're a pain in the ass, Tommy."

"The feelin's mutual I'm sure."

Williams started to go, then stopped. "Almost forgot. You skipped the benefit the other night. Mr. Carnegie was asking for you."

"I wonder what he wants."

"They always want something."

"I'll get back ta him."

"And I'll get on the Coney Island situation. One thing fell our way. She was a Negro."

"Why'd ya even bother? No one's gonna give a damn."

"I like to be thorough. Lovers' quarrel should work."

"Brilliant." Byrnes rolled his eyes, then went back to the paperwork on his desk. But Williams just stood there, staring at him. Finally, Byrnes noticed and looked up.

"Well, are you gonna tell me?" Williams asked.

"What?"

"Who the hell Schopenhauer is."

"It's way beyond yer reach. Ya wouldn't understand."

Williams grunted and left. Byrnes smiled. Truth was he didn't know who Schopenhauer was either. He had heard the name mentioned at one of the society parties he was "required" to attend and liked the sound of it. But it was enough to aggravate Williams, and Byrnes enjoyed that.

~

Mary spent Friday morning into the afternoon reading the transcript of Ameer Ben Ali's trial at the New York County Courthouse, which was also known as the Tweed Courthouse because of the fortune the former Tammany boss had bilked from the public during its construction. There was really nothing in the transcript that added significantly to Superintendent Campbell's version of the case except that it was clear that Ali was a terrible witness. Sometimes he understood the English questions they were asking and sometimes he didn't. Every so often he'd get frustrated and scream out in Algerian Arabic. Mary reasoned that these outbursts must have exacerbated any xenophobic fears the all-white American jury might have had. And Ali's lawyer was either vastly incompetent for putting him on the stand without the proper preparation or Ali was an irrational, unpredictable human being. Of course, a third possibility did exist. Maybe Ali's lawyer put him on the stand because he knew he had no case, knew that Ali was guilty, and was hoping for a miracle.

Mary went from the courthouse to the *New York Times,* where a small bribe to a clerk got her access to old issues of the newspaper with articles about the case. Going through them, she was able to glean more information, some merely a memory jog and some new to her. It all boiled down to this: the case against Ameer was circumstantial. The eyewitness reports were conflicting but Superintendent Campbell was right in that the blood evidence was particularly damning. Carrie Brown had rented room 31 at the East River Hotel and Ameer Ben Ali was across the hall in room 33. There was a blood trail from Carrie Brown's room to Ameer's, and there was blood on Ameer's doorknob and also on one of his shirts. There were also contents from her stomach found in his room. Circumstantial? Yes, but hard to ignore. One of the new facts she learned was that a year ago Ameer had been transferred from Sing Sing prison to the Matteawan State Hospital for the Criminally Insane. She knew she needed to speak with him. That involved a train trip up to Matteawan, and she planned to do it sometime in the next few days.

It was now Friday night, and that meant only one thing to Mary: dinner at her parents' house. Dinner with her parents had evolved over the years from her mother, Elizabeth, picking on her about her not being married to Elizabeth picking on both her and her brother, Sean, about not being married. Mary had had two serious relationships and had even been engaged once, but she had broken it off. Sean's situation was different: his fiancée was brutally murdered four years earlier, and he hadn't gotten over it. He was still filled with guilt that he, a Brooklyn policeman, couldn't protect her.

Elizabeth thought it had been more than enough time.

"One day, Sean," Elizabeth would say, "you're going to wake up and discover you're forty, alone, and miserable."

Sean never responded to his mother's harangues, mainly because he wasn't good at verbal jousts. Mary was. "He doesn't have to wait until he's forty, Mother," she'd often quip back. "You're already making him miserable. You have a talent for making us all miserable."

On a particular Friday after a rough week at work, Sean finally struck back. "If being alone means I never have to suffer through another Friday night dinner, then you're wrong, Mother. I'd be very happy, thoroughly ecstatic!"

Surprised at Sean's pluck, Mary gasped and then had to quickly suppress a giggle. Being the peacemaker in the family, their father, Jeffrey, tried to get Sean to apologize, but Elizabeth called him off. She resorted to giving both Sean and Mary the silent treatment for the rest of the dinner. That was fine with them. Of course, the next Friday she was back to her old self.

Mary and Sean were convinced nothing would ever change Friday night dinner and sometimes wondered why they kept attending. However, they always reached the same conclusion. Family was a lot like poker. You had no power over the hand you were dealt, and you were stuck with it.

Surprisingly, that evening did turn out to be different. Elizabeth made an announcement. "You children should know that your father will soon be out of a job."

Jeffrey Handley had worked at the same butcher shop

for thirty-two years. He had gotten the job around the time Sean was born. His not working there was unthinkable. Almost in unison, Mary and Sean uttered a very incredulous "What?"

Jeffrey jumped in. "There's no reason to get the children all riled up, Elizabeth. Nothing is definite yet."

"Stop fooling yourself, Jeffrey," Elizabeth said, then turned to Mary and Sean. "Mr. Flanagan is retiring, and he's going to sell his business."

Jeffrey turned to his children and explained, "He hasn't sold it yet, and he said that he'd make a deal with whoever buys it for me to keep my job."

"For how long?" Elizabeth chimed in. "Until Flanagan is out the door?"

"Now, Elizabeth—"

"You're much too trusting, Jeffrey. These are businessmen. The buyer may say yes to complete the deal and then he has a son, a nephew, or a cousin and you're out."

Jeffrey sighed, partially because he was tired of this argument that they had been waging for days and partially because he was afraid she was right.

Mary spoke up. "There's no need to fret about something over which you have no control. We will find out in time. I think Father's right."

"You would," Elizabeth snapped back. "You're a dreamer just like him."

"Yes, Mother, and you've always belittled my dream. Yet, I seem to have created a very nice career from it."

"None of it means anything without family."

"If by 'family' you mean someone who criticizes your

every move and declares your life's ambitions utter garbage, then I can do without it, thank you very much."

Elizabeth did a slow burn as she rose from the table. "Jeffrey, did you hear what she said? Are you going to let her talk to me like that?"

This time Jeffrey opted not to be the peacemaker. "What do you want me to say, Elizabeth? What did the girl say that wasn't true?"

By now, Elizabeth was livid. "For once in your life, show some backbone. You've always let these children step all over you." With that, Elizabeth stomped out of the dining room to her bedroom and slammed the door. Stunned, Mary, Sean, and Jeffrey sat in silence for a moment until Mary broke it.

"Are you okay, Dad?"

"I'm fine. Thanks, Mary. It's time your mother learned that she can't speak to us like that without consequences."

"If I didn't see that with my own eyes . . . ," Sean said in awe. "It's always Mary who charges out of here in anger. Never Mother."

Mary sighed. "Don't get too optimistic. I'm sure she'll be back to her old self in no time. She defines 'wet blanket.' "

"Actually, I believe the term was invented because of her," Sean said, kidding.

"It originated in the seventeenth century, but I'm sure they were anticipating her birth."

Mary and Sean started to laugh. Jeffrey couldn't help smiling, too.

"Ease off a bit on your mother. She's so frantic about my job she's not herself."

"It's a fine distinction, but I do see what you mean,"

Mary said, then looked at her father with sympathetic eyes. "Do you think you have anything to be concerned about?"

"I don't know." For the first time in their lives, Mary and Sean saw their normally upbeat and positive father look worried and a bit scared. They both moved toward him, hoping their closeness would soothe his upset. It didn't.

5

Ameer Ben Ali wasn't Mary's only case, and the one involving Colleen Murphy had certainly become more personal. Sarah and Walter lived in the affluent residential section of Williamsburg. Since Sarah was her best friend, it was easy to invent an excuse to stop by her house, not that any excuse was really needed.

Sophie, the live-in maid, let her in, and after the usual pleasantries she informed Mary that Sarah was in the backyard. As Mary headed in that direction, she spotted Walter on the telephone in his home office, wearing a Norfolk jacket and tweed trousers, indicating to her that he had either just finished or was about to be involved in some outdoor activity. He smiled and waved at Mary, then shut the door. His secretive nature prompted Mary to suspect he was arranging a clandestine liaison with Colleen. It was possible her imagination could have been running a bit wild, but she doubted it.

Sarah and Walter's home reflected how well his law practice was doing. Custom furniture from Europe adorned the spacious house and so did paintings from minor yet recognized artists. Sarah and Mary had grown up on the same street in Brooklyn and servants like Sophie had been as far from their imaginations as were charity balls and formals, which Sarah now regularly attended. The Coopers' wealth was nowhere near the rarefied atmosphere in which the Rockefeller family or the Vanderbilts resided, but they were financially comfortable.

Mary did find Sarah in the backyard, miraculously managing her four children. She viewed it as a miracle, because although she loved children and, in spite of her mother's constant diatribes, wanted to be a mother one day, she didn't know how any one person could keep four children of different ages occupied and happy for any length of time. Somehow Sarah was able to do it and make it look simple, while still remaining calm and beautiful.

God, Mary hated Walter!

Sarah was on the back porch playing house with little Lucy, at the moment pouring fake tea for their imaginary guests, as she kept an eye on Ginny, Harry, and James, who were engrossed in a game of tag. When she saw Mary, she quickly rose and went to hug her.

"Mary, what a nice surprise!"

Mary was Ginny's favorite adult in the world except for her parents, and when she heard her name she immediately stopped to look, allowing James, who was "it," to catch her.

"Gotcha," screamed a very happy James. "You're it!"

"It doesn't matter. I'm not playing anymore."

"That's not fair. I've been 'it' forever, I finally catch you, and—"

"Can't you see? Aunt Mary's here."

Ginny's words instantly stopped James's complaint. In

no time, all four children were huddled around Mary. Their adoration wasn't completely selfless. Her presence usually meant they would be off on a fun outing like Coney Island or the park or something of that ilk. As the children jumped up and down declaring their preferred destinations, Mary immediately responded.

"I'm sorry. I'm working on a case, I was in the neighborhood, and this is just a quick visit." Their disappointment was instantaneous and quite vocal, but Sarah soon put a stop to it.

"You heard Aunt Mary. You all know she's an important detective."

"Yes," Ginny piped up, "very important, and I'm going to be one, too, someday."

Sarah turned toward Mary, making sure the back of her head was facing her children, and whispered through her smile, "You see what you've done?" They both laughed.

"Do only girls get to be detectives?" James asked. "I want to be one, too."

"Enough, children. Go back to playing while Mary and I chat for a bit."

Ginny, James, and Harry returned to playing tag, the three of them arguing over who was "it," while Sarah suggested that Lucy bake a scrumptious apple pie. Excited, Lucy nodded and walked four steps to her imaginary oven to bake her imaginary pie.

"So, what case is the famous Mary Handley working on?"

"You know I can't divulge too much," Mary replied. And in this instance she really couldn't. She decided to mention her other case. "I don't know if you remember it but about three years ago Carrie Brown, an old"—Mary stopped, looked to make sure none of the children were close, and whispered—"prostitute was murdered in lower Manhattan."

"Oh yes, of course. Some crazy Arab did it." And that was the crux of the uphill battle Mary was facing even if Ameer Ben Ali was innocent. Sarah didn't have a prejudiced bone in her body, and yet even she identified him as a "crazy Arab." It was almost impossible to undo an image the press had so firmly implanted in people's minds.

"I'm not sure how crazy he is but yes, Ameer Ben Ali."

"Is it possible that he's innocent?"

"Anything is possible, but I'm not far enough along to have an opinion as of yet. Besides, what I've discovered I can't discuss, nor would you find it of much interest."

The conversation about Mary's work was dropped, and they went on to their usual friendly chatter about what was happening in their lives. Mary was trying to glean if there was a hint of upset or unhappiness with Walter. There was none that she could perceive. It made her feel worse that Sarah was completely oblivious to his deception. It also made it harder for her to tell her about it. She was beginning to work up to it when Walter emerged from the house and headed for them. He had abandoned his rugged, outdoors outfit and was now wearing yet another fashionable summer suit, not unlike the one he'd worn at the Oriental Hotel. The same straw hat was tucked under his left arm.

He held out his hand. "Mary, so good to see you. I'm sorry about earlier. I was on the telephone with a client."

As they shook, she replied, "No need to apologize, Walter. I know how important clients are." Mary was being facetious, but he showed no sign of recognizing it.

"Walter, darling, why are you so dressed up?" Sarah asked. "You haven't forgotten that you promised to take the children hiking?"

"No, I haven't, dear, but unfortunately, some nasty business has arisen, and I must leave."

Yes, monkey business.

"But, Walter, this is Saturday. Surely whatever it is can wait until—"

"It can't, Sarah. I'm sorry."

You ass!

He shrugged. "The life of a lawyer."

If he's a lying, cheating prick!

"Oh well, the children will be disappointed, but business is business. Hope it goes well." Sarah kissed Walter on the cheek, then he bid both of them good-bye and left.

Mary did her best to hide her anger for Sarah's sake as she expressed her regret that she, too, had to get back to work and also left. She felt some comfort in the fact that she wasn't lying. Walter was her work.

~

It was a bright and sunny Saturday. The temperature had already hit eighty-five degrees a few minutes before eleven A.M. People had come to Coney Island in droves to enjoy the beach and the amusements. Children's laughter and screams of excitement permeated the air along with the sounds of parents issuing words of caution and barkers beckoning people to their booths.

Edgar Jefferson was also in a jovial mood as he strolled

along the beach near the midway. After all, he was a working actor, and he knew how difficult that was to accomplish. It wasn't the type of role that excited him, but it was a job, and each time he went before an audience it was a learning experience. He was twenty-seven, and he knew that he might have to spend years before he achieved his heart's desire, which was to perform Shakespeare in London and Europe like his idol Ira Aldridge. Aldridge had died decades earlier but not before he had achieved fame and considerable notoriety for his Shakespearean roles in London and throughout Europe. This was considered a great accomplishment, not because he was an American, which he was, but because he was black.

Edgar was also black, and he had been born on the day Aldridge died, August 7, 1867. He felt Aldridge's spirit had somehow passed into his body. He wasn't consumed by this notion or the least bit warped about it. It was just a feeling that kept him going. After all, he had Aldridge's deep, melodious voice, and there was no question he had the talent. Opportunity was another thing. In his day, Aldridge had had New York's African Grove Theater in which to cut his teeth on Shakespeare, but that theater had closed decades before. Even though it was very popular, a bunch of rowdy white bigots had forced them to shut their doors.

As he walked along, Edgar received waves, nods, and friendly hellos from the majority of the regulars who worked at the park. He had a very pleasing personality and a hearty laugh, which helped him transcend color and made him well liked by his coworkers. Much of Brooklyn, New York City, and the rest of the United States were not nearly as accepting.

Edgar entered the arcade area and saw Arthur, the short, pudgy, balding white man who had hired him, pacing nervously. When he spotted Edgar, he heaved a large sigh of relief.

"Stop cutting it so close, Edgar. You're giving me heart failure."

"Please, the ungodly amount of food you ingest will get to you way before I do." Edgar's tone was friendly and Arthur's anxiety quickly dissipated into a smile. "Besides," Edgar continued as he posed in a theatrical stance, "you will never have to hold the curtain for me. Edgar Jefferson is a professional and is always on time."

"Good. Get out there and earn your money."

"As always, I will have them in the palm of my hand."

Edgar turned and went to work. He stuck his head through a hole in the canvas before him and saw the crowds passing by. Suddenly his voice became high pitched and he assumed the cliché accent and language that reflected how the white world thought all black people spoke.

"Well, if dat don't beat all. My massah said dere was all dese white folk out dere waitin' fer me. I didn't believe 'im. I shoulda. I always listen to my massah, except when it comes to white women. I loves them white women." Then he licked his lips.

Edgar had already drawn a crowd, most of them appalled at his words. At this point, Arthur stepped in front.

"All right, ladies and gentlemen, which one of you is going to silence this savage from the wilds of Africa?" He pronounced it "Ah-free-ka." "Step right up and kill the coon."

Edgar continued baiting the crowd and a line began to

form. Arthur handed out three balls and collected a nickel apiece to give each of them three shots at the coon.

~

Mary was very good at tailing a suspect, and Walter seemed completely unaware of her. She reasoned that it was probably due less to her ability than to his being blinded by his lust. She hoped that he was leading her to a boring meeting with a client but soon abandoned that hope when she found herself on a train heading to Coney Island. She had to control the anger she felt to avoid getting sloppy. Walter was in the next car, and it all would become a jumbled mess if she allowed him to see her.

Coney Island was the end of the line, the last stop in Brooklyn. After that, there was only water. Moving quickly, Walter popped out of his car and made a beeline for the Oriental Hotel. He did pause a few times and looked around as if checking to see if he was being followed, but Mary was too good at what she did to be detected. *The bastard!*

She had to wait a few minutes outside the hotel after Walter entered in order to avoid bumping into him and Colleen. She wanted to catch them in their hotel room together, so there was no chance they could feign innocence.

It turned out Mary was able to spend that time judiciously. There was a store advertising the Kodak box camera. A photograph of their rendezvous would be irrefutable. She detested the voyeur element that it added, but this was her best friend and she needed solid proof. Mary bought the Kodak along with a roll of film.

It was the Saturday of a holiday weekend, and the lobby

of the Oriental Hotel was naturally buzzing with people. Seeing no trace of Walter or Colleen, she figured they had already gone up to their room. Last time they had been in room 424, and the clerk had seemed to indicate that Walter often took that room. She needed to be sure.

A nicely dressed man in his midthirties was already at the hotel desk and the male hotel clerk was thumbing through the reservations book. Mary got in line behind him. Then the blond-haired man whom Mary had seen a couple of days before with Austin Corbin approached the desk in tennis attire, holding his racquet. He called to a female hotel clerk.

"Barbara, my dear, please make a seven thirty dinner reservation tonight at the hotel restaurant?"

"Certainly, Dr. Lawrence. For how many?"

Dr. Lawrence smacked his forehead. "Yes, that would help. Four."

"I'm sure it's fine, but I'll check and be right back."

"That's sweet of you, Barbara. Take your time."

She left as the male hotel clerk said, "Ah yes, here's your reservation. Two nights, Mr. Burke." And he pushed the reservation book over for the man to sign.

"That's it. Except my name is spelled B-e-r-k, not B-u-r-k-e. When my father came to the United States, the immigrant officers didn't understand his name and shortened it from Berkowitz. I've had to explain that over and over again my whole life."

Just as Mr. Berk was about to sign, the hotel clerk pulled back the reservation book. "I'm sorry, but this reservation is clearly for a Mr. Burke. B-u-r-k-e, not B-e-r-k."

"Yes, I've explained that—"

"Sorry, sir."

They went back and forth a few times, but Mr. Berk could see he was getting nowhere. "Okay, forget about my reservation. I'd like a room for two nights."

"Unfortunately, we're sold out. It's a very busy weekend."

"I know. That's why I made the damn reservation in June!"

"There's no need for profanity, sir."

"I beg to differ."

Hoping to avoid any unpleasantness, the hotel clerk abruptly turned and disappeared into the back. At this point, Dr. Lawrence felt a need to interject himself.

"Dear fellow, are you not aware that this hotel is restricted?" Mr. Berk didn't respond or even look at him. "Surely you know what 'restricted' means."

Mary couldn't help commenting. "Of course he does. It means only people with less than normal intelligence are allowed to patronize this hotel. Happily, Mr. Berk doesn't qualify."

Mr. Berk looked at Mary, then at Dr. Lawrence, shook his head, and stomped off.

Dr. Lawrence turned to Mary. "He could have avoided all this unpleasantness if he had simply checked in advance. Typical of his kind, but I applaud your humor. It was a valiant effort to deflate a messy situation."

"I was merely stating a fact."

"I do believe you're pulling my leg, Miss—"

"Handley. Shortened from Handelstein."

"Nice try, but your Irish heritage is too apparent."

"There are no Irish Jews?"

"None who are female private investigators in Brooklyn."

"So your superior Aryan savvy didn't give me away, but rather the daily newspaper."

"Why do I feel like we're in a boxing ring?"

"That wouldn't be fair. You're overmatched."

At that point, Barbara returned. "You're all set, Dr. Lawrence. Four at seven thirty tonight."

"Thank you, Barbara," he said with a smile, then turned to Mary. "Hopefully, my wounds will have healed by then." And he walked off, leaving Barbara a bit puzzled.

Mary decided to take advantage of her befuddled state. "Hello, Barbara, I'm supposed to meet Walter Cooper here. Is he in room four two four?"

Barbara looked at the hotel register and confirmed that he was. "Thank you," said Mary. "And don't mind Dr. Lawrence. He's a renowned joker."

"Really? Dr. Lawrence?" Barbara remained befuddled as Mary headed for the elevator.

While she made her way down the corridor of the fourth floor, Mary decided on a plan of action. After all, knocking on the door was one thing. Getting them to open it was another.

"Who is it?" Walter asked, sounding concerned.

You should be concerned, you . . . But Mary responded in a very civil tone, using her best Irish accent, "Room service, sir."

"We didn't order anything."

"I know, sir. Champagne, compliments of the hotel."

There was a pause, then Walter opened the door and said, "Thank you. That's very kind—" He stopped, completely flabbergasted when he saw Mary standing there with her Kodak box camera in hand and ready to shoot. "Mary, what the—"

But Mary didn't pause, nor did she respond. She knew she would get upset and never get the photo she needed. She pointed the camera and hurriedly took the shot. When she looked up, she didn't know what to make of what she saw.

Besides Walter and Colleen, there were two other men in the room. Mary's righteous anger quickly dissipated. What was going on?

The room was spacious and nicely furnished. Besides the bed, there was a large carved mahogany sofa with red upholstery embroidered in gold, a black and red velvet Burmese club chair, and a mahogany writing desk with a chair.

Shortly after Mary had entered she'd realized that one of the other men was Joseph Hodges Choate, a celebrated New York lawyer who had argued before the Supreme Court against the racist Chinese Exclusion Act and had been involved in many landmark cases. She didn't recognize the third man, who was in his midthirties and had a thick crop of brown hair. His nose was larger than most but fit into his face nicely. Needless to say, this was no romantic rendezvous.

"What in blazes are you doing here, Mary?" Walter demanded.

"Mary Handley?" Colleen said, finally recognizing her. "I haven't seen you in years."

"All I can say is that I am on a case."

"Who hired you? Was it Sarah?"

"Was it Brian?"

"Was it the Marquis de Sade?" asked the third man in the room.

"The Marquis de Sade?"

"You barged into a hotel room brandishing a camera. It's something the marquis would do."

"I highly doubt it. He wasn't around when they invented the camera, because he's been dead for eighty years."

"Still client material for you. You look like the séance type."

"And what is that?"

"Essentially, it means you have a screw loose, madam."

As Mary stepped toward her tormentor, Walter quickly placed himself between the two. He knew he'd have to calm the waters in order to find out anything useful.

"Mary, let me introduce you. You obviously know Colleen." Mary nodded to Colleen, which prompted her to once again ask if Brian had hired her. Mary wisely didn't respond and Walter continued. "This gentleman is—"

"Joseph Hodges Choate. I'm a great admirer of your work, Mr. Choate."

"Really?" queried Choate. "I'll take that under advisement and decide later whether I should consider that a compliment or not."

"I hope to prove to you that this situation is an anomaly and that my opinion is worthy."

"That will take a lot of proving," chimed in the third man. Mary's head whipped around sharply in his direction, and Walter once again felt the need to intercede.

"Mary Handley, this is Harper Lloyd."

"Ah, that explains your sour disposition: two names that

can easily be switched. I'm sure just as many people call you Lloyd Harper as Harper Lloyd. It must drive you quite mad."

"I bow to your expertise, for you are as mad as Lewis Carroll's Hatter."

"You can read? That's a surprising development."

"Stop it," Walter demanded. "I declare a cease-fire to all hostilities, at least until we get to the bottom of this." He took out his wallet. "Mary, if we hire you, might I assume you will keep the same confidentiality you afford to all your clients?"

"Yes, of course, but—"

"Here's five dollars. Consider yourself hired for a few hours."

"Walter, I can't take money from you."

"You have to."

"But, Walter—"

"Enough, Mary, it's done. If it makes you feel better, buy something for the children." Mary quieted, knowing any further protest would be useless. "Now, I'll tell you what we're doing here on the condition that you tell us if it has anything at all to do with why you're here."

"That sounds fair, as long as I don't have to reveal who my client is."

Harper flinched. "You can't trust her, Walter. This woman's too loosely tied together."

"Which name is real," Mary shot back, "Harper or Lloyd, or are they both phony?"

"I trust Walter," Choate said.

"Thank you," Mary replied.

"Not you. Him." Choate pointed to Walter. "Besides, Miss

Handley, if you violate our trust, not only will I put an end to your detective career, but I will also sue you to a point where your great-grandchildren will still be paying my estate."

"Is that even possible?" Mary asked, and they all looked at her. "Just wondering. Okay, I'm on board, aye-aye, sirs . . . and lady." Mary paused. "Sorry, that was a bit too flip."

Harper gestured to Walter. "See what I mean?"

Walter pulled out the desk chair and suggested that everyone be seated. As he sat, Mary and Choate chose opposite ends of the sofa; Colleen sat on the club chair and Harper on the edge of the bed. Walter then explained that one of Joseph Choate's clients was William Laidlaw, the man who had been found on top of Russell Sage in the Henry Norcross bombing.

"I'm aware of the case," Mary said. "The accounts in the newspapers are hard to miss. Mr. Laidlaw claims that when the bomb went off, Mr. Sage grabbed him and used him as a human shield. Mr. Choate, I have read some of your cross-examinations of Mr. Sage in the newspaper, and I commend you on exposing the selfish, cowardly nature of that old skinflint."

"'Skinflint' is a relative term, Miss Handley," Choate said. "Sage doesn't care that William Laidlaw will be in pain and infirm for the rest of his life. He's determined not to pay him a cent, no matter how much it costs him in legal fees. As you probably know, I have won judgments against him, yet he keeps on appealing."

"Mr. Choate," Walter continued, "has many obligations ahead of him, including some very important arguments before the Supreme Court. He has brought me on as co-counsel in case those obligations draw him away from this case.

Then I will take over. But for now my involvement is a private matter, the reasons for which are not important to this discussion."

"I understand. Why would you want Russell Sage and his Wall Street cronies on your back if you're not definitely taking over for Mr. Choate?"

"Walter is being very generous by donating his time," said Choate. "William Laidlaw has no money and Walter will not get any remuneration unless we secure a permanent judgment. I see no reason to throw him to the wolves any sooner than is necessary."

"That's lovely of you, Walter," said Mary, feeling incredibly guilty at what she had suspected.

Walter smiled. "Let's just hope the wolves don't get their way."

"But how is Colleen involved?"

"I saw it, Mary," Colleen said.

"Saw it? You were there?"

Colleen nodded her head. "I was looking for a job. It wasn't just for the money. The children are wonderful and I love them, but I needed to be around adults for a while. I tell you, Mary, never marry a sailor. They're never there to help."

"There's nothing wrong with working. You don't have to make excuses, Colleen."

"My mother agreed to watch the children. I got dressed up and went down to the Wall Street area thinking I'd go from floor to floor asking if anyone was hiring. That's how my friend Lorraine got her job with Mr. Sage."

"Your friend works for Russell Sage?"

"She did, and I was going to meet her for lunch when a man passed me in the hall carrying a bulky satchel and entered the offices. He announced he had a letter of introduction from John D. Rockefeller, so I waited outside, not wanting to interrupt important business."

"As you probably realize, Mary," Walter added, "that man was Henry Norcross."

"Yes," said Colleen, "and then Mr. Sage came out of his office. It turned out the letter was not from Mr. Rockefeller but rather a demand for one million two hundred thousand dollars. Can you imagine? I didn't know there was that much money in the world."

"I assure you," Mary replied, "that Russell Sage has that sum many times over."

"Amazing. That kind of money." Colleen shook her head, processing it. "Anyhow, Mr. Laidlaw arrived and Mr. Sage motioned for him to come over. Then after some more talk, there was a second, maybe less, where he saw the man was going to drop his bag and he pulled poor Mr. Laidlaw to him."

"You actually saw Russell Sage do that?"

"Like I said, it was a split second, but yes."

"Oh my God."

"My sentiments exactly," said Choate.

"You look okay," Mary said. "I mean, you avoided getting—"

"Just small cuts and bruises. Lucky, I guess. Some boards covered my body. Maybe they protected me. I don't know. The office was completely destroyed. I checked on Lorraine. She had a bad glass cut on her leg. Others were hurt worse, but she was my friend and I helped her downstairs.

The ambulances had already arrived, they took her, and I went home."

Mary slowly absorbed this information. "I can't imagine. That must've been awful."

"So now you know," Walter said, "why we've chosen such an out-of-the-way, clandestine meeting place. It's not just for my sake. It's also for Colleen's."

Choate clarified it further. "Her eyewitness testimony will not only put an end to any thought Russell Sage might have of appealing but also secure us a very generous judgment. It's essential that Sage and his cohorts know nothing about Colleen, so that she won't be subject to their bullying tactics."

"What about Lorraine? I'm sure they'll question her if they haven't already."

"She quit her job after that," Colleen answered. "Then her husband lost his. Her uncle in Ohio offered him a job and they moved."

"So, after all this," Walter said, "does your case have anything to do with ours?"

"Not in the slightest. You have nothing to fear."

"That's a relief."

Harper stood up. "That's it, Walter? You're just going to accept that?"

"I've known Mary for years and—"

"Who are you, anyway?" asked Mary.

"I'm a reporter."

"I should have known. Obnoxious, egotistical—it all fits."

Choate laughed. "She's got you pegged, Harper."

"Actually, Mary," Walter interceded once again, "Harper

is one of the good ones. He was concerned about William Laidlaw, did some fine investigative work and found Colleen."

Colleen leaned over toward Mary. "What do you think, Mary?"

"About what?"

"Should I testify? These men keep telling me I have a duty to perform, that these rich, megalo—something—"

"Megalomaniacs. It means they're power crazy."

"Yeah, they have power and I don't. I'm afraid what they can do to me and my family."

"Now, Colleen," Choate said. "We've discussed this many times—"

"I want to know what Mary thinks."

Mary leaned in toward Colleen. "It's your life. I can't tell you what to do. All I can do is relate what I've experienced. I once had in my possession something a very powerful man wanted. He even tried to have me killed for it. But once I got it into the right hands and exposed him, he stopped trying to kill me. I no longer had what he wanted."

"He completely stopped? He didn't try to punish you for—?"

"There are vindictive people in this world, but these men are businessmen. They see no percentage in committing a crime from which they won't profit."

"How do I know that Russell Sage is not one of the vindictive ones?"

"You don't, not with complete certainty, but it's also possible if you don't testify that Russell Sage could find out about you and make sure you never let the information out."

Colleen shook her head. "It doesn't sound good no matter what I do."

"When in doubt, Colleen, it's never wrong to tell the truth."

"Thanks, Mary." And Colleen sat back, thinking about her words.

Harper decided to take advantage of the situation. "Since it's never wrong to tell the truth, maybe you can tell us why you were here."

"To be honest, it was a mistake, and I am quite embarrassed about it." Mary felt comfortable saying this. She didn't see it as a lie but rather as a half truth.

Harper's look told her he could see right through her. It was disconcerting.

7

It was the Saturday of Labor Day weekend and Russell Sage was working. His only concession to the holiday weekend was that he was at home. Work was his life, and the money he derived from it was sacred. It was hard to determine which of the two he valued more, but since one begat the other, he'd never have to choose.

There was a knock at his office door. Any interruption of his work annoyed him, and he wasn't too shy to show it.

"What is it?" he snapped.

From the other side of the door came Olivia's voice. "Your lunch is ready, dear."

"Tell Beatrice to serve me in here." Beatrice was their maid, one of several servants. She was his favorite because she never tried to engage him in what he called "mundane chatter." She did her job and got out. He admired anyone who was efficient. Food itself was a necessary evil that pried him from his work but until a viable substitute was found, he was stuck with it.

Olivia opened the door. "We so rarely dine together during the day. I thought it would be nice to do so on this holiday weekend. That is, if you can find the time, dear."

Sage knew his wife well. She didn't make these demands unless there was something she wanted to discuss, something she needed. Marriage was no more than a business deal to him, and as in every business deal there were certain give-and-take moments. Olivia had been a dutiful wife who had always lived up to her part of the deal, so this was one of his "give" moments.

"That's a lovely idea, darling. I'll be there shortly."

She smiled and left. True to his word, he joined her in the dining room a few minutes later. After they greeted each other, Beatrice, a fleshy, even-tempered woman, emerged from the kitchen, silently placed their lunch plates in front of them, and immediately left. Sage smiled, pleased with her performance.

"I hope you like the watercress salad, dear," Olivia said. "I made it myself and I tried something different."

"It's quite good. Nice job," Sage said as he chewed away. He didn't notice any difference, but saying so would probably distress her and he didn't want to risk that over a watercress salad. What concerned him more was that she'd made the salad instead of the cook. It meant this "give" moment would be significant. He waited for her proposal. It didn't take long.

"I'm glad you like it. I so wanted you to." She smiled and took a bite herself. "How is your work going?"

"Demanding but fine. The usual."

She nodded and smiled. "I spent a few days this week at the New York Women's Hospital. They're doing wonderful work there."

"Good to hear." His praise stopped there. More would enhance the sales pitch.

"They're having a terrible time with funding. There's nothing pleasant about turning away the infirm."

"Yes, a nasty business."

"Russell—"

"No."

"But, Russell—"

"We've had this discussion many times, Olivia. I work very hard for my money—"

"These people aren't loafers. They're—"

"And just because I'm smarter I should support them? No, Olivia, I sweat for every penny that I earn and I'm not giving it away."

"Andy Carnegie and John Rockefeller have seen fit to be more understanding when it comes to charity. I think—"

"If Andy and John want to throw away their fortunes, it makes me ill but it's their prerogative. I choose not to."

"I'm not suggesting you do it on the same scale. I would never suggest that. What I am asking is but a mere fraction. It's so infinitesimal you'll never feel it."

"But I will, Olivia. I assure you I will. Now, I don't want to hear any more of it."

"Russell—"

"I mean it. End of discussion."

At this point their butler, Gregory, entered. "Inspector Byrnes is here to see you, sir."

"Show him into my office, Gregory. I'll receive him there." Sage stood. "Sorry about the interruption, dear. Lovely salad." And he followed Gregory out of the dining room.

Byrnes was sitting in a leather club chair when Sage entered his office. He rose and they shook hands.

"Good to see you, Tom. Are you working on this Labor Day weekend?"

"Six days a week fer the city and seven days fer ya." He indicated Sage's desk. "I see yer workin', too."

"People mistakenly view this weekend as a vacation. In order to honor labor, I intend to labor even more." Sage then emitted a loud guffaw. Byrnes wasn't amused, but it was Russell Sage and he felt obligated to also laugh.

"That's a good one, Russell."

"Yes, and people think I'm humorless." He went to his desk and sat. "So, to what do I owe the pleasure of your company?"

"Have ya spoken with Mr. Carnegie lately?"

"Andy? It's been a week or so. We had some business, and he came to my office."

"Andrew Carnegie went to yer office. That's a real testament to how big ya are, Russell."

"It was business. I don't think of it that way." He obviously did. Humility wasn't his strong suit.

"I saw Mr. Carnegie today on another matter. He was at the fund-raising event for Carnegie Hall when he was approached by a Miss Elizabeth Cloverfield."

"Ah yes, Betty. Quite a little tigress."

"Apparently, she more than fits that title. She made it clear to Mr. Carnegie that if she doesn't hear from ya soon, she's goin' public with an affair she alleges she had with ya."

"That certainly sounds like Betty. She loves drama."

"Can I be of assistance?"

"Not necessary, though I am getting too old for this nonsense."

"Don't tell me yer finally laying down yer sword?"

"Wouldn't dream of it. I already have a new interest. I just need to be more specific in where I concentrate my energy."

"Ya keep givin' me more reasons to admire ya, Russell."

"Leave Betty alone. She can't cause much harm. Olivia and I have an understanding."

"Yet another reason I tip my hat ta ya."

"Sorry you had to come over here for something like that."

"It's not just that. Some other information came to my attention." Sage leaned forward, resting his arms on his desk, waiting for the news. "It's William Laidlaw, Russell."

"What is it now?"

"He told his nurse—and these're his words, not mine—that he has evidence that'll 'turn that ol' miser's pockets upside down.' "

"And you naturally assumed 'old miser' meant me?"

Byrnes paused, concerned he might have inadvertently offended Sage. After a moment, Sage burst out laughing.

"Got you there, Tom. See? I can be quite the prankster."

Byrnes was annoyed but hid it. "Yup, ya got me, all right."

"So what is this ridiculous evidence?"

"I don't know yet, but his nurse is an ally and you'll know as soon as I do if it's the morphine they're giving him or it's real."

"Thank you, Tom. It pays to have resourceful friends." Sage opened a desk drawer, took out an envelope full of cash, and tossed it across his desk. "I was going to give this to you next week but as long as you're here, you saved me the price of a messenger."

"I value yer friendship, too, Russell." He disliked the old coot, but it was hard to dislike the envelope he was stuffing into his jacket pocket.

"Would you like something to eat or drink? I can have Beatrice bring it in." Protocol required Sage to ask, but he wasn't fond of socializing and besides business, he felt he and this policeman had little in common.

"No thanks. Gotta keep my lovely Irish nose to the grindstone."

Sage was relieved, even more so when Byrnes left and he was able to get back to work.

~

The gathering in room 424 of the Oriental Hotel was still going on when Mary left. They were preparing Colleen for her testimony, and Mary had no reason to stay. As she exited the hotel and was passing an outside dining area where hotel guests could enjoy a meal or drinks with a view of the beach and ocean, she heard a familiar voice.

"There she is, Austin. That's the woman who beat me senseless." Dr. Lawrence was sitting with Austin Corbin, both of them sipping mint juleps. When Mary saw him approaching, she visibly sighed. Needless to say, Dr. Lawrence was oblivious.

"Miss Handley, I'd like to apologize for our earlier altercation and invite you to have a drink with me and my good friend Austin Corbin."

"I'm sorry, Dr. Lawrence, but I do have a pressing engagement."

"We won't take much of your time. Fifteen minutes at the most."

Mary could see he was not going to give up. She decided it would take much less energy to acquiesce and spend a few minutes with them than to argue the point. More importantly, she didn't want to call attention to herself. Someone might ask why she was there.

"Austin Corbin, Mary Handley."

Corbin rose. "How nice to meet you, Miss Handley. Please join us. Chester has been talking nonstop about you."

"Chester, is it?" said Mary as she sat. "I'd use 'Dr. Lawrence' whenever I could."

Dr. Lawrence laughed. "See what I mean, Austin? She's an absolute pistol." Corbin also laughed. Their tone was condescending, as if they were saying, *How cute it is that this woman dares to be so cheeky.*

"Can I get you something to drink, Miss Handley?"

"Yes, thank you," she replied, and Corbin summoned the waiter. Mary never responded well to condescension, so she looked at their leafy summer drinks and decided to make a direct assault upon their masculinity.

"I'll have a whiskey. Neat, please."

"Neat? That's awfully strong," cautioned Dr. Lawrence.

"It's all I drink." It wasn't, but they had sounded the call to arms.

"Did you get some nice pictures of my hotel?" Corbin asked.

Mary had almost forgotten she was carrying the camera.

"Yes, yes, beautiful property. I was on my way down to take some photographs of the amusement area, too."

"Make sure you stay far away from the Gut. It's no place for a decent woman."

"Really?"

"There's a seedy element. You know, Negroes and other types."

"I was under the impression Negroes weren't welcome there."

"They're not welcome, but they're not forbidden," said Dr. Lawrence. "There is a significant difference."

"So you contend they go there not to have a good time but just to make white people uncomfortable?"

"I contend they have no sense of boundaries, like that Mr. Berk today."

Mary's drink arrived and she downed it in one large gulp. "I'll have another and please leave the bottle next time."

"There's no sense in arguing with Chester about the Gut. He's there all the time and knows all about it."

"I'm surprised, Dr. Lawrence, that you, of all people, would want to mix with inferior types."

"Being a doctor, I'm curious what makes these people tick."

"What kind of doctor are you?"

"My specialty is endocrinology, but my main focus the last number of years has been a study, a scientific one devoid of the bleeding-heart claptrap found in Jacob Riis's *How the Other Half Lives*."

"In Riis's book, there are actual pictures of the squalor in lower Manhattan. Is it your contention that he staged them?"

"I wouldn't put it past that Jew," said Corbin.

"Lutheran," said Mary.

"What?"

"Riis. He's a Lutheran from Denmark."

Corbin turned to Dr. Lawrence. "We really need to limit who's allowed to come into the country. Some sort of vetting would be nice."

"Why don't we limit immigration to only wealthy white men who are content with their homeland?" Mary quipped. "That ought to put a significant dent in the rolls."

The waiter returned with another whiskey for Mary and left the bottle. She smiled. "Thank you." She quickly downed the second whiskey, then poured herself a third.

"Be careful, Miss Handley," warned Corbin. "You're drinking potent stuff."

"Nothing to be concerned about. You know what they say about us. 'Irish' is synonymous with 'whiskey.' Or is it 'potatoes'? Oh, well." She downed the third drink.

Anxious to discuss his work, Dr. Lawrence turned to Mary. "In my study, I'm more concerned with the why. For instance, I find it fascinating how Negroes compensate for their lack of brain power by immersing themselves in the pursuit of pleasure."

"Yes, I've noticed how being dragged over here as slaves, then being denied a proper education and decent job opportunities have made them such a fun people."

"It's all for the best. Having smaller brains, they're built for manual labor."

"If you're referring to the study by Dr. Samuel Morton, the only small brain present there was his." She poured a fourth drink.

Corbin jumped in. "You can't seriously believe those animals are our equals?"

She gestured toward their surroundings. "You obviously do."

"Either the drink has impaired your thinking or you're filled with mindless female jabber. I'm leaning toward the latter."

Mary defiantly downed her fourth drink and poured a fifth. "This beautiful hotel, which you spent millions to build, is designed in a Moorish style. Moors are black and personae non gratae here. So that begs the question: are you hypocritical or just plain stupid? I'm leaning toward the latter."

Corbin stiffened as Mary gulped her fifth drink and then stood. She was a bit wobbly but did her best to present a sober appearance. "Thank you for the whiskey and for tolerating my mindless female jabber. Good day, gentlemen."

Mary walked off as steady and as straight as she could manage, then Dr. Lawrence turned to Corbin and commented, "Well, that wasn't much fun, was it?"

"Fun? I say, Chester, I'm beginning to worry about you."

"How so?"

"One moment you're a serious scientist, and the next—well, I was in the office late last night when I saw you come in with blood on your shirt."

Dr. Lawrence paused for a moment, then burst into laughter. "Austin, my good friend, it wasn't blood you saw but rather cheap red wine a jockey spilled on me in the Gut."

"A jockey? I would think it would be on your pants, not your shirt."

"He was standing on a stool making a toast."

This time Corbin joined Dr. Lawrence in his laughter.

"Thank God! I was afraid you were becoming like that person. You know, the one in that Stevenson book."

"*Dr. Jekyll and Mr. Hyde*?"

"Yes, exactly!"

The two of them laughed even harder as they picked up their drinks, clinked glasses, and sipped away. What Corbin completely missed was the look of relief on Dr. Lawrence's face that he had avoided a problem.

~

When Mary got to the train station, she found Harper Lloyd also there, waiting for the train. "Well, well, if it isn't the very secretive lady detective. Have you finished investigating whatever case you were on?"

She approached the smug reporter, intent on putting him in his place. Instead, she threw up all over him.

Mary felt terrible about the mess she had made. She got an old rag from the man who sold the train tickets and started wiping Harper's shirt. Needless to say, he was not happy.

"My God, Miss Handley, you are a walking catastrophe."

"Mary."

"Huh?"

"You might as well call me by my first name. We're a bit more familiar now."

Harper shook his head as Mary finished working on his shirt.

"I've cleaned as much as I possibly can. May I suggest you give me your shirt? I'll take it back to my apartment, wash it, then return it to you."

"And I'm supposed to walk around Brooklyn bare chested?"

"Don't tell me this is your only shirt?"

"The only one I'm wearing. I'm not in the habit of wearing two at a time, but maybe I should change that policy now that I've met you."

"I'm sorry. I'm still a bit wobbly from the whiskey."

"A drunkard, too. Makes for an interesting résumé."

"Not my norm. I was trying to show up a couple of rich bigots. A fruitless effort, I might add. People with those beliefs have thick heads."

"As opposed to people with your beliefs?"

"I admit to having a thick head, but I'm right." There was a pause, then they both laughed, cutting the tension. "Let's go to wherever you live, and I will wash your shirt there."

"That's really not necessary."

"I insist. I always correct my mistakes."

"That must leave you very little time for anything else."

The train arrived, and Mary decided to ignore his wisecrack. The smell emanating from Harper's shirt was strong, so the passengers in their car sat as far away from the two of them as possible. Some decided to change cars. It was uncomfortable for Harper and amusing to Mary. For his sake, she tried to stifle her grin.

Harper's apartment wasn't far from Mary's, about a half a mile, and it was about the same size as hers. That's where the similarities ended. It was completely utilitarian and spotlessly clean. There was a bed and a small dresser in the bedroom, where the main living area contained only a sofa and a desk with a chair. There was no dining table, so Mary reasoned that if he ate there at all, he dined at his desk.

"This is the apartment of a man who is rarely here," she said.

"To the contrary," he replied. "I am here quite often." He pointed to the typewriter on his desk. "This is where I write."

"Well then, this is an apartment of a man who—" Having soiled his shirt, she saw no reason to hurl an insult at him, so she changed course. "Needs his shirt washed."

Harper took off his shirt and put on a fresh one. To her surprise, he showed her to a wooden tub and washboard. He even had soap. She had pegged him for a man who took his clothes to a Chinese laundry and had fully expected to have to go to her apartment in order to properly wash it. She found that odd for a single man, then stopped herself. All her life, she had fought stereotypes about women and decided not to foist one upon a man. She filled the tub with water, added some soap, and started scrubbing.

"I should be done in no time," she said. Harper didn't respond. He was already engulfed in reading some typewritten pages. She was quiet for a while but found the silence to be uncomfortable. "Is that the article you're writing about Colleen?"

"Oh, no. Tit for tat and you go first. Is Walter's wife your client?"

"Absolutely not. She's my best friend."

"Then it's obviously Colleen's husband."

"You get only one. Time for the tat."

"I suppose that's fair." He indicated the pages. "This isn't about Colleen. I can't write about her or let anyone know about her until after the trial. And that goes for you, too."

"By now you should know I don't reveal secrets." She picked up his shirt. "Where's your clothesline?"

"Lay it on the sink. I'll take care of it."

As Mary did just that, she casually asked, "So, how did Walter find you?"

"He didn't. Choate had asked my friend Jacob Riis to get involved. He was too busy and he recommended me."

"Jacob Riis. I'm a great admirer of his."

"I'll tell Jacob. I'm sure he'll be absolutely thrilled."

"Are you aware that sarcasm often hides a little boy wanting to be hugged?"

"No little girls?"

"We're stronger and more direct."

"You couldn't have gotten that from your friend Austin Corbin."

Mary was embarrassed. "You saw me with that insufferable man."

He told Mary that he was through soon after she left and that the rest was lawyer work. He saw her on the way out. Mary related her conversation with Corbin and Dr. Lawrence.

"I'm not surprised at Corbin's lack of subtlety. I expect no less from the man who said—and I quote—'If this is a free country, why can't we be free of the Jews?' "

Mary couldn't help smiling. "Yes, I remember reading it in the newspaper. A total non sequitur. It defies any sense of logic."

"Did his friend Dr. Lawrence chew your ear off about his study?"

"You know him?"

"It's my business to know every loon in Brooklyn and New York."

"Why do wealthy white men feel the need to justify their privilege?"

"Pardon my French, but it's as clear as what's missing between their legs."

"That's an affront to women."

"Never thought of it that way. Sorry."

"Accepted. More accurately, it's because their tiny dicks are larger than their brains."

Harper reacted with mock affront. "Miss Handley, such raunchy language!" Then he began to laugh.

"Corbin thinks Lawrence is being brave by mixing with the riffraff in the Gut."

"He isn't all wrong. A Negro prostitute was killed there Thursday night."

Suddenly, Mary became serious. "Really?"

"The papers didn't carry it. I'm sure they thought she wasn't important enough to be newsworthy— What?"

"Nothing. I just realized I have to be somewhere. It was nice meeting you. Sorry about the shirt." She headed for the door.

"You can't leave. I've filled you with information, and you've told me nothing."

Mary turned, a twinkle in her eye. "And I thought it wouldn't hit you until I was gone."

He watched her as she left, impressed.

~

Edgar found out about Meg Parker's murder late that afternoon. News like that spread rapidly among the workers on the midway. Taking a break from getting pelted with balls by angry white people, Edgar could hear snippets of conversation about a murder as he strolled along, enjoying the ocean air. At first, he paid no attention to it. Violence was an everyday occurrence in Brooklyn. Murders were committed so frequently that Edgar, like most people in the world, had steeled himself against them. It's not that he was unsympathetic, but they were faceless people and taking time to mourn for them all would make it impossible to accomplish anything in life—and he wanted to accomplish a lot.

Then, through the gossip, through the fearful concerns for their own safety, the name Meg shot out from someone's mouth. He stopped, at first thinking he had misheard it. Then he heard it again . . . and again. But there were many Megs, and there was no reason why this one was necessarily his. He would find out. He had to.

Edgar went to Jess Carver, the man who ran the carousel. Jess knew everything that happened on the midway and all of Coney Island. He was a good listener and people liked to confide in him. While Jess was taking tickets and the band organ blasted out John Philip Sousa's march "Sound Off," Edgar tapped him on the shoulder.

"Who was killed here the other night?" Edgar asked.

The music had drowned out some of Edgar's words. "Hi, Edgar. Sorry, couldn't hear you."

He spoke louder. "I said, who was killed here the other night?"

"Oh, that." As Jess turned to tell Edgar what he knew, a young boy tried to sneak past him onto the carousel. Jess grabbed him. "A ticket or no ride. Get outta here before I call the cops." The boy scampered off as fast as he could and he proudly turned to Edgar. "Scared the daylights out of that one."

"Jess—"

"Right, the woman who was killed here."

"It *was* a woman?"

"Yeah, Meg. You probably know who she was. Everyone does. God knows she's been around for years."

"Meg who?"

"Huh?" asked Jess as he put his hand to his ear.

Edgar was almost shouting now. "Meg who?"

Jess shrugged. "Can't remember. You know, Meg, that old Negro prostitute. Guess the life finally got to her."

"Meg Parker?"

"Yeah, that's it. Meg Parker." At that point, the band organ had stopped while changing songs, and since Jess was practically shouting, "Meg Parker" rang out through the crowd as loud and clear as a siren. No one seemed to be affected by it except for Edgar and the few people who snickered at Jess's being caught yelling when it wasn't necessary.

Edgar stood there, motionless. It was only for a few seconds, but he no longer had any sense of time. It could have been minutes or hours. He was numb.

"Edgar. Edgar, are you all right?"

Edgar didn't answer. He slowly turned and started walking. He didn't know where he was going, but he needed to get away from the crowds. Soon he found himself on the sidewalk near the beach. His knees gave way and he sunk to the ground. As the band organ started playing Sousa's "O, My Country," the emotion swept over him—the sorrow, the regret, and the pain. By then Edgar was wailing.

The predominantly white people out for a stroll gave this crazy man a wide berth. They were afraid he might hurt them, and his color only increased their fear.

All his emotions gradually merged into one: a profound anger that soon became rage. Edgar now had a mission. He would find the man who killed Meg and get revenge.

On Sunday, Mary met Sean at Lilly's, a restaurant not far from Second Street Station, where he was on duty. There was plenty of overtime available for policemen, and since the death of his fiancée, Sean had taken as much as he could.

"You know," Sean mused after they ordered, "it wasn't too long ago that you'd come begging to me for lunch money."

"If it hurts your male pride, feel free to buy lunch."

"No, I kinda like being treated."

"So what did you find out?"

"Only her name, Meg Parker."

"Did you get the file?"

"That's the problem. It's sealed."

"Sealed? That doesn't make sense. Why would they seal a file on a murdered prostitute in Coney Island?"

"It's hard to understand everything they do. They must have their reasons."

"It also helps that their own men don't question it."

"I can see where this is going. Does it mean you're not buying lunch? Because if it does, I want to change my order."

Mary ignored Sean's humor. Too many thoughts were racing through her head. "I need you to do something else for me."

"I'm not stealing any records, Mary. My brother obligations stop there."

"I'd never ask you to steal. How could you say such a thing?"

"But. I know there's a but." There was a short pause. "Go ahead. You might as well have out with it."

"I need you to check the files of all the prostitutes who have been killed since Carrie Brown."

"Are you insane? That's over three years of cases."

"You didn't let me finish. I only want the files that have been sealed."

"So, you only want me to check the cases that I can't check?"

"Exactly. It would be wonderful if you could get me the names and the dates. Places would also be helpful."

"Just when I think I'm beginning to understand you—"

"Always keep them guessing."

"I'm not 'them.' I'm your brother."

"And that's why I'm sure you'll catch up. Until then, I'm treating you to Lilly's, your favorite restaurant."

The waiter arrived with steak and potatoes for Sean and a chicken salad for Mary. Sean's eyes lit up when he saw the steak, and he immediately started to carve away.

"I'm going to savor every morsel because in the long run I'm sure you're going to make me pay for every ounce and more."

Mary looked at him playfully. "Why, Sean, what a terrible thing to say about your favorite sister."

"You're my only sister," Sean replied with his mouth full. "That's why I have no choice."

Mary smiled. "I knew you'd catch on." Then she took her first bite of her chicken salad.

~

There were six Leo's Meats shops. Five were in Manhattan. The one in which Basem worked was the first in Brooklyn and the newest. It was a typical butcher shop with beef suspended from the walls on hooks, and a counter with smaller meats displayed covered by a glass shield.

Mary entered shortly after opening on Monday. She intended to catch a train to Matteawan that morning to speak with Ameer Ben Ali and she needed to see Basem first. The man behind the counter was wearing a butcher's apron. In his late thirties, he had a pleasant but nondescript face and was completely bald, the top of his head having the sheen of a cue ball. Some men grew facial hair to offset this look, but not this man. He seemed proud of it.

"Welcome to Leo's Meats. I'm Leo. How may I help you?"

"Funny. I had envisioned Leo would be in an office somewhere, managing the finances of his many holdings."

"I believe in the hands-on approach to business. I work in all my stores, and this being a new one, I will be here for a while."

"That's a very sound business philosophy. No wonder you've done so well."

Mary soon regretted those words. Thrilled with his success, Leo had the annoying habit of launching into his life story at the slightest provocation, sometimes with no provocation at all. He told Mary that he was penniless and orphaned at fourteen. Soon after he joined the Barnum and Bailey Circus as an acrobat and toured the world. Eventually, Leo saved up enough money to buy his first butcher shop. "I am a living example of the opportunities America gives a man if he is able and willing."

"Very impressive, and I know a little bit about the meat business. My father has worked in a butcher shop for thirty-two years."

"Which one?"

"Flanagan's, over on Fulton."

He nodded his head in recognition. "I've been looking at that shop. Flanagan is selling."

"Well, if you decide to add Flanagan's to your meat empire, rest assured that you won't find a better or harder worker than my father."

"If I do, I would love to have your father stay on. It's good business. I'm sure he knows all the customers."

"You're a smart man, Leo." She extended her hand. "I'm Mary Handley."

Leo wiped his hand on his apron, then shook Mary's. "Leo Cosgrove. Ah, Mary Handley. You're the female Sherlock Holmes who's helping Basem."

"I hope I can live up to that title. Have you read Arthur Conan Doyle?"

"I love everything literary, especially plays. I adore the theater."

"A butcher with a penchant for the arts. I'm even more pleased to meet you, Leo."

"Well then, before I disappoint"—Leo turned toward the back—"Basem, your detective is here."

Basem entered, his apron almost completely covered in red. There were some spots on his shirt, too. It made him look like he had been immersed in blood, so the smile on his face seemed incongruous. "It's good to see you, Mary. I'd shake your hand, but I'm afraid I'd get blood on you."

"It's not blood, Basem," Leo said. "It's a liquid that comes out of the animal's muscles. I don't know what it is but it doesn't have the same consistency or the same texture as blood." He turned to Mary. "I'm teaching Basem the business. I'm sure your father knows this."

Mary nodded her agreement, but she really didn't know. She'd always thought it was blood and was never curious enough to ask if it was anything different.

"So," Basem said, "what news do you bring?"

Before Mary could answer, a woman entered the store. Leo waved his hand. "Talk to Mary, Basem. I'll take care of this customer." Then Leo greeted the woman like he had Mary.

"You have a great boss," Mary whispered.

"Yes, I know. Like I said, he is very understanding." But Basem's mind wasn't on his boss. It was on his brother. He anxiously looked at Mary, hoping for a miracle.

"There's not much yet. I'm looking at the prostitutes who have been killed since Carrie Brown to see if there is a connection. It's nothing solid, just a hunch."

"You're the professional. Sometimes hunches work, right?"

"Sometimes they do and more often they don't. Basem, I am going up to Matteawan today to see your brother. It would be extremely helpful if you gave me a letter of introduction. I don't want to travel all the way up there just to be turned away by the institution or by your brother because neither one has heard of me."

"Like I told you, he doesn't know English very well."

"Then write it in Algerian Arabic. I'm sure he'll understand that." Mary had come prepared with paper and pen, and she handed both to Basem.

While he was writing the letter, she looked at Leo, who smiled back as he was helping his customer. She sincerely hoped he would buy Flanagan's. Then her father would keep his job, her mother would calm down about money, and they all could go back to their normal family insanity.

10

Matteawan, New York, and Fishkill Landing were two small towns close to one another about sixty miles from Manhattan. They were best known not for any industry but rather for nearby Mount Beacon, where, during the Revolutionary War, the patriots would set fires to warn George Washington if the British were coming. There was a movement afoot to merge the two towns into one city, but at the moment they remained separate.

The trip up on the Hudson River Railroad was pleasant enough and not too long. The Hudson River Railroad was owned by the Vanderbilt family, and it spurred Mary to reflect on the luxurious train trips she had taken with George Vanderbilt four years earlier. She had long since gotten over the disappointment of their broken engagement, but it did take a while. Even though she was the one who'd initiated it, she'd had to wait for her emotions to catch up with her intellectual reasoning.

The train station was in Fishkill Landing, and Mary took a trolley to Matteawan, which was only about a mile and a half away. Since Ameer Ben Ali had been transferred to a hospital for the criminally insane, his condition weighed heavily on Mary's mind. She didn't tell Basem, but she viewed his letter more as a device. If he was presently living in some fantasy world, maybe the letter would momentarily shake him into a reality where he could answer some questions. Maybe. It was possible he had shut down all communications and nothing could be done.

The letter gained her entrance, and Mary was ushered into an activity room where everything seemed quite peaceful. Patients were at various tables, some reading, others playing checkers or cards. One heavyset woman sat in a chair knitting while she gazed out at the grounds. Matteawan was a model institution that engaged patients in farmwork, cooking, and other normal activities as part of their therapy.

In no time, Ameer was escorted in by a muscular male nurse and sat down at her table. He looked different than the sketches Mary had seen of him during his trial. He now had a full, straggly beard and longish hair, which gave him the appearance of a crazy man. The male nurse stood behind Ameer. Mary looked up at him.

"Can we have some privacy please?"

"I don't think that's wise, madam."

"I'll be fine. Thank you."

"Do you know what this man did?"

"I know what they say he did, and I'm perfectly capable of taking care of myself."

He raised his hands as if surrendering. "I warned you." He pointed. "I'll be in the corner, just a scream away." He went to the spot he had indicated, folded his arms, and waited.

Mary turned back to Ameer, who uttered his first words: "Who are you?"

"Your brother Basem sent me." She gave him the letter and as he read it, she studied his face. His unkempt appearance betrayed a deeper problem. As she looked into his eyes, she saw a man who had given up hope, or rather had had it beaten out of him. Neither necessarily meant that he was innocent. It could have meant that he felt great sorrow and despair over the consequences of his actions. She needed to find out.

Ameer looked up from the letter. His English was marginal, and he had learned to speak slowly and deliberately. "How is Basem?"

"He's very concerned about you or he wouldn't have hired me."

Ameer shook his head. "But how is he?"

"What do you mean?"

Frustrated, he mumbled in Algerian Arabic before slamming his fist on the table. The loud sound prompted the male nurse to head in their direction. Mary saw him coming and waved him away. Ameer cooled off as quickly as he had gotten mad.

"Sorry. My English no good."

She spoke slowly. "It's much better than my Arabic or my French. Try. I will help."

"Basem not happy with America when he leave. Now he is back."

"He came back to help you, and he is fine. Basem has a good job." Ameer seemed to absorb this information and accept it. Mary decided to move forward. She needed to find out his version of what happened the night Carrie Brown was killed, without the pressure of a trial. She hoped she would hear something that would be helpful. She doubted it, but she had to try.

~

As Alexander "Clubber" Williams entered Second Street Station, hushed whispers shot through the halls announcing his arrival. Everyone wondered who he was there to see and why, each one hoping it wasn't them. He had openly taken bribes and mercilessly beaten people, including a fellow policeman, yet every time he was brought up on charges his guardian angels on the Board of Police Commissioners saw that he was set free. Even though the Lexow Committee was currently investigating him for police corruption, the prevailing feeling was that he'd once again avoid any punishment. Williams strutted up to the desk sergeant, Billy O'Brian, a pleasant Irishman who was pushing sixty and loved his work; he vowed that they'd have to carry him out on a stretcher. Billy was afraid of no one.

"Where can I find Sean Handley?"

Billy had known Sean and Mary Handley since they were children, and if he wasn't a second father to them, he definitely had uncle status.

"Why are you lookin' for Sean?"

"None of your business."

"That's not very sociable of ya, Alex."

"I'm not the social type. You should know that by now, old man."

"Yer not exactly a young whippersnapper yerself."

"Button it."

"Oooh, sent the shivers right through me." He mimed shaking from the cold, then continued. "Now, why do ya want Sean?"

Williams was frustrated. "Ahh, I'll find him myself." He then turned around and started shouting. "Handley. Sean Handley, get out here. I'm lookin' for you."

"Might be a good thing to add who ya are. Just so he knows."

"Everyone knows who I am."

"Sometimes it's hard to hear through all that wind and bluster."

Williams had had enough of Billy. He frowned, turned openly toward the rest of the police station, and shouted, "Sean Handley, get your arse out here. Alexander Williams is lookin' for you."

Hushed whispers of Sean's name whipped through the halls of the station like the hissing of a snake. Pretty soon Sean stepped out of one of the back offices and faced Williams.

"Are you looking for me, Captain Williams?"

Billy turned to Williams and shrugged. "All ya had to do."

Sean welcomed Williams into his office, a tiny box with just enough room for a small desk and chair.

Williams looked around the room, then said mockingly, "They must think an awful lot of you here, Handley."

"How can I be of service to you, sir?"

"You can answer me one question. What the hell do you think you're doin'?"

"Excuse me. Doing what, sir?"

"Don't play coy with me, boy. I've been 'round the block and then some."

"If you could just tell me—"

"You've been requesting files of murder cases that aren't yours and not even under your jurisdiction."

"Oh, that."

"Yes, that," Williams said, then jiggled the infamous club at his side, an obvious intimidation tactic. "Speak up. Let's hear it."

Sean had already rehearsed what he was going to say if someone asked him a question like this, so he had prepared an answer. Still, Williams made him nervous. He made most people nervous. "Well, you see, Captain, I heard about the Margaret Parker murder—"

"Meg Parker."

"Meg Parker. Of course. I wanted to see if there was any evidence in other prostitute murders that might connect the murders and help us find the killer."

"There's no connection."

"You already found that out?"

"I said so, didn't I? Do you not have enough work here, Handley? I can give you more. Speak with your captain, have you walking a beat again."

"That won't be necessary, Captain Williams. I have no more interest in the Meg Parker case."

Williams leaned toward Sean, his hand on the top of his club. "You sure?"

"Positive."

"Smart boy, Handley." He patted Sean on the back and opened the door. "Learn how to play team ball and next time I see you, maybe you'll have a real office instead of a rat hole."

"I don't have an office. I'm using Bailey's while he's on vacation."

"Not good enough for a rat hole." Williams shook his head, and his loud, bellowing laugh echoed through the halls as he left.

~

It took time and patience for Mary to extract information from Ameer, but it did result in a possible lead or two. He maintained that he was with a Spanish woman named Maryann Lopez that infamous night and the person with Carrie Brown was a blond-haired man with a mustache. He was adamant that Maryann had lied on the witness stand when she had testified that she wasn't with him and he had no idea why. He also didn't know how Carrie Brown's blood and the contents of her stomach got on his shirt or in his room. He had come home drunk, passed out, and the next thing he knew he was being arrested.

Ameer might have been lying, but his bewilderment and frustration seemed sincere. Mary decided to verify his story. At least she now had something to verify.

"Ameer, how did you get from Sing Sing to here?"

He looked her in the eye and innocently replied, "The train."

"No, no, no," said Mary, holding in her urge to laugh. "I meant why did they move you?"

"Ah, why." Ameer scratched his beard as he thought. "I'm different. Different not good in America. Worse in prison. Get beaten every day. If I stay, I die."

"So you faked being insane?"

Ameer nodded. "It better here. Not good but better." He paused as Mary watched a deep sadness come over him.

"You've run into some bad luck. We're not all like that, Ameer."

"I want to go home." His eyes welled up and he began to cry before burying his head in his arms on the table, every once in a while mumbling, "*Allah yusaeiduni*," which meant "God help me" in Arabic.

Though Ameer's tears were real, it didn't necessarily mean he was innocent. He could have been a good actor, or profoundly sorry for the murder he committed, or merely upset over the consequences he was suffering. Regardless, his pain was compelling, and Mary was moved. She promised him she would do everything she could to get at the truth. He was very grateful; blessing her through his tears as the muscular male nurse led him away.

Mary slowly rose and looked at her watch. Because they were made for women, they were called wristlets. Pocket watches were thought to be more masculine, so few men wore watches on their wrists. Mary didn't care about image. It would be inconvenient to dig into her pocketbook whenever she wanted to know the time, so the wristlet worked for her. Having checked the train schedule, she knew that there was a train due into Fishkill Landing bound for Manhattan in about an hour. Her work was done, and she decided she might as well make her way to the station. On the way out, she heard a familiar voice.

"Mary, it's so good to see you."

Mary turned and was astonished at what she saw. The heavyset woman whom she had seen from behind earlier, the one who was knitting, had risen from her chair and was facing her. Though she had put on twenty-five or thirty pounds, she recognized the woman immediately. Mary had known her as Kate Stoddard, though she had eventually discovered her real name was Lizzie King. They used to be very good friends. Six years earlier, they had worked in the same hat factory and had lived in the same building. During Mary's first detective case, she'd discovered that Lizzie was a killer, and she was sentenced without a trial to the State Hospital for the Criminally Insane at Auburn. Mary had heard they had recently transferred many of the patients at Auburn to Matteawan. She was convinced that, unlike Ameer, Lizzie's insanity was very real.

"Hello, Lizzie. You're looking well."

"You're looking well, too."

"Thank you." There was a moment of silence where Mary wasn't sure what to say. Finally she spoke, "I expect you're getting some good help."

"Oh, I am, lots of it."

Mary had always known that deep down, underneath whatever sickness had taken over Lizzie's mind, there still existed that sweet country girl from Haddonfield, New Jersey, who was innocent, optimistic, and her good friend. She hoped that Lizzie was on her way back to becoming that girl.

"I'm so happy to hear that. I'm sure that one day they'll declare you cured and you'll be set free."

"It'll be a lot sooner than we both think."

"That's wonderful, Lizzie. Have your parents been able to visit?"

"Her mother is very supportive," a broad-shouldered female attendant named Wendy interjected as she was passing by. "She's visited three times in the three months Lizzie has been here. Hasn't she, Lizzie?"

Lizzie nodded, smiling.

"And now she has you visiting her. Pretty soon they're going to be lining up, Lizzie." Wendy looked at Mary as if to say, *See how well she's doing?* and continued on her way.

"It was so good to see you. Now, if you'll excuse me, I'm sorry but I have to catch a train." Mary extended her hand and they shook.

Just as Mary turned to go, Lizzie stopped her. "Mary, remember that conversation we had when we last saw each other?" As Mary raced through her mind to remember, Lizzie continued in a matter-of-fact tone.

"I am going to kill you."

Mary had definitively found out that Colleen was not having an affair, and it was time to let her husband know. She met Brian on Tuesday morning, the day after she returned from Matteawan, at a coffee shop in downtown Brooklyn.

"Are you sure?" Brian asked.

"Positive. I followed her everywhere and nothing led to an affair," Mary replied.

"Then why is she acting so strange?"

Mary knew why but couldn't tell him. "Brian, I don't have a crystal ball into your relationship. Have you tried sitting Colleen down and having an honest heart-to-heart talk?"

"You're joking."

"Not in the least. Talk to her, Brian. Ask her what's going on. No accusations: just tell her that you love her and that you're afraid you're losing her."

"Mary, I can't—"

"It's the truth. Tell her."

There was an uncomfortable silence as Brian tried to digest Mary's advice. Then he said, "How much do I owe you?"

"Nothing. You're friends of the family."

"Really?"

"Really. Just promise me you'll speak with Colleen."

"I'll try, Mary. Maybe not exactly what you said but I'll try."

At this point, Harper Lloyd arrived at their table with his tongue firmly implanted in his cheek. "Well, if it isn't the extraordinarily famous detective Mary Handley, sitting at a coffee shop with us common folk."

"I'd never think of you as common, Harper Lloyd. Possibly trashy, but never common."

Harper looked at Brian. "She's too good. I can never compete with her."

Brian started to rise. "Well, I have to be going."

"Mary, where are your manners? Aren't you going to introduce me to your friend?"

As Mary hesitated, Brian stuck out his hand. "Brian Murphy, nice to meet you."

They shook. "Harper Lloyd, nice to meet you, Mr. Murphy." Then he turned toward Mary with an impish glint in his eye. "Very nice."

Brian thanked Mary for her help and left as Harper sat down in his chair.

"Okay, now you know who my client was. Gloat away to your heart's content."

"Is it any consolation that I had already figured it out, and because I thoroughly investigate my stories, I knew who he was before we were introduced?"

"Absolutely none. I hate being transparent."

"So do I. Let's just call it a draw: one for you and one for me."

"This is my business, Harper Lloyd, not some baseball game."

"Good, because baseball games rarely end in a draw, and I'm not looking to declare a winner."

"What are you looking for?"

"In spite of your tendency to discharge the contents of your stomach on innocent bystanders—"

"Not so innocent."

"I probably deserve that. Anyhow, you mentioned a fascination with Jacob Riis. I'm meeting him tomorrow night for dinner. Would you like to join us? Provided, that is, that you refrain from disgorging yourself on him."

"You've used that joke once too often."

"Sorry. I'm told I have a tendency to do that."

"And I have a tendency to point it out."

"So, what is your reply?"

"First things first. Is this your roundabout way of asking me for a date?"

"I don't see it as roundabout at all. It's quite straightforward. Do you or don't you?"

Mary elongated his question. ". . . Want to go out on a date with you?"

"Yes, yes, it's most definitely a date."

"That wasn't so hard, was it?"

"I once had a tooth pulled. That was easier."

Mary couldn't help laughing. In spite of how they'd started out, Harper Lloyd seemed smart and witty and it didn't hurt that she found him attractive.

"Okay, Harper Lloyd, it's a date."

"Great. One favor though: please call me by my first name."

"Which one, Harper or Lloyd?"

"I see there's no statute of limitations on your jests."

"I don't think I'll ever tire of it."

Harper smiled. "Would it be all right if I pick you up at seven o'clock?"

Mary responded that it was, and always having a pencil and paper in her pocketbook, she wrote down her address and gave it to him. He stood.

"Before you go," Mary said, "I have one last question for you. I know you didn't accidentally bump into us here. How did that come about?"

"Don't worry. Your detective instincts are intact. I didn't follow you. . . . I followed him."

"Ah, thank you."

"Now, answer me one last question. Do you put all men who ask you out on a date through the same rigorous torture which you just made me suffer?"

Mary looked up at him until their eyes met. "Only the ones I like."

Her spirit intrigued him.

~

Thomas Byrnes was not a fan of classical music or opera, and thus rarely had any desire to go to Carnegie Hall. But on this day, he had been summoned by Andrew Carnegie, and when Carnegie requested his presence, he knew it wasn't merely a request.

The philharmonic orchestra was rehearsing Beethoven's Ninth Symphony as Byrnes entered. All the seats in the hall were empty except for the one occupied by Carnegie in the middle of the last row, where he was humming and waving his right hand as if he were conducting, slowly and more in reverence than in enthusiasm. Byrnes made his way to him and sat, leaving a seat between him and Carnegie to avoid an errant slap in the face in case the steel magnate's conducting suddenly became more frenetic.

Byrnes was about to speak when Carnegie signaled him to remain silent. Carnegie held music in high esteem and refused to spoil it with talk. They remained there a full five minutes without uttering a word until finally the orchestra took a break.

"Beautiful piece, simply magnificent," said Carnegie.

"Yes, quite lovely. Now—"

"Gustav Mahler is currently working on it. Making improvements, he says. I ask you, how do you improve on perfection?"

"Seems . . . futile."

"Good point, Tom. Destructive, too. People with massive egos can do a lot of damage in this world. They must be stopped."

Coming from Carnegie, it was at the very least ironic, but Byrnes only smiled inwardly.

"Do you know why you're here?" Carnegie asked.

"Ya asked me to come."

"That doesn't answer why."

"I figure yer'll tell me. Yer not one to waste time."

"That I'm not. No, that I am not." He reached down under his seat, came up with a thick stack of letters, and handed them to Byrnes. "Death threats, dozens of them. Can you imagine? People want me dead." As Byrnes glanced at the letters, Carnegie continued, "Where have you been? I left two messages for you. Did you not get them?"

"I did. I was busy, and they didn't sound urgent."

"Are you not satisfied with our arrangement?"

"I'm very satisfied, sir."

The expression on Carnegie's face was enough. Byrnes didn't need Carnegie to clarify his threat with words. "I'll get on it right away. I'm pretty sure ya have nothin' to worry about. Probably a bunch of crackpots."

"Like the anarchist crackpot who attacked Henry?" Henry Clay Frick was Carnegie's partner at Carnegie Steel. Two years before, a confirmed anarchist named Alexander Berkman had barged into Frick's offices, shot him three times, and stabbed him several more. Miraculously, Frick survived and Berkman was now in jail.

"If you like, I know some very good men, and I can get you protection."

"No. I refuse to live like Jay Gould. For a year after the Russell Sage bombing, he hid in that fortress of his, wearing a disguise whenever he dared to venture out. He lasted only a year, and mark my words. The fear had as much to do with his death as the tuberculosis."

"I'll find out who's behind these." He held up the letters, hoping that was his exit line. It wasn't.

"Don't these people know I'm giving all of my money to charity? I'm their friend, not their enemy."

Carnegie had written "The Gospel of Wealth" five years earlier, in which he proposed the theory that people who spend their lives accumulating great wealth should spend their latter years donating it to charitable causes. Even though he was still working, he was already putting that plan into action, backing up his words.

Byrnes knew that Carnegie's rationalization involved skewed logic. He had destroyed scores of people with his ruthless business practices over the years. The families of workers who were killed when he sent in armed Pinkertons to crush a strike didn't care if he made token contributions. But Byrnes would never mention these thoughts. He liked their arrangement.

"Dontcha worry. Yer no Jay Gould. I'll get the fellas behind this."

"Thank you, Tom."

They shook hands and Byrnes stood up. "Can't have anything happen to America's greatest benefactor, can we?"

The orchestra was returning from its break, and Byrnes left with the letters in his hands. They were most probably from many different people, which presented him with a problem. How the hell was he ever going to satisfy Andrew Carnegie?

12

Maryann Lopez was a dead end. Finding her was easy enough. All Mary had to do was to go to the lower Manhattan area where the East River Hotel was located and ask around. Many of the locals knew Maryann, and one of them was able to point Mary to the flophouse where she frequently stayed. Mary had found her outside that flophouse sharing a bottle of cheap whiskey with her friend Solly. To Maryann, a friend was defined as anyone who could raise enough money to share the cost of a bottle. A close friend was someone who had his own bottle and invited her to share. Solly was somewhere in between. Drunk as they were at ten in the morning, they boldly announced that Maryann had traded sex for booze. Both seemed happy about it.

The life had taken its toll on Maryann. Besides having a hacking cough that conjured up a bloody mucus symptomatic of several serious illnesses, she had trouble remembering the day before, much less three years earlier. Ameer's name didn't ring a bell and neither did Carrie Brown's. It didn't matter whether she might eventually remember their names or what might happen if Mary could catch her in a sober moment. No court would ever grant an appeal based on the word of a drunk. Mary had responsibly suggested that Maryann see a doctor, and had gotten the response she had expected. She could still hear their bellowing laughter when Mary was a block away and on her way to the East River Hotel.

Mary's expectations were not high. Her hope was that the scene of the Carrie Brown murder might reveal something. She had no idea what that might be, but it had to be better than what she currently had, which was nothing.

The hotel catered to people who were spiraling downward or had already hit bottom. Because it had a bar on the ground floor that turned into a lively honky-tonk at night, some people called it a resort, which was an extremely kind description. Most of the people who slinked upstairs to the rooms during the night were either prostitutes with their johns, those who were too drunk to go home, or those who were down on their luck and could only afford the seedy, rundown rattrap that was the East River Hotel.

As luck would have it, and this was the first bit of it Mary had encountered, Eddie Harrington, the same clerk who was there in 1891 when the murder took place, had kept his job. Daytime was always slow, and he was more than happy to escape the dreariness of his job in order to show Mary around. She had told him she was a private detective, and that had made it even more exciting for him. The Carrie Brown murder was the hotel's one brush with fame. It had become their own personal tourist site, and his behavior was not unlike that of a guide at the Statue of Liberty. When he got to room

31, he went into his speech about Carrie Brown with a theatrical flair.

"This is the room where Carrie Brown was slaughtered that terrible night back in 1891. Old Shakespeare didn't deserve such a fate. In case you didn't know, that's what they called her: Old Shakespeare, because she loved to recite the bard."

"That's fascinating." Mary would have loved to have told him to skip the tourist rhetoric and just open the door, but the last thing she wanted was to offend him. She would have questions to ask, and she wanted him primed and ready.

Harrington opened the door. "There have been rumors that Old Shakespeare once had a husband and children, lived a respectable life until demon drink took over. For a full year after the murder, people would request this room, wanting to stay in the place where Carrie Brown had spent her last night." They stepped inside.

The room wasn't any different than what she had expected. It could have been one of any number of rooms in that type of establishment. There was a rickety old bed, a small chipped dresser, and a slightly rusted sink with a threadbare towel hanging on a hook next to it. A door hid a tiny closet on the wall opposite the bed.

"I understand you found the body."

"Yes, it was awful," said Harrington, playing on the melodrama as if he was reliving it. "There was poor Old Shakespeare. It looked like she had been gutted, disemboweled, body parts everywhere, and her eyes—her eyes wide open as if still in disbelief."

"It must have been awful."

"'Awful' would be mild," he replied with increasing intensity. "It was disastrous, catastrophic, apocalyptic. And then—then I saw the cross etched into her thigh." He turned toward Mary in true ham actor form. "The sign of the Ripper."

The Jack the Ripper controversy was Mary's main hope in proving Ameer's innocence. If, in an attempt to make good on his boast about Jack the Ripper, Thomas Byrnes rushed to judgment, then maybe, just maybe, Ameer really was innocent. But she was well aware that so far there was no evidence to prove such an allegation and she needed something very solid in order to go up against Byrnes.

Mary turned back toward the open door and pointed across the narrow hallway to room 33. "And that was the killer's room, Ameer Ben Ali?"

"Yes. If I had known he was capable of such a dastardly deed—"

"Ameer Ben Ali wasn't a violent person?"

"He stayed here a lot and did get into his share of scuffles, but never anything that could suggest a savage murder."

"From the carnage you describe, it's easy to see how there was a blood trail from this room to Mr. Ali's."

"Yes."

Harrington's behavior had changed. Instead of his multiword, expansive answers, this was a mere one word, and said in a clipped tone. There was something he was hiding.

"You did see the blood, didn't you?"

"Of course."

"It must have been very telling—a thick trail of blood from Miss Brown's room to Mr. Ali's, blood on the doorknob of his door—"

"To be truthful, Miss Handley, I never saw any blood."

"But you just said she was disemboweled. How could—"

"In this room, yes. It was covered in blood, but I saw nothing in the hallway and definitely nothing on Ameer Ben Ali's doorknob."

"But how could that be? All that blood and Ameer Ben Ali didn't carry any over to his room. I could swear I read that at the trial there were traces—"

"I didn't say there wasn't any blood. I said I didn't see any. Mr. Byrnes explained that I was obviously at a heightened emotional state and may have missed certain details."

"Really, Mr. Byrnes suggested it?"

"Yes. Makes sense, too," Harrington replied, nodding his head. "I was down at the police station for hours. I felt like I was going through his famous third degree. Imagine me, a killer. Impossible, I don't have the stomach for it." He shuddered.

"I know exactly what you mean. I don't either." Mary paused. "Didn't Carrie Brown—excuse me, Old Shakespeare—have a visitor that night?"

"Yes, C. Nick, a blond-haired man with a mustache."

"What does the C stand for?"

"I have no idea. At this establishment, I'm lucky if they sign in at all."

Mary was finished with her questions and was soon on her way. No reason to dawdle. A little bit of the East River Hotel went a long way. She did feel better about the possibility of Ameer's being innocent. Maybe there was no blood trail from Carrie Brown's room to Ameer's and either the police investigators had tracked the blood across later or it was planted. She now had something to work on. The problem was, how was she going to prove any of it and how was she ever going to find C. Nick?

~

The Home for the Incurables, formerly St. Barnabas Hospital, on Third Avenue and 183rd Street, was established in 1866. Despite being built with the best of intentions, the home was crowded and had fallen into disrepair. Since the bombing in 1891 at Russell Sage's office, William R. Laidlaw couldn't work and was in constant pain. For a while, his sisters supported him, but they could no longer foot the bill, which was why he was now residing in the Home for the Incurables and would continue to do so unless he was blessed with a windfall. At that moment, his only possible windfall had Russell Sage's name on it.

Laidlaw was wheeled into the crowded activity room in his wheelchair by his nurse Emily. Waiting for them were Choate and Walter. Choate greeted him with a cheery disposition.

"How are you feeling, William?"

"Do you really want to know?"

"Let's save that for later. We have matters to discuss. Let's go for a stroll." He looked at Emily. "We'll return him to you shortly."

"You don't need to bother. I'll push him. It's my job."

"Take a break. You've earned it."

"I've just come back from one."

"Be my guest. Take another."

"I really don't mind."

"But he does, Emily," Laidlaw interjected. They all looked at him. "I'm just stating the obvious."

Emily relented, Choate took over, and Laidlaw, Choate, and Walter headed outside, where there was an absence of plant life or anything green and it was still quite warm even though it was late in the afternoon. Laidlaw was the first to speak.

"What's the bad news?"

"Who said I have bad news?" Choate answered with another question.

"It's all over your face. You have that Joseph Hodges Choate glum look."

"Okay, is this any better?" Choate smiled broadly.

"Oh, God no! You look like a circus clown, a very unconvincing one."

"Then let's start at the beginning. William, I want you to meet Walter Cooper."

Choate turned the wheelchair so that Laidlaw was facing Walter, who stuck out his hand. "How do you do, Mr. Laidlaw?"

"How do you think I am? I'm broke, in agony, and living in this dump. Besides that, everything's just peachy."

"All right," Choate said. "Get it all out, William, all the venom, because until you settle down, we can't discuss business."

Laidlaw paused and took a deep breath. After a few seconds, he said, "I'm sorry, Mr. Cooper. With everything that's happened in the last few years, it sometimes becomes too much. We win, we get reversed, we win again, and we get reversed again. I feel like I'm living on a seesaw."

"It's perfectly understandable, Mr. Laidlaw. You've shown amazing fortitude and drive. I doubt whether I would hold up as well under your circumstances."

"You would. What other choice is there?"

Choate began pushing Laidlaw again. "You remember when I told you that there might come a time when I'd have to step back for a bit?"

"Oh, my God, you're dropping me!"

"William—"

"What am I going to do? This, for the rest of my life. I can't do it. I just can't do it!"

"Stop the dramatics, William, I am not, repeat, am not dropping you and never will."

Laidlaw tried to pull himself together. "Okay, then what is going on?"

"I have been asked to argue a case before the Supreme Court in the hope that I will get them to throw out the income tax act that was passed last month. It's an important case that will affect a lot of good people and will take considerable preparation."

"Okay, so if you're not dropping me, what does this mean?"

"It means I have brought Walter on to help out. He is a terrific lawyer with a great record, and I'd trust him with any of my cases."

"Well, that's easy then. Have him do the tax case, and you stay with me."

"I am staying with you and will continue to be the lead counsel. Walter will report to me everything that is going on, and I will have my input. I just can't be present as often as I have been."

Laidlaw put his head down. "I understand."

"Mr. Laidlaw," Walter said as he got in front of the wheelchair, stopping its forward progress. "I am a good lawyer, a very good lawyer. Mr. Choate and I have spent days deposing your new witness, and I assure you, once she gets on the stand, I could be the worst lawyer in the world and you'd win this case going away."

Laidlaw looked up at Walter. "Are you a racehorse enthusiast?"

"Huh?"

"You used the term 'going away.' It's a racehorse expression."

"No, I don't like to gamble, but there's one thing you should know. I'd bet on your case all day long."

Laidlaw turned to Choate. "You should have brought him around sooner. I'd have fired you a long time ago."

They all shared a laugh, and Choate guided the wheelchair back toward the building as the conversation turned to the mundane. Walter wasn't used to boasting, and he knew he shouldn't have made such a strong proclamation. But he knew he had Sage. He could feel it.

There were considerable afternoon shadows, but if they had looked they would have seen the outline of Emily standing at a window staring out at them.

13

It was midafternoon when Mary entered Lazlo's Books, seeking the peace and quiet of her office in order to ascertain her next move. The store seemed empty until she heard laughter from what sounded like two people coming from the back. One person was clearly Lazlo, who rarely laughed. When he did, it was open, full throttle, and loud, so there was no mistaking it.

"Lazlo, you devil, consider putting a cap on your laugh unless you want to awaken every baby in the neighborhood."

He emerged from the back still chuckling, but mildly. By his side was the lady browser Mary had met a few days before who clearly had her sights set on him.

"Can you believe it, Mary? Gerta here has the same fascination as I do with my triumvirate."

Mary knew all about Lazlo's triumvirate. It consisted of Benjamin Franklin, Lord Byron, and Aristotle, three men whom he idolized for their respective brilliance. Her instincts told her that Gerta's fascination with it, real or not, paled in comparison to her fascination with him. But why put a damper on what she viewed as genuine feelings?

"Isn't that lovely? Two peas and so forth. Gerta, it's a pleasure to meet you. Mary Handley." Mary stuck out her hand and Gerta shook it.

"It's a pleasure to meet you, too, Mary. Lazlo brags about you all the time."

"All the time, huh?" Mary responded with a smile on her face. She had been busy with her case and hadn't realized that Lazlo and Gerta had been spending that much time together.

"Not all the time," said Lazlo. "I'm not a gusher."

"Don't worry, Lazlo," said Mary. "Your reputation as a malcontent is safe with me. My lips are sealed."

Gerta joined in. "So are mine."

At that point, Sean entered the shop. "Mary, I'm glad you're here." He then spotted Lazlo and Gerta. "Hello, Lazlo and . . ."

"Gerta," volunteered Gerta.

"Nice to meet you. Mary, can you spare a few minutes?"

When they were alone in Mary's office, Sean unloaded what was on his mind.

"I got an unscheduled visit from Clubber Williams."

"Because of my request?"

"He only knows it's from me, but it wouldn't take a genius to determine that you might be involved."

"I don't want you to get in trouble, Sean. Time to cease and desist."

"I've already done that. Clubber thinks it's at his request, but in reality it's because I've already gotten all the information I'm able to get from sealed cases. Your instincts were correct. There is a pattern." Sean handed her a piece of paper with the information. "After Carrie Brown was murdered, there were five more that year in lower Manhattan, five the next in Long Island City, and then five more the following year in upper Manhattan. Meg Parker was the first this year, and I guess that means we're due for four more."

"And all in Coney Island," Mary added as she studied Sean's paper. "Your writing is not easy to decipher. Very much like chicken scratchings."

"I had to do everything quickly. I could have been caught."

She pointed to the paper. "What is this?"

"A nine."

"And this?"

"Thirty."

"One more."

"An eight."

"Thank you," Mary said, then studied the sheet one more time. "My goodness, except for Carrie Brown, all of these murders were committed on the same month and day in each successive year."

"That's a problem, sis. It separates Carrie Brown as an isolated murder Ameer Ben Ali could have committed."

"I'm not ceding that possibility yet. Anything is possible with a mass murderer running free. I need to find more information."

"I already told you—"

"Not from you, Sean. You've done enough." Mary paused. "Though there is one more thing I would like you to consider."

"No."

"I haven't said anything yet."

"I can tell from your tone I'm gonna hate it."

"What tone?"

"The same one you've always used when you want me to do something I absolutely, positively don't want to do."

"I have a tone like that?"

Sean nodded.

"Try to block out the tone and just listen to my words. They're what's important." Mary carefully considered how she was going to phrase what she needed to say, then decided to just blurt it out. "I hate to echo Mom but it's time you concentrated your energies on courting."

"You're right. The words are worse."

"Sean—"

"Et tu, Mary?"

"I hope you're not trying to convince me you've actually read *Julius Caesar*?"

"I was trying to get through to you in a language you'd understand."

"I mean it, Sean," Mary said, her infamous tone turning very heartfelt and earnest. "It's time to stop mourning. Find yourself someone to love. I loved Patti, too, but she's been gone for a long time and I know she'd want you to be happy."

"Don't be so sure. She was a redhead, and you know how jealous redheads get."

Sean and Mary shared a wistful smile, then his faded. It was hard to tell if he was sad or lost in deep thought.

"Well, I said what I needed to say." With that, she walked out of her office.

"Where are you going?" Sean followed Mary into the main part of the bookstore.

Besides having a keen interest in all things intellectual, Lazlo also had a fascination with the abnormal behavior.

It wasn't that he found any enjoyment in such things, but rather that he was curious what caused someone's mind to become so twisted. It turned him into a bit of a pack rat when it came to newspaper or magazine articles on the behavior of diseased minds. Since Ameer Ben Ali's sad journey had begun with a Jack the Ripper–style killing, Mary had decided to start there. She found Lazlo reading Lord Byron's "She Walks in Beauty" to Gerta.

And on that cheek, and o'er that brow,
So soft, so calm, yet eloquent,
The smiles that win, the tints that glow,
But tell of days in goodness spent,
A mind at peace with all below,
A heart whose love is innocent!

Gerta was thrilled. "Brilliant! What beauty! And might I add, what a talented reader."

"Thank you. Byron lived for passion, and I try to bring that out when I read him."

"There's no question that you do. It's quite overwhelming. I hear they're doing a reading of his poetic works at the Columbia Theater on Washington Street next week. We should go."

"Most certainly. It's a date."

Gerta was more pleased with the words "It's a date" than any part of Lord Byron's poem. Lazlo himself was a bit surprised at his proclamation but definitely not unhappy with it. Mary saw this as a good opportunity to interrupt.

"I hope I'm not intruding, Lazlo, but I know you had a collection of the Jack the Ripper newspaper and magazine articles. Might I have a look at them?"

"Would that I could. If you remember, we had a bit of a fire a few years back, and they went up in the proverbial puff of smoke."

Lazlo was referring to a fire that was set by a villain Mary was chasing in one of her cases. Luckily, they both survived, but he had to move to a different location and certain things like newspaper clippings were irretrievable.

"I don't know how I could have forgotten. I've certainly apologized for it ad infinitum."

"Unnecessarily so, I might add. You can probably go to the *Brooklyn Daily Eagle* or the *New York Times* or any number of newspapers. They all keep archives. It will take longer but—"

"I'll help you, Mary," Sean chimed in.

"No, Sean, you've done plenty. I don't want you taking any chances with your career. I'll do it on my own."

"Mary—"

"I mean it. I'm tired of my family and my friends"—she nodded toward Lazlo—"getting hurt simply because they tried to assist me. I will have no more of it."

"Then maybe I can assist you with information that will limit your work," Lazlo said. "The year Jack the Ripper's Whitechapel murders took place was 1888. That should narrow things down significantly, and it was also a noteworthy year for you." Mary paused to think. "The year of your first case, Mary. I can't believe you forgot it. I never will."

"Just a momentary lapse," Mary responded. "I certainly will never forget it. In fact, I saw Lizzie King the other day."

Sean was concerned. "Did they let her out? I'll talk with my captain—"

"No, Sean, it was nothing like that. I saw her up at Matteawan when I was visiting Ameer. But you're right. She still holds an awful grudge."

"Then I'm even happier New York has her locked up for the rest of her life."

Mary realized that whatever solitude she was seeking would not be possible at Lazlo's. She said her good-byes. Sean wanted to walk her home, but they parted ways and Mary went directly to the *Brooklyn Daily Eagle* offices. Lazlo was right. Knowing the year made searching for the Whitechapel murders much easier, and the information she attained was quite revealing. All the prostitute murders since Carrie Brown had been committed on the exact dates of the Jack the Ripper killings. Each successive year hit the same dates: August 31, September 8, two on September 30, and another on November 9. She was confident in her assumption that Clubber Williams and probably Thomas Byrnes had sealed these cases to save face, not wanting the public to know that a Ripper-like killer or the Ripper himself was still at large. She wasn't sure yet how she could use this information to help prove Ameer's innocence. Since he had been locked up, he couldn't have killed these other women, but as Sean had pointed out, that alone didn't prove he didn't kill Carrie Brown. After all, there could be two killers or four or any number. Jack the Ripper was famous, and the information pertaining to his killings was available for any sick mind to see. There was one more fact that was even more troubling.

If this killer followed his pattern, the next killing would be on September 8, which was only a few days away.

14

It was early the next morning when Superintendent Campbell returned from the offices of the two Brooklyn police commissioners. No conflict there. They were allies, men he had put in place to make his job easier. Waiting for him in his outer office was Mary Handley. She had a look about her he had seen many times. It seemed as if she was agitated, but he knew it was just excitement. She was standing, and Campbell immediately concluded she probably had been the whole time she had been there. She approached him, her piercing blue eyes at their widest and focused completely on him. His secretary, Miss Carroll, knew that Mary was a friend and had carte blanche to visit whenever she so desired.

"We need to talk, Chief."

"Hello, Mary, how are you? I'm fine, thank you. My, you look lovely this morning. I do, too? Well, if you say so."

"Okay, I understand. I'm missing my manners this morning. Now—"

"Miss Carroll, feel free to take a break and get some coffee," he said to his secretary. "I believe I can handle this visitor all by myself."

Miss Carroll grabbed her pocketbook, promptly rose, and left. As soon as the door closed, Mary said, "Chief, you won't believe what I found out."

"Somehow I think I will. Shall we?" He gestured toward his office, and they went inside, he sitting behind his desk and she still standing. She began pacing as she spoke.

"I need your help, Chief—"

"Mary, I have been superintendent for five years now, and every time you come to visit me, invariably, the first words out of your mouth are that you need my help."

"That's not true. Last time I commented on how impressed I was that you were keeping your weight off, which, by the way, it does look as if you have slipped in the last week and need to regather your willpower. Might I suggest—"

"Stop it, Mary. You win. You know I'd rather listen to anything than how to limit the few indulgences I have left in the world. Congratulations, well played."

Mary smiled, not only because she had successfully navigated the conversation back to the subject she preferred, but also because it came with a compliment from Superintendent Campbell. She relished any nod he gave her even if it stemmed from her being annoying.

"Thank you. So here it is. I checked the sealed cases of female murders since Carrie Brown and it just so happens that all those sealed cases occurred on the same days in the same months Jack the Ripper committed his Whitechapel murders in 1888—"

"Yes, I know."

"Suspicious, ominous, whatever you care to call it, it is . . . You know?"

"I relish rare moments like these when I appear to be a step ahead of you. That is, before you ruin it, and I realize I am a step behind."

"What prompted you to look into those cases? I didn't ask you to."

"It may not look like it, but believe it or not, we do actual police work here."

"I profusely apologize if I have offended you in any way whatsoever. Now would you please explain to me what happened?"

"You got me thinking about the Carrie Brown murder. She was on my mind when I heard there was a prostitute by the name of Meg Parker who was killed in Coney Island early in the morning on August thirty-first."

"One of my women."

"I decided to check into it, not because I thought it had any connection to the Carrie Brown murder, but because your visit dredged up ancient feelings about Old Shakespeare and how vulnerable these poor women are."

"Glad to know I can have that effect on you, Chief."

"You depressed me, Mary."

"It spurred you into action, didn't it? I bet you didn't think once about food."

"Wrong. It made me think more. You know, life is short, et cetera. But that's beside the point. I found it odd that Meg Parker's case was sealed in my jurisdiction. After all, as much as I detest this job, I am the head man here. I asked my police commissioners, and they hadn't ordered it. Then they checked all the way down the line until they found out from the beat cop that Alexander Williams ordered it under the authority of Thomas Byrnes."

"I knew Byrnes was behind it all. His mammoth ego couldn't withstand the possibility of failing on his promise to catch Jack the Ripper in thirty-six hours."

"That doesn't mean your client is innocent."

"I know that."

"Do you also know what I am about to tell you?"

"That you already did what I came here to ask you to do: unseal Meg Parker's case. You can't unseal the others because they are out of your jurisdiction. Meg Parker is not. You unsealed her case and found out what I suspected. She was killed in a very similar style to Carrie Brown."

"Do you also know the name of my third cousin once removed on my mother's side?"

"No."

"Thank God I have some secrets I can hide from you."

"Actually, no. Her name is Hannah. I didn't say it straightaway because I didn't want to upset you."

"And then you decided it was perfectly fine to upset me."

"I remembered you had mentioned her before. Since I didn't discover her name by means of deduction or investigation but rather through you, I thought you wouldn't mind."

"You're right. I don't, and I feel much better."

"You're welcome, Chief."

He took a folder out of his drawer. "Here is the Meg Parker file. Feel free to read it, but only while you're here. This file is not leaving my office."

She started leafing through it immediately. "Thanks, Chief."

"Now, where was I?"

"I think you're finished."

"No, I'm not. Is it possible I have discovered something that the great Mary Handley knows nothing about?"

She looked up from the file. "Of course, Chief. You're my mentor and always will be."

"Thank you, Mary. I hope you know I've been joking. Since taking this job, I have developed a sarcastic sense of humor. It helps me while away the hours."

"Never a problem. I enjoy it when you're joking." She wanted to add *which is so rare* but decided not to antagonize her friend.

"Since Byrnes and his Manhattan group meddled in my affairs, I decided to return the favor. The Carrie Brown case is not sealed, and I went over it with my commissioners. It seems that the man who went to Carrie Brown's room with her that night—"

"Her customer, C. Nick?"

"That is him. He was spotted on a Central Railroad of New Jersey train to Cranford that night by a conductor, but no one ever followed it up because they already had their killer."

"Do you by any chance have the name of that conductor?"

"Do you think I would have brought it up if I didn't?"

"No, but I know how much you enjoy imparting new information, and I didn't want to spoil your fun."

"You just did."

"Come on, Chief, I know you're not that sensitive."

He wasn't. Superintendent Campbell gave her the name, Klaus Kastner. She thanked him, and she left, hoping Klaus Kastner was still employed by the Central Railroad of New Jersey and that he had a good memory.

~

Having been summoned, Byrnes found himself in Russell Sage's Wall Street office at nine o'clock in the morning. He was getting tired of being at the beck and call of these rich, spoiled millionaires, but their pay made his salary from the New York City Police Department look anemic. So, he was there and even managed a friendly smile.

"What do you have for me?" asked Sage, a man who wasted no time getting to the point.

"Excuse me?"

"You mentioned that Laidlaw had some damaging evidence. What is it? Surely you've found out by now."

It had only been a couple of days since their conversation on Labor Day, and Byrnes wanted to tell him to stop making ridiculous demands and to shut up. Detective work progressed at its own pace, and though money helped and entitled Sage to an accounting, it didn't create fuckin' miracles. Of course, he didn't say that. He wasn't stupid. Besides, he did have some news. In his euphoria, Laidlaw had let something slip to Nurse Emily.

"Good question, Russell. Although we're not there yet, we do know the evidence will take the form of an eyewitness. Now, think. Do ya have any idea who that might be?"

"An eyewitness?" Sage mused as Byrnes could almost physically see him searching his mind. "The only ones there besides Laidlaw and Norcross were my employees. I have spoken with all of them, and none would dare testify against me."

"Russell, I'm sayin' this as a friend to be helpful. Ya need ta be careful how ya phrase sentences like that. It makes ya sound guilty."

"I'm only speaking like that because I am talking to a friend. I'm not an idiot."

"I'm sayin' it fer yer own good. I've been a detective fer a long time and have interrogated more than I can possibly remember. If ya get in the habit of making statements like that, ya might slip when it counts and there's no takin' it back."

"I appreciate your concern, Tom, but I honestly don't know who it might be—unless good ol' Bentley Norton ripped the typewriter off his face and has risen from the dead."

"Benjamin, *Benjamin* Norton," Byrnes corrected Sage. "And you just did it twice. I know yer not foolish enough ta make a joke about the deceased Mr. Norton on the stand, but please get his name right or it won't matter if yer guilty or not. The jury will think yer an unfeelin' boss and the suckin' sound yer'll hear will be yer money leavin' yer bank account."

That got Sage's attention. There was nothing he held more precious than his money. Olivia was not going to get any of it for her infernal charities, and he'd be damned if Laidlaw got one penny. Any desire to be cavalier or flip about it had been wiped from his being.

"Let me think about it some more. Maybe I can come up with something."

"Terrific. And ya know I'll do my part."

"Never had any doubt. Thank you, Tom."

They shook hands and Byrnes left, glad it was a brief visit. He had more important things on his mind. Williams had told him that someone had had the Meg Parker file unsealed. He needed to find out who that was and why.

15

Because of its proximity to the Rahway River, Cranford had attained the nickname of "the Venice of New Jersey." Mary had never seen Venice, Italy, but she doubted this little New Jersey farming community had much in common with it. At the moment, she was nowhere near the river and found herself in front of a farmhouse dismounting a horse and buggy she had rented at the train station. It was the sixth farm she had visited that day in search of the elusive C. Nick.

Finding Klaus Kastner had turned out to be the easier part of this journey. He was still working on the Central Railroad of New Jersey line from Manhattan to Cranford and back again. Mary caught up with him on the platform for the outbound train to Cranford. When she expressed relief that she was able to locate him, he responded in his German accent.

"Why would I ever leave this job? Good pay, good hours. I'm lucky man."

"You also sound like a sensible man and from what I hear, observant, too. I know it was a long time ago, but could you please tell me everything you remember about the man you saw on your train the night of April twenty-fourth, 1891, after Carrie Brown was murdered?"

"I remember like it was last night."

"You must have a great memory."

"Sometimes good, sometimes not so good. But that night I will always remember."

"Why?"

"It's not often I get passengers with blood on their hands."

"C. Nick had blood on his hands?"

Klaus nodded. "Lot of blood. I saw his ticket. He said the C stood for Curt. He told me he was German like me and spoke to me in German. He was no native. Maybe his parents were—"

"Can you describe him?"

"Around thirty-seven years old, blond hair, mustache, blue eyes, my height—one and three quarter meters. Seemed pleasant."

"How long did you speak with him?"

"Not long. I have job to do. He said a glass broke in his hands. Had cloth wrapped around them, but it didn't stop the blood. I offered to get help, but he didn't want any."

"Where did he get off the train?"

"Cranford. He said he worked on one of the farms, and he would get help there. When I saw newspapers next day, I went to police. They thanked me, but I never hear from them again."

"You may hear from me again."

"No problem. I want to help. I love this country," Klaus said. "Now I have to collect tickets." He started to enter the train, then stopped. "One other thing. He was bleeding, in pain, yet he had smile on face as if he like it. Strange man. That's why I call police."

As Mary stood in front of her sixth farmhouse, the Mitchell farm, she was beginning to wonder if C. Nick had lied to Klaus about his job. It was plausible that he would, especially if he was really the killer. The Mitchell farm was not large, probably small enough for one family to handle, and the only saving grace about it being late afternoon was that there was a good chance they would be done with the day's field work and be home.

Horace Mitchell answered Mary's knock on his door. He was a robust fifty and was eating an apple.

"What can I do for you, young lady?" he asked. Mary was now thirty years old, ancient according to her mother. She wasn't used to being called a young lady anymore, but she found it refreshing and saw no reason to contest it. She explained to him who she was and why she was there, asking specifically about C. Nick. He verified that C. Nick had worked there, that the C stood for Curt, and his description matched Klaus Kastner's.

Mitchell seemed very friendly and invited Mary inside. He was living there alone and worked the farm by himself. His wife had died five years earlier, and his two sons wanted nothing to do with farming. One was now living in New York and the other in Philadelphia.

"They're working longer hours making money for somebody else. I don't get it, but it's what they want." He shook his head, then took another bite out of his apple.

The house was simply furnished in a utilitarian way and only had a few remnants that suggested a female had once lived there, one being a doily on a club chair that looked oddly out of place. Mary followed Mitchell to one of the bedrooms. "This was Lincoln's room, my oldest boy. It was where Curt stayed when he worked for me, which wasn't long."

"Did you fire him?"

"God, no. At that time I thought I needed help. I've since found I can do it all myself." He looked at Mary as if still bewildered by C. Nick's behavior. "He said he found out he wasn't cut out for physical labor, got up, and just left. No notice, no nothing."

"Was this the day after April twenty-fourth when he came home with cuts on his hands?"

Mitchell nodded. "He left some things behind. Why? I don't know. Maybe he was in a hurry, but I'm sure he would like to have them back." He went to the closet and took out a bloodstained shirt that was on a hanger.

"This was his?"

Mitchell nodded again, then he went to a chest of drawers, removed a small paper bag from the top drawer, and handed it to Mary. "This was also his."

Mary opened the bag. Inside was a bloodstained key with the number 31 on it, Carrie Brown's room number that fateful day at the East River Hotel. Mary couldn't believe it.

"Did you show this to the police?"

"Of course. I may be a farmer but I do read the newspaper. It's how I get through dinner." He took a final bite of the apple, which was almost down to its core, and chewed away.

"What did they say?"

"They sent a man all the way out from New York. I could tell he wasn't happy about the trip. His name was Billy . . . Will . . . I don't know. Something like that."

"Williams—Alexander Williams."

"Yes, that's it. He kept showing off a big nightstick he was carrying. He was very proud of it." Mitchell shrugged, indicating that he didn't understand why.

"What did Williams say?"

"Nothing, really. Just that my evidence was unimportant because they already found the killer and had more than enough to convict him. I was surprised later when I found out their killer wasn't Curt Nick."

Mary was surprised, too. At the very least, he had to be an accomplice or a material witness. Most probably, though, he was the killer.

"Would you mind if I kept these things?"

"I've been holding them for over three years hoping someone would come back and ask about Curt. You're the only one and probably the last, so they're yours."

"Thank you, Mr. Mitchell. Do you have any idea where Curt went?"

"Couldn't say. He lit out of here so fast."

"I see. Well, thank you so much. You've been a tremendous help."

Mitchell escorted her outside, stopping only to throw the apple core into the garbage can under the kitchen sink and to give Mary a larger paper bag to hold the bloody shirt. They shook hands and Mary climbed back into the buggy she had rented to ride back to the train station.

"I just thought of something else," he said. "I don't know whether it will help or not. He may have been joking or lying or just making excuses for being a lousy farmhand."

"What?"

"When he said he wasn't cut out for farmwork, he said

he had never done manual labor before, that he was a doctor and doing some crazy study about what groups were suited for different types of work. Whatever that means."

"I think I know what it means," said Mary, who immediately had a certain doctor in mind.

~

Ever since Edgar had found out about Meg's murder, he had spent every waking hour scouring the midway and the Gut for information about her killer. He had told Arthur he would have to get someone else to replace him, at least for a while.

"I can't get someone on such short notice," Arthur complained.

"I'm sorry, Arthur. I'm a professional, and I hate to do this to you, but I have no choice."

"You're a good kid, Edgar—"

"I'm far from being a kid. I'm twenty-seven."

"Anyone under forty is a kid to me."

Edgar chuckled. It was his first smile in days.

"Anyhow, this is what I'm going to do. I'm going to shut down Kill the Coon for the next three days while I look for your replacement. If you're finished with whatever you're doing at that point, you're welcome back. If not, I have to move on. Understand?"

"That's more than fair. You truly are a prince, Arthur—a bit of a rotund one, but a prince nevertheless." They exchanged warm smiles that only true friendship could elicit. Arthur became very earnest. "I wish our venture together was *Hamlet* instead of what it is."

"So what you're saying is, you wish you could replace me in *Hamlet*?"

Arthur waved his hand in the air. "Get out of here before I change my mind."

The Coney Island insiders had taken to Edgar. It's not that bigotry was absent among the people who worked there, but there was a camaraderie that often trumped it. They adhered to a silent code where they helped their own but were deaf and dumb when it came to anyone from the outside, especially the police. Edgar knew there were a lot of lowlifes who hung around the Gut who were capable of killing Meg without a second thought. That would have made finding her killer nearly impossible, but other factors were in play that narrowed the field.

A midway worker had been with a prostitute in the room next to Meg's at the Elephant Hotel. When he left he saw the door was ajar and peeked in. He had reported the crime to the police and was also one of the few people who knew the details. Hence, it had spread to a handful of others, midway stalwarts who felt comfortable giving Edgar information.

Once Edgar knew how Meg was killed, he was able to put a plan into action. He began to question everyone he knew on the midway and in the Gut. He tried every type of description but in the end he was essentially asking if they had noticed some sick freak hanging around. He was smart enough to know that deviants like this man often hid their feelings. It made them better predators. Edgar had a vast knowledge of Shakespeare, and many of his tragic heroes—King Lear, Hamlet, and Macbeth, to name a few—were driven mad. He had extensively studied madness because his major goal in life was to play all of those roles. There was always some piece of behavior, no matter how small, that stood out and made them odd.

He was going to find the odd ones, narrow them down, and then do to Meg's killer what he had done to her.

16

On her way back from Cranford, Mary couldn't stop thinking about Dr. Chester Lawrence. She realized it might be a little early for her to assume he was C. Nick without more corroboration, but it was hard to ignore that certain facts were falling into place. C. Nick told Horace Mitchell that he was doing a study that sounded very much like the one Dr. Lawrence was doing. Dr. Lawrence was also an endocrinologist, which made him an expert in the organs that had been extracted from Carrie Brown's body.

Mary felt that pointing the finger at Dr. Lawrence should have no bearing on her doing her job for her client. She had a bloody key, a bloody shirt, Horace Mitchell, Klaus Kastner, and Eddie Harrington. That should be enough to set Ameer's conviction aside, or at least get him a new trial. Since Inspector Thomas Byrnes was the one pulling the strings, there was no point in seeing anyone but him. After arriving in Manhattan, she went straight to his office. It had been over three years since Ameer had been convicted, and it was time for his nightmare to end. She was hoping Byrnes's ego wouldn't be as wrapped up in the case as it had been back then.

"Miss Handley," he greeted her as he was sitting at his desk. "I was expectin' ya sooner or later. Yer kinda on the sooner side. Have a seat, why don't ya."

Mary sat, facing him. "You were expecting me?"

"Did ya really think ya could investigate one of my cases and I wouldn't find out?"

"Of course. How could you not know? You have great influence, Inspector Byrnes, and that's why I've come to you."

"You can blow as much smoke as ya want. If this visit has anythin' to do with Ameer Ben Ali, yer barkin' up the wrong tree."

"Maybe you won't feel that way after I've said my piece. I've uncovered some very compelling evidence, sir." Mary then told him everything that she had. Byrnes listened, or at least seemed to be attentive, as she went through all of it without one interruption.

"Excellent, Miss Handley. Ye've done some very fine detective work. Unfortunately, it won't do Ameer Ben Ali a lick of good."

"Why not, Inspector? This evidence clearly casts doubt on his guilt."

"The problem yer facin' is a jury of his peers already found him guilty, and accordin' to law, the evidence had ta be more than compellin'. It had ta be beyond a reasonable doubt."

"Some of my evidence directly refutes what was presented at trial."

"So ya say, but it's all circumstantial."

"Ameer Ben Ali was convicted on circumstantial evidence."

"There was also a confession."

"Which he later retracted. Your third degree is very grueling."

"That's a polite way of sayin' I beat it outta him. Is that what yer sayin', Miss Handley?"

"I'm not saying you did anything, just what might have been possible."

"Ya do a nice little jig around the issue. The point is, if ya hadn't committed a murder, would ya admit ta it even if someone was beatin' ya?"

"I may not, but every person has a different level of tolerance."

"Especially when they've done the crime. Believe me, I know these scum."

"Maybe this is a waste of my time. Maybe I should take my findings to the district attorney's office."

"Do what ya gotta do, Miss Handley." He wasn't the least bit concerned, which meant he knew it was futile.

Mary was getting frustrated. "Inspector Byrnes, there have been sixteen other murders since Carrie Brown, all done the same exact way. Does that not mean anything?"

Byrnes leaned forward on his desk. "Really? And how do you know this?"

Byrnes had called her bluff and Mary quickly backtracked. "I only definitely know of one, but I'm sure the others are—"

"Yer bein' reckless and emotional, girl. Now, ya dug a hole fer yerself. You have a brother on the force with a bright future, I hear. Ya wanna dig a hole for him, too?"

Mary didn't want to get Sean in trouble. Even though Byrnes was in Manhattan, his influence was far-reaching.

"I'm sorry if I offended you, Inspector Byrnes. Apparently, I'm a little too wrapped up in proving my client's innocence. Please excuse me."

"It's okay. I'll write it off to a particular time of the month."

Mary bit deeply into her lip. "I hope you don't mind answering one more question."

"Go right ahead."

"What would I need for you to consider reopening the case?"

"Don't waste yer time. We already have the right man."

"Please humor me. What would I need?"

He shrugged. "Bring me the man ya think killed Carrie Brown, and if yer right, yer client goes free."

She wanted to tell him that she would do his job for him and better than he could ever do it, but she didn't. Mary rose and started to leave.

"Tell me, Miss Handley. Why'd ya take this case? I mean besides the fact yer bein' paid."

"To be honest, at first it was just to do a fair examination of the facts. I never thought I'd wind up believing he was innocent."

"Why does it make a difference?"

"Excuse me?"

"If it wasn't this crime, he'd have committed another. These immigrant mongrels are ruining our city."

"Lest you forget, we're a nation of immigrant mongrels, Inspector Byrnes. Look how we Irish are treated. Surely that must give you some sympathy for the others."

"Ya can't seriously compare the Irish to the Eastern European scum that's invaded us. They're trash. They live like animals."

"Funny. That's exactly what they say about us." There was nothing more for Mary to do or say, and she left.

Burdened with having to actually find the killer, Mary's thoughts wandered back to Dr. Lawrence and whether he might be the infamous C. Nick. There were quite a few similarities, but proving his involvement would not be easy. A lot of her theory depended on whether C. Nick had told Horace Mitchell the truth about who he was. It kept coming back to her though that C. Nick had no qualms about telling Klaus Kastner who he was and the truth about where he was working. He also had no problem leaving a bloody hotel key and shirt at Horace Mitchell's farm. This seemed like a man who was sure of himself and did not fear capture. Why would he all of a sudden want to lie about who he was or his profession to Horace Mitchell? He most probably wouldn't and was almost daring someone to catch him. She hoped to oblige him.

On her way home from the subway station in Brooklyn, Mary passed Leo's Meats. It was closing time, and she owed her client an update, no matter how depressing that might be. It was Basem's money, and he would have to decide if he wanted Mary to continue.

"Of course he wants you to continue," Leo interrupted Mary and Basem after Mary had given Basem the news. "Tell her, Basem."

Upset, Basem was still absorbing Mary's words. "It seems useless," he finally said.

Leo quickly jumped in. "You're wrong, Basem. There's always a chance."

"Our justice system has flaws," said Mary, "but it's the best in the world. You will see, Basem, when Ameer is set free. And I'm going to make sure that happens whether you're still my client or not."

Basem's words stopped Mary on her way out. "Miss Handley, I want you to continue."

"Basem," said Leo, "did you not hear her? She will do it for free."

"I won't allow it. I believe in paying my debts."

"You're a very honorable man, Basem, and I assure you I will do everything I possibly can to help Ameer."

"I know you will. Let's hope it will be enough."

Leo told Basem to lock up and followed Mary outside. "Thank you, Miss Handley."

"I meant every word."

"Basem isn't as strong as he looks. I'm afraid any more bad news could break him."

"My intention is to bring him good news."

"I have faith in you," said Leo as he shook her hand, confirming his belief. "I should tell you, I just bought Flanagan's Butcher Shop. Closed the deal today."

"Really?"

"Don't worry. Your father's job is secure. In fact, for the short time I've known the two of you, it seems as if you have a lot in common. You're both hard workers and fiercely loyal."

"Good Irish working-class values."

Leo corrected her. "American, Mary. American."

"You're right, Leo. My mistake."

He smiled. "Well, I'm off to the theater. I'm going to see *As You Like It* at the Brooklyn Academy. I love Shakespeare. Don't you?"

"He was a brilliant playwright."

"My sentiments exactly. In this production, I understand they dress up in marvelous costumes, and you can't tell the actors without a playbill. What fun!"

They said their good-byes and took off in opposite directions. After a few steps, Mary remembered that she had a date with Harper and she was already late.

17

When Mary arrived at her apartment, she found Harper waiting outside. He had been there for over forty minutes.

"I'm so sorry, Harper. I've been in New Jersey all day on a case and just got back."

"Don't feel sorry for me. You were the one in New Jersey."

Mary smiled, appreciating that he joked about her tardiness rather than being upset.

"Maybe you should go on without me, and we'll do this another time. It'll be a while until I clean up and change."

"No need for that. Come as you are."

"I can't go like this. It's embarrassing."

"If you can refrain from throwing up on anyone, it'll be a major improvement."

Harper won. Mary liked men with a good sense of humor. She didn't mind being the subject of a barb as long as it was a good one. Harper had arranged to meet Jacob Riis at Carl Luger's Café in Williamsburg and had borrowed a horse and buggy for the evening.

With Harper at the reins and Mary sitting next to him, it

didn't take long for him to ask what Mary had in her paper bag. She had only known Harper for a short time, but she somehow felt she could trust him. By the time they had gotten to the restaurant, Mary had told him everything about her day.

"Did you really think Byrnes was going to let his prize catch go without having a sacrificial lamb to take his place?"

"I was hoping he'd have some sense of justice. I realize that's naïve when dealing with the New York City Police Department, but somebody must have some somewhere."

"You need to tell Jacob about this."

"I can't meet Jacob Riis for the first time, say hello, and then dump my problems on him."

"Why?"

"Because it's rude, and besides, he's Jacob Riis."

"Do it, Mary. It's okay. Believe me, I know Jacob." He seemed earnest enough, but Mary decided she'd see how the evening went before bothering Riis. Then Harper asked the question she had been expecting. "Do you really think Dr. Lawrence is the killer?"

"He fits some of the parameters, but I would need more evidence to be sure."

"Can I see that key again?" Mary handed it to him. "That's what I thought."

"What?"

"It looks like a thumbprint."

"I know what you're thinking, and the problem is that identification by fingerprints has never been used in the United States for a criminal case."

"Juan Vucetich used a bloody fingerprint to nab a killer two years ago."

"I know all about Vucetich. Unfortunately, he's in Argentina, and I have neither the time nor the resources to go down there."

"What would you say if I told you I know a man named Ivan Nowak who worked closely with Vucetich and is now living here in Brooklyn?"

"I'd say thank you. Thank you very much."

"Why? I said I know him. I didn't say I'd introduce you."

"So you mentioned Nowak just to torture me?"

" 'Torture' is such a nasty word. I prefer 'frustrate.' " He smiled, then told her he'd arrange a meeting with Nowak when she had gotten Dr. Lawrence's thumbprint.

Mary didn't know how Byrnes would react to the thumbprint, even if it matched Dr. Lawrence. Yet, if it did, it would be another piece of evidence in Ameer's favor and possibly something she could use to scare Dr. Lawrence into a confession. The next thing she had to figure out was how to get Dr. Lawrence's thumbprint without his knowing what she was doing.

As they rode on, the conversation turned personal as they shared life stories. Mary found out that Harper was an only child whose mother died in childbirth. His father was a factory worker who logged twelve-hour days. That might have been a problem if his father didn't come from a large Catholic family who believed in looking out for one another. They made sure they were always around and Harper felt loved.

"So that's why you do what you do," said Mary. "You're looking after others because others looked after you."

"No, it's because I get to be alone and finally have some peace and quiet."

They were laughing as they pulled into a stable near Carl Luger's Café. The café specialized in steaks. It had opened in 1887 and was owned by Carl's uncle, Peter Luger. Since they were so late, Mary expressed doubt that Jacob Riis would still be there. Harper assured her that he would, that they had the kind of relationship where if one of them didn't show up, after a while the other would start combing the hospitals for him. Harper was right. They found Jacob Riis at a booth, dutifully nursing a scotch as he waited for his dinner companions.

Riis was forty-five, had graying hair with a mustache and wore glasses. After Mary and Riis were introduced, they mollified their stomachs by ordering, then settled in.

"I am a great admirer of your work, Mr. Riis," Mary said.

"Please call me Jacob."

"Thank you. Jacob, I hope you don't mind, but I've always wanted to ask you a question and now that I've met you, I can't let that opportunity pass."

"Go right ahead."

"You portray the plight of the poor immigrants in our city with such hopelessness and despair. Other groups who have come even earlier seem to have assimilated well. Why do you think this group will be different?"

"Good question, Mary."

"I don't bring you dumb ones," Harper quipped.

"Ones? I'm a generic one?"

"I meant you were smart, a thinker. But now that you point it out it does sound—"

"Condescending?" He grimaced and she mercifully let him off the hook. "I'm just toying with you, Harper."

"And you do it so well."

Riis smiled. "This isn't different, Mary, but it is infinitely more difficult. Our industries are growing at an astounding rate, yet most of the money is going to a handful of people. It's cheaper for them to bribe police and politicians than to pay their workers a decent wage."

Mary nodded. "And then they send in armed Pinkertons to break up peaceful strikes and blame the workers when violence erupts."

Riis shrugged. "It's what everyone believes. Read any newspaper."

"And who owns the newspapers?" Harper asked. "It's nonsense. My father's union is full of men who don't want to bomb anyone. They just need a little more to survive."

"If a lie is repeated often enough," Riis said, "people begin to think it's true."

Mary looked at Harper, who reacted defensively. "What? I haven't lied to you."

"I was just looking at you. You must have a guilty mind."

Riis laughed. "I like her, Harper. You've finally found a woman who's capable of dueling with you."

"I get the feeling that if it ever did come to a duel, I'd be Alexander Hamilton to her Aaron Burr."

"I'd never kill you, Harper. Just maim you a bit to keep you in line."

Harper shrugged toward Riis, as if to say, *See?* All three had a good laugh, then Harper said, "Actually, Jacob, this is our first date."

"Really? You behave as if you have been doing this for a while. As the Buddhists say, you must have met in another lifetime."

The dinner arrived, steaks for everyone. After they

oohed and aahed over the generous portions and how delicious it was, Harper surprised Mary by saying, "Jacob, Mary is working on a case she'd like to discuss with you."

"I told you I didn't want to bother Jacob with—"

"It's Ameer Ben Ali."

Riis nodded. "I know that case well. He was convicted on flimsy evidence."

"It's more than that," Mary responded. Then it all flooded out of her mouth almost involuntarily. She told him about Eddie Harrington, the key, the bloody shirt, and her conversation with Byrnes.

Riis leaned in toward her. "There's something you might be interested in, Mary. Teddy Roosevelt is a friend. He will be in town next week from his ranch in the Dakotas on his way back to Washington, D.C. A group of us are trying to convince him to return to New York and become president of the New York Police Commission. I can't think of a better man to clean up our police department, and I believe your story will help our efforts."

"If you're asking me to join you, count me in."

Both Harper and Mary felt infused with a positive energy on the ride home from dinner with Jacob Riis. When they got to her apartment, Harper walked her to the front door.

"I had a very nice time, and thank you so much for introducing me to Jacob."

He almost said, *I know you're frustrated and I wanted you to see there are a lot of us who feel the same way you do. You're not alone.*

Instead he kissed her. It was the right move.

18

Byrnes had to placate Carnegie and Sage, the former about murder threats and the latter about the Laidlaw suit. Both were incredibly spoiled men who were used to getting their way and expected unreasonably quick service. He decided to focus on the most serious situation first, and though Sage might have viewed a financial threat as equivalent to one on his life, the stack of letters Carnegie had given him took precedence.

In spite of his questionable police tactics and massive ego, Byrnes had excellent detective skills that he had honed over the years. He looked at the stack of letters that Carnegie had given him and determined pretty quickly that, although there was an effort made to make the handwriting look different, they had probably been written by the same person. To be sure, he gave the letters to a handwriting expert who supported his suspicion. Even though they were postmarked mostly from two distinctly different neighborhoods in New York City, he decided to check with Pittsburgh first. It was the center of Carnegie's steel empire and also the site where two years before he'd had his most infamous confrontation with workers. The Homestead Steel Strike was the result of Carnegie and his partner Henry Clay Frick deciding to lower already low wages. It escalated when they sent in Pinkertons, police, and eventually the militia to break the strike and to destroy the union. Needless to say, violence erupted. No one knew exactly who fired the first shot, but when the dust cleared, besides the wounded, several Pinkertons and workers were dead. The most obvious suspects would be among the workers. Byrnes found the Pittsburgh Police Department to be extremely cooperative. When asked if any of the wounded or families of the deceased had moved to New York City, they could only come up with Pauline Rutter, the wife of George Rutter, a worker who had been shot and killed by Pinkertons as they arrived on their barge and fought their way onto land.

It didn't take long for Byrnes to find out that Pauline Rutter lived and worked close to the two places where most of the letters had been mailed. He had policemen pick her up, and in no time she was in an interrogation room experiencing Byrnes's famous third degree. In Pauline Rutter's case, there were no beatings necessary. After some intense questioning, she exploded with the truth as if it were a cathartic event she welcomed.

"Andrew Carnegie's a stinkin' murderer!!" she screamed.

Byrnes moved in closer. "So ya wrote those letters?"

"Arrest him! He killed my husband, George!"

"Ye've got it all wrong. Mr. Carnegie wasn't in Homestead during the strike."

"His armed thugs were. George didn't have a weapon and they shot him like a dog!"

"So ya wrote the letters?"

"I don't know what you're talking about!"

Byrnes got right in her face and demanded an answer. "Mrs. Rutter, did ya or did ya not write those letters?"

"I wrote 'em all right! That bastard deserves to die. He killed George!" She broke down and started crying.

Byrnes gave her a moment. As she calmed, he opened the door to the interrogation room. Two officers came in and handcuffed her. He had gotten his confession. He saw no reason to keep badgering her, so he softened his tone.

"Mr. Carnegie didn't kill yer husband, Mrs. Rutter. He was trespassin' on private property."

She looked up, her face showing a combination of bewilderment and anger. "Trespassing? George worked twelve-hour days, seven days a week. How come he wasn't trespassing then?"

Byrnes signaled the two officers and they escorted her out. He then called Carnegie who had instructed his secretary to ask if the news was good or bad. When Carnegie was told it was good, he made arrangements to meet Byrnes for lunch at the Old Homestead Steakhouse on Ninth Avenue between Fourteenth and Fifteenth Streets. Byrnes wondered where they would have met if he had said it was bad. But he hadn't and that was enough for him.

When Byrnes got to the Old Homestead Steakhouse, a message was waiting for him. The maître d' delivered it.

"Mr. Carnegie apologizes for the inconvenience but some business has arisen. He's not sure when he will be finished but certainly in enough time to have lunch. He asks you to meet him at Russell Sage's office on Wall Street, after which the two of you will go to Delmonico's."

Delmonico's was in the Wall Street area and closer to Russell Sage's office. Byrnes was certain the only person's convenience Carnegie had in mind was his own. Byrnes headed downtown, consoling himself with the fact that at least his restaurant had been upgraded.

~

In spite of having spent a very nice evening the night before with Harper and Jacob Riis, Mary hadn't slept well. Getting a clear thumbprint from Dr. Lawrence for Ivan Nowak to examine would not be an easy task. Dr. Lawrence couldn't know what she was doing, and she would somehow have to trick him. Mary had read enough about the science of fingerprinting to know that the thumbprint would have to be clear and very visible. It couldn't be as simple as taking a glass Dr. Lawrence had held or a book he had touched. After agonizing over what to do, she decided to get a thumbprint that would be as close as possible to the type she already had.

That morning she went to the former Flanagan's Butcher Shop, which was now one of the ever-growing line of Leo's Meats stores. She had decided to purchase the bloodiest piece of meat they had and wrap it in white paper, hoping to get a clear thumbprint from Dr. Lawrence. And since she was going to buy meat, she thought she might as well give her father's store the business.

"I've taught you better than that, Mary," Jeffrey cautioned her. "Bloody isn't necessarily the best meat. Let me get you a really good piece."

"For me, really good is really bloody."

"I don't understand."

Leo was there, as he was with all new stores for the first few weeks. He saw what was going on and jokingly added his two cents. "Don't quarrel with the lady, Jeffrey. Give the customer what she wants."

"We're not quarreling," said Mary. "This is a normal Handley discussion. You really don't want to see us quarreling."

Leo laughed. "I've got some really bloody chopped meat. Is that okay?"

"Sure."

"But remember what I told Basem the other day. It's not really blood. It's—"

"It may not be, but 'blood' gets right to the point."

"Duly noted. How much would you like?"

Mary hadn't even considered that. "About a pound will do."

"I know where it is," Jeffrey said, and started to go for it, but Leo stopped him.

"I'll get it, Jeffrey. Spend the time with your daughter." He disappeared into the back.

Mary moved closer to the counter and Jeffrey, then whispered, "How do you like Leo?"

"He seems like a very nice and fair man."

Mary smiled. "I'm glad it worked out."

"Did you know he was in the circus?"

"He told me. I didn't need to know, but he told me."

"Yeah, he does that. . . . Now tell me what this bloody meat business is about."

"It's nothing. I have a friend who likes the reddest—"

"I'm your father. I know when you're up to something, Mary."

She relented. "It has to do with a case. I have to get someone's thumbprint."

"And the blood—"

"Exactly."

Leo returned with the chopped meat wrapped in white butcher paper. It was oozing blood. "Here you go, Mary. Is this bloody enough for something that is not really blood?"

"Absolutely perfect."

Leo put the wrapped meat into a bag as Jeffrey turned to Mary. "That will be twenty cents."

As Mary opened her pocketbook, Leo said, "Your money's no good here, Mary."

"She can afford it," said Jeffrey.

"I can, Leo."

"I'm sure you can, but your father's my newest employee, and I feel like being magnanimous."

"That's very generous," said Mary. "Thank you." She took the meat and left.

While sitting on the train on the way out to Coney Island, Mary tried to plan exactly how she was going to get Dr. Lawrence to handle the bloody meat and leave his thumbprint. She decided she would have to figure it out when an opportunity presented itself. First, she had to make sure he would even talk to her after the tongue-lashing she had given him and Austin Corbin. She was so lost in thought that she was unaware they had reached the last stop and everyone had exited the train. When others began to enter for the trip back, it finally dawned on her and she got out just in time.

The Oriental Hotel was just as busy as it had been during her last visit there. Mary walked around the hotel inside and out looking for Dr. Lawrence and didn't spot him anywhere. After two hours of scouring every inch of the place, she was contemplating leaving when she saw Austin Corbin at the front desk finishing a conversation with the hotel manager. She headed toward him. Corbin served a dual purpose. If he didn't know where Dr. Lawrence was, he could provide a good rehearsal for when she did meet up with him.

"Mr. Corbin."

He reacted coldly. "Miss Handley."

"Please hear me out. I behaved terribly the other day, and I feel awful about it."

"Somehow I doubt that."

"I can completely understand how you might feel that way, but the truth is I haven't been able to sleep. My apologies to you, sir, and to Dr. Lawrence. My conduct was outrageous. I could blame it on the whiskey, but that's too easy an excuse."

"Well, that's refreshing to hear. Kudos to you, Miss Handley, for not taking the easy way out. I'm sick and tired of people who blame their poor behavior on demon rum."

"Of course, that doesn't make my behavior less heinous."

"No, but it does show a certain level of self-awareness that is rare today."

"How kind of you to say so. As you most certainly know, I can be completely intransigent, so it is with considerable difficulty that I confess the following: I have reviewed our conversation many times over, and I have to admit you made some very interesting points."

"Really, which points?"

Mary had known he would test her sincerity. Even so,

it took a moment for her to gather herself before she could spew out a hate ideology she abhorred. Luckily, she got a reprieve.

"It really doesn't matter. You know what they say about the three stages of truth. First, it's ridiculed, then it's violently opposed, and then it's accepted."

"I didn't know you read Schopenhauer, Mr. Corbin."

"As a businessman, I'm aware of anything that supports my way of life. So your particular stage doesn't concern me. If you're a rational being and listen to reason, you will eventually have to accept the truth or deny nature."

"Well put, sir."

"Along those lines, I am on my way to a luncheon, and I invite you to come with me. Dr. Lawrence and I have joined with a group that has some very exciting ideas on how to strengthen America and bring it back to its original purpose."

"I'm always open to new ideas. Will Dr. Lawrence also be there?"

"He's speaking, and I implore you to keep an open mind."

"Oh, I most definitely will," said Mary, suppressing her excitement.

~

Byrnes viewed anxiety as a weakness. That explained his grumpy disposition as he sat in Russell Sage's outer office. Peter Ramsey, Sage's loyal secretary, who had suffered through the bombing three years earlier and still returned to work, would occasionally look up from the mound of paperwork on his desk and smile reassuringly at Byrnes. In return, Byrnes would nod back at him while thinking, *Stop smiling, ya baboon. Ya have no idea what I'm thinkin', so stop pretendin' ya do.*

After a ten-minute wait that seemed infinitely longer, Andrew Carnegie emerged from Sage's office. Sage had remained inside, which meant Byrnes wouldn't have to face him without having solved his problem yet. His reprieve prompted an inner sigh of relief.

"Tom, so glad you could make it," said Carnegie, loudly and expansively.

Byrnes spoke in a lower voice, hoping that Carnegie would follow. "Lunch with ya at Delmonico's is an invitation I could never refuse."

"So, it's all done?" Carnegie hadn't taken his cue.

"The culprit's locked up and the key thrown away."

Carnegie grinned, a rare event to be sure, but any pleasure Byrnes derived from having pleased Carnegie soon evaporated when Carnegie turned back toward Sage's office. "Russell, come out and say hello to Inspector Byrnes. He just did a magnificent job for me."

Sage stepped out of his office and Byrnes greeted him. "Hello, Russell."

"Hello, Tom." Sage was not shy when it came to getting to the point. "Any progress with the matter we discussed?"

"I'm workin' on it and expect to have a solution soon."

"I suppose you'll have more time for it now that you've solved Andy's problem. Nice to see you, Tom." Sage went back inside his office and closed the door.

Byrnes had made no attempt to respond. Nothing would appease Sage outside of handing him Laidlaw's witness, which he now had to do sooner than he had expected if he was to keep his relationship with Sage intact. An outburst of *Spoiled rich fuckers* ran through his mind.

"Well, Tom," said Carnegie. "I don't know how you like your steaks, but I'm partial to well done."

As Byrnes exited the Sage offices with Carnegie and got into the elevator, he didn't want his anger to show, so he decided to start a conversation, the more mundane the better.

"How did yer meeting go?"

"As expected. Russell wants me to join forces with him in competing with J. P. Morgan and Jim Hill for the Northern Pacific Railway. Management overextended themselves during the stock market panic last year and it's available."

"I thought ya were cuttin' back on yer business obligations."

"I am. Russell wants me for the Northern Pacific. I want him to help me fund some libraries. It's a process that will take a while."

"So that's why Andrew Carnegie goes to Russell Sage's office instead of him going to yers."

"That is my sole concession to him. Russell just doesn't know it yet."

The two of them exited the elevator and went out of the building, heading to Delmonico's. Also exiting the elevator was a short, brown man from Algeria. People like Basem Ben Ali were nonentities to the Carnegies and Byrneses of the world, so little attention was paid to them unless a crime was committed. Basem knew that, and for that reason he also knew that following Byrnes would be easier than when he followed Mary Handley. He had decided that Mary's method of playing by the book might not be enough to get his brother out of Matteawan. He needed to catch Byrnes in something illegal, or at the very least embarrassing, and trade that for Ameer's freedom. That was all men like him understood.

When Basem saw Carnegie, it took every ounce of his self-restraint to keep his anger in check. If there was one man in the world he hated more than Byrnes, it was Andrew Carnegie. In order to avoid a useless outburst that would only expose him, he channeled his anger toward devising a plan. As he lit one of his hand-rolled Turkish cigarettes, Basem wondered whether there was some way he could get both of them and still free Ameer. Wouldn't that be nice?

19

"I have passed the halfway mark in my study," said Dr. Lawrence, who was dressed in a fashionable cream-colored suit. He stood by his center chair at the dais in one of the banquet rooms of the Oriental Hotel. "So far, the results are very encouraging."

An occasional "ahh" coupled with more prevalent satisfied smirks rippled through the room. Mary was sitting next to Austin Corbin at a luncheon for the Immigration Restriction League where Dr. Lawrence was the keynote speaker. The league was an organization that had been formed by Charles Warren, Robert DeCourcy Ward, and Prescott Farnsworth Hall, three Harvard graduates who viewed immigrants from eastern and southern Europe as racially inferior and a threat to the American way of life. Their goal was to drastically reduce immigration from that part of the world. As opposed as Mary was to the organization's credo, it did do her a service. She was self-educated and had silently harbored an inferiority complex because she hadn't received a formal education. This league demonstrated that even Harvard graduates could be colossally stupid.

"When I have finished collecting all my data," continued Dr. Lawrence, "I feel confident that our goals can no longer be ignored. Politicians will not be able to turn a blind eye to the facts. After all, we didn't invent a pecking order of the races on Earth. The Lord, our God, did."

Dr. Lawrence sat to an enthusiastic round of applause as waiters emerged from the kitchen and served dessert. Mary turned to Corbin, wanting to assure him that her conversion to his side of the fence was ongoing.

"Dr. Lawrence is an excellent speaker."

"Once his study is revealed, our government will have no choice but to yield to our demands."

"The best of luck to you."

Corbin's look clearly said he still doubted the sincerity of her sudden conversion, but he didn't see the harm in her hearing Dr. Lawrence speak. His attitude was simple: the more people that heard their message, the better.

Mary knew she sounded phony. She just hoped to keep Corbin at bay long enough to get to Dr. Lawrence. She looked around the room, which was filled with white males. The only other woman present besides herself was a fairly large redheaded lady seated a couple of tables away from her. She seemed a bit overdressed for the occasion, not the least of which was a necklace featuring a huge diamond and gold heart locket. Her flaming red hair reminded Mary of Patti, Sean's deceased fiancée. The woman noticed Mary staring at her and gave her a nod of camaraderie. Maintaining her cover as a recent convert, Mary nodded back, not wanting to cause any ripples. She had to keep her focus on the prize: Dr. Lawrence and his thumbprint.

People were surrounding the dais, congratulating Dr. Lawrence on his speech, and Mary saw an opportunity. She took her bag of meat with her as she slowly insinuated herself into the middle of the crowd at the dais. When she got close to Dr. Lawrence, she faked being tripped, stumbled toward him, and made sure the paper surrounding the meat unwrapped, spilling its contents into his lap.

The blood from the meat covered the crotch and thigh area of his cream-colored pants, some of it splashing onto his jacket, with a dot or two on his cheeks. Dr. Lawrence immediately jumped out of his seat and started brushing his pants, his hands turning red with the blood.

"Miss Handley, what in God's name—"

"I am so sorry, Dr. Lawrence. I tripped coming to congratulate you and—"

"Why would you . . . ?" Rendered speechless, he pointed to the bloody meat, which was now on the floor next to the wrapping paper.

"It's a piece of chopped meat I was bringing to my friend. Then I bumped into Mr. Corbin and he told me about this luncheon and your speech—"

"Enough! Just get it out of here before it does any more damage."

"Of course. I am so sorry. Could you hand it to me, please?"

Dr. Lawrence harrumphed, then reached down with his bloody hands and scooped up the meat with his left hand as he held the wrapping paper with his right. Mary didn't want to touch it, so she opened her bag, he dumped it inside, and she took note of where his right thumb was placed on the paper. At that point, Dr. Lawrence was deluged with waiters armed with water and rags to get the stains out of his clothing, which in all likelihood was a hopeless cause. As he was surrounded by people patting him down, Mary took the opportunity to leave.

"It was a brilliant speech, Dr. Lawrence. Keep up the good work."

Annoyed, he shook his head as Mary made her way through the disapproving crowd to the exit, all the time hoping the thumbprint on the key was from his right hand. She figured she had a 50-50 chance.

~

Edgar was getting closer. He was looking for weird, probably perverse, and though no one person could corner the market on those qualities, especially in the Gut, his discussions with the midway workers and Coney Island regulars had narrowed down the field. The majority of them agreed that no ordinary lowlife could have fooled Meg even if he had a wad of cash.

"Meg was a pro. There's no chance in hell she would've been caught nappin' by one of them regulars."

"I've seen her in action. If some ordinary Joe made a move, he'd be eatin' dirt, not her."

"It had to be someone different, someone she wasn't used to."

"Probably a rich guy, one of those highfalutin' types who thinks his shit doesn't stink."

"Hadda be a dandy in order to fool Meg."

Edgar agreed. It seemed reasonable it was someone with whom she wasn't used to interacting. Meg might have been impressed with a person from a richer, more refined class, mistakenly thinking the money, education, and expensive clothes made him better than her. He questioned every bartender, shopkeeper, and con man in the Gut and came up with a number of well-dressed, wealthy gentlemen who had recently been cruising the bar and beach area. He spent day and night in the Gut, found these men, and followed them. It didn't take long for him to narrow it down to less than a handful.

Being an actor, Edgar considered himself an expert on human behavior. Their cocky own-the-world attitude didn't fool him. Crazy was crazy. The only question in his mind was whether the murderer had fled Coney Island, never to return after killing Meg. That would involve knowledge that he had done something wrong and fear that he might get caught. Every instinct he had told Edgar that a maniac like the one who killed Meg had no fear and no conscience. He would wait for the killer to strike again. If he returned, he was a sick fuck who couldn't stop. Edgar would make sure that he did.

20

Mary kept pounding on Harper's door, but he didn't answer. She had heard voices inside, at least one of them a woman.

"Harper, I don't care if you have ten women in there and you're all naked," she shouted through the door. "I have to see you. It's important."

Harper finally cracked open the door and spoke in a low voice. "It's not a good time, Mary. Can you come back later?"

"Take a short break from your orgy and listen for a minute. I have it." She held up the bag and changed to a whisper. "The print. I need Ivan Nowak's address."

"Ivan doesn't know you. I have to be there, and I won't be free for a while."

"Oh, come on," she said, then shouted past Harper, "Ladies, put your clothes on and have a smoke. Casanova will be back soon." She turned to Harper. "See? Simple as that."

"That was incredibly rude. You—"

"Harper," a female voice called from inside, "let her in. It's okay."

Harper reluctantly opened the door wider, and Mary

walked in. To her surprise, the only other person there was a conservatively dressed elderly lady who was sitting on Harper's couch.

"Mary Handley," Harper said as he closed the door, "meet Mrs. James Norcross."

Mary immediately put it together. "You mean—"

"Yes. She's the mother of Henry L. Norcross. Mrs. Norcross is in town from Massachusetts this week and has been kind enough to give me an interview for my article. Of course, I'm not sure how she feels about it now that you've barged in."

"It's perfectly all right, Harper," said Mrs. Norcross. "I know all about jealous women."

"Jealous? Me, of Harper? Please, you couldn't be more wrong."

"You heard a female voice and you didn't think she might be a relative or part of his work, but rather jumped to the conclusion that Harper was having an affair, not only with her but with multiple partners."

"I was joking."

"That's an excellent way of avoiding the truth."

Mary turned to Harper. "Who is the investigative reporter here, you or her?"

"I'm leaving this investigation in Mrs. Norcross's lap," said Harper, enjoying every second of it. "She's doing a fabulous job, and I can't wait to see where it goes."

"Nowhere, Harper, absolutely nowhere."

"That's it, my dear," said Mrs. Norcross. "String him along until he's completely helpless."

"That will not be difficult. When I met him, he was completely helpless."

Harper quickly jumped in. "Not exactly how I remember it."

Mary started to answer but Mrs. Norcross beat her to it. "You two can continue your lovers' spat after Harper has finished our interview, unless, of course, you are finished."

"I'm not. Mary, could you please come back in a little while?"

"She can stay. I'm not going to say anything the world won't be able to read in your article."

Allowing a reasonable amount of space between them, Mary also sat on the couch as Harper picked up a pad and pen, then plopped down on a chair facing Mrs. Norcross. "Did Henry ever express a hate for Russell Sage?"

"Not specifically against Mr. Sage. He did say he thought it was unfair that a few Americans made ungodly amounts of money while many were starving, but I've heard a lot of people say that and none of them did what Henry did."

"So he never gave you any indication of why?"

Mrs. Norcross paused, reliving the pain of losing her son. "It's been almost three years, and not a day goes by where it hasn't plagued James and me. We've searched our memories for clues, behavior that would have indicated something. How could we have been so blind?"

She buried her head in her hands and started to cry. Mary quickly took a handkerchief out of her pocketbook and gave it to her. "It's not your fault, Mrs. Norcross. He probably didn't want you to know. I hide things from my parents all the time."

She looked up at Mary in torment, as if she might have an answer. "Why?"

"There are things I don't want them to know. They'll

worry or try to stop me from doing something I'm going to do anyway."

Mrs. Norcross shook her head. "Children."

Harper gave her a moment to gather herself, then asked, "He didn't leave anything behind, maybe a good-bye note?"

Mrs. Norcross reached for her pocketbook, which was next to her on the couch. "I meant to show this to you. He dropped it in our mailbox the night he left." She pulled out an envelope, removed a letter from it, and gave it to Harper. He stared at it, then handed it to Mary. The letter read, "I'm going to New York to get 1.2 million dollars. If I don't return, I love you. Henry."

"And you have no idea why that amount or why he did it?"

"If I had any idea beforehand, I would have lain down on the railroad tracks to prevent his train from leaving the station. At that point though, we didn't know what he had planned, where he was going in New York, and rushing there to search for him seemed futile." Her words were very earnest and heartfelt, her frustration even more so.

Mary felt sympathy for this poor woman. Even though she had just met Mrs. Norcross, she put her arm around her. It seemed natural when this perfect stranger responded by resting her head on Mary's shoulder, seeking whatever comfort she could offer.

~

William Laidlaw's nurse, Emily, had a decision to make. She had done her best, but it wasn't good enough for Byrnes and he had a stranglehold on her. Her younger brother had been out of work since the Panic of 1893 had caused a serious depression throughout the country. Jobs were scarce and often nonexistent. Broke and desperate, he had picked out a rich gentleman on Fifth Avenue to rob. The problem was her brother was a lousy crook. The man gave him an awful thrashing and had him arrested. Byrnes said he would square things with the man and make sure her brother went free if she got him the name of William Laidlaw's witness. Otherwise, her brother would spend years in jail and he'd see to it that she got fired.

Byrnes had just upped the ante by giving her a deadline of two days. Laidlaw was not a trusting soul, and she was beside herself with worry. She had to do something drastic. Her dumb brother and her livelihood depended on it.

The Home for the Incurables was overcrowded, so it took some clever maneuvering for Emily to find an empty room with a bed. She had it for about an hour and that was plenty of time for what she had planned. Laidlaw was usually in a sour mood and it was no different when she wheeled him into the room.

"What are we doing here?" he asked.

"I have a surprise in store for you, William."

He brightened. "A surprise, huh?"

Emily knew he liked her. Truth was, even with her many other patients and duties, she was really the only human contact he had during the day. He didn't like socializing with the other patients. They depressed him. His sisters rarely visited. He did have a fiancée before the explosion, but she left him soon after. He couldn't blame her for not wanting to be tied down to a cripple for the rest of her life. But Emily? She was pleasant and nice, not much in the looks department but who was he to be picky? Her father worked in a bank like he had, and she shared a fondness for numbers with him. He enjoyed Emily.

"I'll help you onto the bed," she said.

"What for?"

"You're always complaining about the pain in your legs, and I thought a massage will do you some good."

"Oh, Emily, you're a saving grace. You're an angel. That's what you are."

He propped himself up by pressing his left hand against the arm of his wheelchair. She locked her arm under his right armpit, and he was lifted onto the bed.

"Lie on your back," she instructed him as she closed the door. "I have some lotion that should be soothing."

She unbuttoned his pants and removed them, leaving his knee-length drawers. Emily then poured some lotion onto her hands, bent over his body, and started at his ankles. Laidlaw immediately began moaning. They were moans of relief.

"That feels so good, Emily. I don't know what I'd do without you."

"I like you, too, William, but sometimes I get the impression you don't feel the same way about me."

"That's not true. I do like you."

As she worked her way up his calves to his knees and he moaned louder, she said, "Like involves trust, and you hide things from me."

"No, I don't. I trust you. I swear."

"Then how come when I ask how your case is progressing, you just say fine? There are particulars."

She worked her way above his knees, her fingers moving under his drawers and up his thighs. He hadn't been touched by a woman in years and certainly not below the waist. His only experience with that was a prostitute on his eighteenth birthday. His fiancée, like most women of the day, had wanted to wait until marriage, a marriage that never happened.

It was hard to hide how excited he was, his penis trying to climb out of his drawers. "Trust me, William. Why don't you trust me?"

He was breathing very hard, his moaning heading toward a crescendo. "I trust you, Emily. I do."

She suddenly removed her hands from his body. "I don't see it. You don't act that way."

"Emily, please, believe me. I trust you. I trust you with my life!"

"You do? I'm touched, William. That makes me feel wonderful." She then returned her hands to his drawers and started rubbing again. He emitted a huge sigh of pleasure. "I was thrilled to hear you have a witness."

"Yes, thrilling." He wasn't thinking about the witness.

"That's strange, after all this time, a witness suddenly stepping forward."

"No one stepped forward. My lawyer found her. Ooooh, Emily!"

"Her? So, a woman. Interesting. Who is she?"

"It's a secret, Emily. I promised—"

She immediately stopped rubbing and stood erect as if she was finished.

"What? Why did you—?"

"I thought you trusted me, but it's okay. We can keep this as a strictly nurse-patient relationship . . . if that's what you want, William."

Laidlaw had been worked into an aroused frenzy. "No, no, it's you who I want. I want you, Emily!"

"I want you, too." She smiled at him and pulled down his drawers. When she put her hand on his erect penis, she could tell by the look on his face that he would soon reveal everything she needed to know and her debt to Byrnes would be paid.

Then, after just a few strokes, he ejaculated and it hit her on her cheek. She hadn't counted on it happening so quickly, and she hadn't gotten the information yet. It was now highly unlikely that she would. As he moaned in postorgasmic pleasure and she grabbed a towel to clean herself, Emily was tortured by the thought that tomorrow she would have to try again. She doubted anything would ever erase the strong feeling of disgust she felt for herself.

~

Ivan Nowak was a tall, thin man who dressed in clothes that didn't fit him and had a thick crop of brown hair that rested on his head in a haphazard way with no noticeable attempt to comb it. His slovenly appearance was deceptive in that he was actually a very sophisticated man who, though he had been born in the United States, had extensively traveled the world. He was lifting his suitcase onto a carriage in front of his house when he turned at the sound of a familiar voice.

"Ivan," Harper called out. "Wait for us." He and Mary rushed toward him.

"Hurry up, Harper. I have to catch a train to Chicago."

"This is Mary Handley. She's a private detective. We need you to examine two thumbprints to see if they match."

"I don't have the time right now."

"Ivan, this could mean getting an innocent man out of prison and catching a man who has committed multiple murders."

"You're never involved in anything small, are you, Harper?"

"Nature of the beast, but this time it's Mary, not me."

"Harper was not exaggerating, Mr. Nowak. This literally is a matter of life and death."

"Please call me Ivan. My father is Mr. Nowak and we don't speak."

"Sorry about that."

"Don't be. It's been a glorious five years and I've never been saner."

"Anyhow, Ivan—" Mary began.

"I've been hired on a murder case in Chicago. While I'm there, I can analyze your prints. I warn you though, with traveling time and the other work they have waiting for me, it will be a good four or five days before I get it done."

"Is there any way you can look at them now?"

"It's not a short process, and I'm already behind schedule. I have evidence they sent to me that I have to examine on the train and have the results when I arrive. I'm sorry, but Chicago is the best I can do."

"Well then, Chicago it is." Mary took the bloody key out of her pocketbook and handed it to Ivan along with the bag of meat as she explained to him the particulars.

"Would it be all right if I got rid of the meat? It might get awfully gamy on the trip to Chicago."

"That's fine as long as you don't ruin the evidence."

Ivan arched his back. "I think I can manage that. It *is*

my area of expertise." He got into the carriage, then poked his head out the window. "Where can I call you?"

Mary pulled out her card and gave it to him. "It's Lazlo's Books. That's where I have my office."

"A detective who reads. Interesting. I'll telephone you in five days. That's next Tuesday at five in the afternoon Brooklyn time. Got it?"

"Got it. I'll reimburse you for the call."

"The Chicago police will be paying for that."

"What's your fee?"

"Nothing for a friend of Harper's." He turned to Harper. "I'm glad to see you have a woman in your life. You're quieter, less bombastic. It becomes you." With that, the carriage took off.

Harper turned to Mary. "Why does everyone think we're a couple?"

"I think we need to focus on something a bit more serious than that," said Mary, looking extremely grave. "Today is September sixth. If the killer stays true to his pattern, he will strike again after midnight tomorrow."

21

Late the next afternoon, Mary was back at her apartment getting ready to go to Coney Island in the hope of preventing another murder and perhaps catching Dr. Lawrence in the act. Harper knocked on the door, and she let him in.

"I don't mean to be rude, but I'm busy. What is it?"

"You can't do this, Mary." She glanced at him quizzically. "I'm not letting you go out into the Gut by yourself to track a killer. It's too dangerous for a whole host of reasons."

She emitted a slight guffaw. "You're not letting me? What makes you think you have that kind of power?"

"You know what I mean. I don't want you to wind up like Meg Parker and the others."

Mary took a deep breath. "I appreciate your desire to protect me, Harper. I really do. My concern is the reverse. I've had experience in these situations, whereas your experience lies in asking questions. I'm sure they're good questions, great questions, questions that have resulted in fabulous articles, but none that ever required you to physically defend yourself."

"Did I ever tell you what happened during my interview with the champ, John L. Sullivan?"

"You didn't interview Sullivan."

"You never read any of my articles. How do you know?"

"Because when you're lying, you blink. I'd stay away from poker if I were you."

"I do?"

Mary nodded. "And I fully intend to read all your work as soon as I get some time. I'm sure you're very talented."

"I can hold my own, Mary."

"I'm sure you think you can."

"I can. I'm deceptively strong." Harper took an erect, defiant pose and puffed out his chest. Mary realized he wasn't going to easily relent. She took a few steps away and faced him. "Okay, take a swing at me."

"What?"

"You heard me. Throw a punch."

"I'm not going to do that. I'll hurt you."

"That's certainly up for debate."

"If you think I'm a harmless bookworm who couldn't hurt a fly, you're mistaken."

"I don't think that. I just think that, unless my back was turned and I was blind, you couldn't do any damage to me."

"You're not going to goad me into this, Mary. I won't hit you."

"Okay, okay, I understand your hesitance, and it's much appreciated. We'll try something else." She paused, then said, "Grab me."

"Grab you?"

"Yes, like you're going to drag me off somewhere. You can do that, can't you?"

Harper thought for a second. "I suppose so. Sure, I can do that."

She beckoned him. "Well then, come on."

When Harper made his move, Mary grabbed his arm, flipped him, and sent him crashing to the floor. Taken completely by surprise, he was a bit disoriented.

"What was that?"

"It's called jujitsu."

"I know that."

"I'm a black belt. Been so for many years."

"How nice for you. You should have warned me."

"Do you think a maniac killer is going to warn you about what he's going to do?"

"Point taken." Harper slowly rose to his feet. "You still need my help."

"Harper, do I have to perform another demonstration?"

"One was quite enough, thank you. But that doesn't change that it will be simple for Dr. Lawrence to recognize you, especially at a place where you don't fit, like a bar in the Gut."

Harper made sense. "You're right. A cramped space like a bar could be tricky."

"You'll stick out at any bar in the Gut, unless you want to dress up like a whore."

"That wouldn't do either. Those masquerades only work in plays. In real life, Dr. Lawrence would spot me and just wonder why Mary Handley is dressed like a whore."

"Then I return to my original premise. You need me."

Mary stared at Harper for a moment. "The only way this is going to work is if you follow everything I say. The last thing I want is a dead investigative reporter on my hands."

"You've thrown up on me, bounced me around, and now you want to protect me. Could this be Mary Handley's own inimitable way of telling me she cares?"

"Maybe. Just a little."

"Define 'a little.'"

"It means I don't want you dead . . . yet."

Her coy smile made him feel good.

~

In spite of still being a bit miffed about his suit being ruined, Dr. Lawrence had a very pleasant dinner with Austin Corbin and the three Harvard men who'd established the Immigration Restriction League. They had all congratulated Dr. Lawrence on his very successful speech and each had a different opinion on what that woman Mary Handley was doing there with a bag of meat. Not one of them was even close to the truth. Corbin told the others that he didn't believe her sudden reformation, but he had seen no harm in her attending the luncheon. He apologized to Dr. Lawrence for that mistake.

At about eleven o'clock, a good two hours after the dinner, Dr. Lawrence exited the Oriental Hotel still dressed in his fashionable evening clothes that he had worn at dinner. In his right hand he was carrying a leather doctor's bag as he got into a hansom cab; he gave his instructions to the driver, and they took off.

Observing this while hiding out of sight nearby were Mary and Harper.

"I wonder what he has in that bag," said Harper.

"I doubt he's going on a house call," Mary replied as they rushed into another hansom cab that was nearby.

Mary instructed the driver to follow Dr. Lawrence's cab at a safe distance, and as they had expected, it led them to the heart of the Gut. They waited for him to disembark and begin his stroll before they ventured outside their cab.

It was the typical lively summer Friday night in the Gut. Mobs of thrill seekers were prowling the streets looking for a good time or for a good score. People from all walks of life—regular workingmen, pickpockets, gamblers, jockeys, tourists, and more—peppered the area, going in and out of the many bars, cabarets, gambling establishments, and houses of ill repute. It was the dark side of humanity, but there was a throbbing pulse to life there that made it seem exciting and had earned it the nickname of Sodom-by-the-Sea.

Mary and Harper followed Dr. Lawrence at a safe distance as he took in the atmosphere, seemingly feeding on it as his gait became more energetic and enthusiastic. He popped in and out of several bars. Mary and Harper's plan was to let Dr. Lawrence roam, but if he ever went into a place and stayed more than five minutes, Harper would follow him in. He did that once and bumped into him when Dr. Lawrence was on the way out. It was fortunate that he didn't know who Harper was, or at least didn't let on if he did.

Finally, Dr. Lawrence entered a place called Les Girls Cabaret. It was one of the more upscale places in the Gut, not that anything in the Gut was upscale. When he didn't come out, Harper went in.

Les Girls Cabaret was pretty much what the sign advertised. There was a small stage where four women were doing an American derivative of the Moulin Rouge cancan dance. On both sides of the stage were boothlike areas where curtains could be drawn and men could get a private dance. There were about twenty tables filled with men ogling the women. About half a dozen hostesses sat at the tables, flirting with the men, getting them to buy drinks from which they got a percentage of the haul. Behind the tables was a bar area that was mobbed with men, again with a few women hustling drinks for the house. One more detail: everyone was white.

When Harper entered, he quickly spotted Dr. Lawrence already seated at a table with a hostess, sharing a bottle of champagne. He went to a part of the bar where he could keep his eye on him. Harper had a feeling that Dr. Lawrence was going to be there for a while, so he ordered an overpriced beer. Everything was overpriced at Les Girls Cabaret, and Harper had already decided he was going to nurse this one for a while.

Outside, ensconced in a nearby doorway with a clear view of the cabaret entrance, Mary waited impatiently. She didn't like trusting anyone else, much less a nonprofessional, to track her quarry, but she really had no choice. The only thing she could do was make sure she was prepared when it was her turn. She checked her pocketbook. There were handcuffs, a gun, and a camera. She'd be ready for Dr. Lawrence when he made his move.

A little after midnight, a black man carrying a beer squeezed into the empty spot next to Harper at the bar. When the other white patrons saw him, they moved away, giving both of them plenty of room. The black man turned to Harper.

"You're not afraid like the others?"

"Afraid of what?"

"That some of my black might rub off on you."

"I'm pale," Harper replied. "I could use some color."

The black man smiled broadly. "My name's Edgar. Edgar Jefferson."

"Harper Lloyd." They shook hands, then Harper looked at his. "No, still white. What good are you, Edgar?"

As Edgar and Harper were laughing, the bartender approached.

"Edgar," he said, "I'm getting a lot of complaints. I have to ask you to leave."

Edgar stared defiantly. "No, Frank, I've got as much right as anyone else to be here."

"They'll just go down the street to the next place and all you'll accomplish is that I'll lose tips. Come on, Edgar."

"I just bought this beer. I haven't even taken a sip yet."

"I'll give you your money back."

"Forget it. My white friend looks like he needs another drink. Here you go, Harper." He put the beer in front of Harper, whose own mug was empty.

"Edgar, is there anything I—"

"Forget it, Harper. I'm used to this shit."

Edgar stormed toward the door. Harper stared at the bartender as he picked up Edgar's beer and took a drink. "So, have I turned black?"

"Cut it. I feel bad enough. Edgar's a friend." The bartender went back to work, and the space next to Harper started filling in again.

It was 12:43 when Mary checked her wristlet. Harper and Dr. Lawrence had been inside Les Girls Cabaret for a while, and she was beyond antsy. Several times she had considered going inside but stopped, reminding herself how easily Dr. Lawrence would have spotted her. Waiting was the worst part of being a detective for Mary. Too many unwanted thoughts ran through her mind, especially with Harper inside keeping track of a dangerous killer. She was not only concerned about his inexperience and the case, but she was also concerned about him personally. In the short time Mary had known Harper, she'd decided she really did like him. He was bright, witty, seemed to have genuine empathy for people, and cared about her, all essential qualities for any man she deemed worthy.

In midthought, Mary saw Dr. Lawrence with his medical bag in hand step out of Les Girls Cabaret and amble down the block. As she watched him go, she waited for Harper to emerge. He didn't, and she was faced with an important decision. Should she go inside and check to see if Harper was all right or should she follow Dr. Lawrence? It was possible that something had happened to Harper but it was less likely in a crowded bar. Chances were, he had gone to the bathroom or was momentarily distracted and missed Dr. Lawrence's exit. When he did realize it, he'd come charging out of the bar, but that might be too late. It was past midnight and already September eighth. Mary felt she had to follow Dr. Lawrence.

A light rain had begun to fall as Dr. Lawrence turned down Surf Avenue and then onto an alley that led to the ocean. The street name was Ocean View Walk, but it was dubbed the Bowery after the area in lower Manhattan with the same name known for the many degenerates, gang members, and criminals who lived there. The street consisted of cheap wooden planks, and there were dives like the St. Dennis Restaurant that made Les Girls Cabaret seem like Delmonico's. Flophouses were in abundance, along with the prostitutes who brought their johns there. Suddenly, Dr. Lawrence's study popped into Mary's mind. She hadn't seen him recording data, and she doubted a serious interview could be conducted in a girlie bar. It seemed like its whole purpose was to provide an excuse for him to prowl the Gut without any questions being asked. Now all she had to do was follow and catch him in the act before he could hurt anyone else.

He approached a black prostitute standing in a doorway. "What's your name?"

"Anything you want it to be."

"Excellent attitude," he said. "I want to see the elephant."

She smiled. She had her john. Now it was just a matter of price.

Mary checked her pocketbook again for the gun and the handcuffs. This was it.

22

The negotiation was brief, just enough time for the prostitute to quote Dr. Lawrence a price and for him to agree. They continued down the street together and turned at the corner, heading toward the Elephant Hotel. As Mary followed, she thought of Harper again, wondering if he was okay or just embarrassed at bungling the job. *If he had bungled it, he'd come out and let me know. That only makes sense. After all—* Mary forced herself to stop thinking about him. That luxury would come later. Right now she was pursuing a killer, and timing was everything. She had to erase that damn Harper from her mind and focus.

They entered the Elephant Hotel, and Mary waited outside a full, excruciating minute before she opened the door just in time to see Dr. Lawrence and the prostitute head for the spiral staircase. As they disappeared into the stairwell and she rushed to follow them, she was stopped by the hotel clerk.

"Where do you think you're goin'?" he called out in a loud voice.

Mary pointed and whispered her response: "I'm with them."

"That'll be a dollar."

"They already paid."

"You wanna do the ol' ménage à trois, fine with me. But there's a two-person rate and a three-person rate." He held out his hand.

Mary was being gouged, but she didn't have time to argue. She quickly plunked a dollar down on the counter.

"All right, give me the key."

"Second key is extra."

"Let me guess—a dollar."

The hotel clerk nodded. His smug grin revealed he knew Mary wasn't with the other two, but this was the Gut. Why kick her out when he could squeeze money out of her?

Mary tossed him another dollar, took the key, and headed for the stairs, suggesting he should switch professions and consider highway robbery.

The room number on the key was 703, which meant it was on the top floor. Mary remembered from the police report that Meg Parker was killed on that floor. She quickened her pace and was out of breath when she got to the top. Ignoring it, she rushed down the empty corridor to room 703 and put her ear to the door.

No sound. Nothing. Had he already killed her? Mary started to chide herself for spending too much time with the hotel clerk when she heard a grunt. It was shortly followed by a high-pitched but low squeal. The second squeal was louder. The third one was even louder, and Mary decided it was time to act. She pulled the gun out of her pocketbook, then opened the door with the key and burst into the room.

"Back away from the woman and put that knife down."

But there was no knife, no woman in danger.

Dr. Lawrence was standing on a chair. A rope was hung from a rafter and tied around both of his wrists. He was bare-chested and barefoot, wearing only cheap, coarse cotton pants. He had a gag in his mouth attached to leather straps that were tied at the back of his head.

The black prostitute, sporting a black leather necklace with spikes and a black corset, had a cat-o'-nine-tails in her right hand. On the floor next to her, Dr. Lawrence's bag was open and looked empty, indicating he had brought all the accessories.

"Get out of here!" she commanded Mary. "This lazy slave didn't pick enough cotton, and I'm gonna teach him a lesson."

She whipped him twice with the cat-o'-nine-tails and blood started streaming down his back. There was no cry for help from Dr. Lawrence but rather a look of total embarrassment.

"I said leave!" the prostitute once again commanded Mary. Then, with Dr. Lawrence's back to her, she signaled Mary to please go. He was paying her a lot for this.

Mary returned the gun to her pocketbook, took out the camera, and snapped a photograph. She wanted to show it to Harper. She was certain he'd say she had made it up.

My God, Harper! What happened to him?

~

Harper had never been so happy. Barefoot, he stumbled through the sand with the cool ocean breeze blowing in his face, feeling like he wanted to be here forever. It was raining, but he welcomed the drops as if they were rays of sunshine warming his body. Suddenly, he stopped, looked toward the ocean, and was overcome with the urge to go for a midnight swim. His motor skills on hold, he was fumbling with the buttons on his shirt, trying to take it off, when he heard someone screaming at him.

"Harper!"

He turned. His vision was blurry, but he could tell that it was a woman.

"Harper!"

It looked like she had blond hair and blue eyes. And she was pretty, all right. Her face was somewhat contorted, though, and wet. She was angry, really angry.

"Where the hell were you, Harper?"

She was marching toward him, sand flying in her wake. Suddenly, his heart filled with happiness, and he went to hug her. "Mary, Mary, Mary."

She deflected his embrace. "You deserted me. What happened?"

Harper almost lost his balance as he looked up. "The sky, Mary. Beautiful."

"You're drunk!"

"Oh, Mary, you're wet. You look so beautiful wet." He went to hug her again.

"Get away from me, you idiot!" Mary pushed him and he tumbled onto the sand. He started to get up but once his hands dug into the sand he became distracted. He lifted huge clumps and laughed hysterically as he let it pour bit by bit back onto the beach.

"Wheee!" he screamed.

"I can't believe I was worried about you."

No sooner did she utter those words than a commotion was heard further down on the beach. Mary decided to investigate, and Harper dutifully stumbled behind her, trying to keep up.

An angry crowd had formed by the bathhouses. Shouts of "Kill the nigger! Hang the black bastard!" rang through the night air. The sea of people reluctantly parted as two policemen pushed through with a handcuffed black man tightly in their grasps. He was covered with blood.

"What happened, officers?" asked Mary, shouting at them in order to be heard.

"I'm really tired," Harper said as he caught up to her.

One of the officers cocked his head toward the black man. "This nigger cut a white woman to pieces down by the bathhouse."

The crowd followed the policemen with cries of "Fry the nigger!" et cetera.

Harper waved happily at the black man. "Hey, Edgar."

Mary turned to Harper. "You know him?"

Harper yawned. "He's my friend."

"Your friend? Harper—"

"Tired, so tired." Harper lay down on the sand and passed out.

"Harper, wake up! What do you know? What the hell is going on? Harper!!"

She bent down and shook him, but nothing was going to wake him up in his state. As the policemen loaded Edgar into a paddy wagon just off the beach with the angry mob still cursing at him, an overwhelming sense of helplessness washed over Mary. She had been convinced Dr. Lawrence was the killer. Without him, she would have to start all over. Assessing the situation made it worse. She had nothing but depressing news to report to Basem and Ameer. Involving Harper was a complete mistake for which she could only blame herself. And who was Edgar? He certainly didn't fit the description of the man with blond hair and a mustache who was on the train and at the Mitchell farm after the Carrie Brown murder. Would she have to throw out all her work? Could she have been that far off, that wrong?

Mary plopped down on the sand next to Harper. She checked his pulse. He seemed fine. That frustrated her even more. It was possible he knew something about Edgar, and it was equally possible he had been drunkenly ranting. All she could do was wait for him to wake up. She decided to get comfortable. Ignoring the rain, she lay down next to him on the sand.

"Damn you, Harper," she said, then tried to go to sleep.

23

Waking up in soggy clothes on a deserted beach is a harsh way to greet the morning. Mary furiously rubbed her eyes, trying to keep any grains of sand from sneaking inside. That's when the events of the previous night once again rushed through her brain, making her relive the disappointment and confusion. The one positive was that the sun was shining. Her head began to throb as she turned toward Harper, who, much to her dismay, was sleeping peacefully. She leaned over him, shook her hair, and watched as the sand particles landed on his face. He began to stir, lazily smacking his lips before waking in a start and spitting out sand with Gatling gun precision.

"Good morning, sleepyhead," Mary said, oozing sarcasm.

"What happened?"

"That's such a complicated question. Do you mean before you got drunk and left me alone with Dr. Lawrence or afterward?"

"Huh?"

"Or do you mean your decision to sleep on the beach

when every other derelict in the Gut was smart enough to seek shelter from the rain?"

The cobwebs were still casting their net over Harper's brain and he was slow in processing the information. "What happened with Dr. Lawrence?"

"I'll explain it to you on the train ride back."

She helped him get up and brush the sand off his clothes, then they began the trek to the train station.

"Did you call me a derelict?"

"Indeed I did." She pointed at him. "Self-explanatory."

It was very early in the morning and though there were only a few people traveling, Mary made sure she picked a car that was empty so they could talk privately. Harper was just starting to grasp some lucidity.

"The guy's a pervert?" an incredulous Harper bellowed out.

"Much to my chagrin."

"Wow!"

"Don't get so high and mighty, Harper, after what you did."

"I keep telling you. I had two beers."

"I've heard that before."

"I don't know what happened. I've never experienced anything like it. The world was wonderful. I felt so . . . happy."

"I'm thrilled for you. Tell me about Edgar."

"Edgar?"

"The Negro you waved to last night, the one who killed a woman."

"Edgar killed someone?"

"Who is he, Harper?"

"I met him at Les Girls last night. He gave me his beer."

"Did you count that in the two or was it your twentieth?"

"I swear to God I only had two!"

"That doesn't hold much weight coming from an atheist."

"I never said I was an atheist. I'm a lapsed Catholic."

"What does that make you, a Protestant?"

For the first time the two of them saw some humor in their situation and they laughed.

"No, Mary, I'm still a Catholic, just not enthused about the many rituals." He shook his head. "Believe me, I'm no Goody Two-Shoes. I've been drunk before and I know what drunk feels like. This was different."

"You felt happy. All that tells me is that you're a nasty drunk."

"I thought you were serious about this."

"I just spent a miserable night on a wet beach because of you, not to mention all the worry about your safety until I found your worthless carcass. I deserve the right to give you a hard time now that I've figured out what happened."

"You were worried about me?"

"That's all you derived from that? You're hopeless, Harper."

"Okay, I'll play the game. What do you think happened?"

"Not think; I *know* that your buddy Edgar spiked your drink, most probably with opium."

"Opium? Impossible, I would have noticed it."

"Not if it was in a high concentrate laudanum mixture. I've read about almost every drug there is, and your pathetic behavior fits all the signs of an opium high."

"Why would Edgar do that to me?"

"That's what we have to find out."

Lazlo's Books was approximately halfway between their two apartments, so Mary and Harper agreed to meet there in two hours after they had cleaned up and changed clothes. Mary had gotten ready sooner than she had expected. She didn't mind being early. She wanted to call Superintendent Campbell before Harper got there. She needed another favor.

On the way, she once again passed the grocery with the offensive sign still in the window: HIRING. DOGS AND IRISH NEED NOT APPLY. Her frustration with her case, along with her lack of sleep, propelled her into the store, where she approached the grocer.

"I would like to apply for the position you have available."

"Sorry, miss, no."

"Why can't I apply?"

"Because I'm hiring and you're not getting the job."

Mary became indignant. "What do you have against the Irish?"

"You're Irish? I didn't know. I turned you down because you're a woman."

Mary experienced a rage she hadn't felt before and in a rare moment of losing control, she kicked a display of teas, which tumbled to the floor. Everyone in the store turned toward her. Embarrassed, she tossed a couple of dollars at the grocer and hastily exited.

She walked half a block, then stopped and took a few minutes to gain control again. By the time she had gotten to Lazlo's she had calmed considerably. The store was fairly crowded with browsers and Mary was happy that Lazlo's business was doing well when it wasn't "Snail Thursday." Lazlo was in the center of the store, having just directed a woman to the mystery section. He motioned for Mary to join him. As she approached, she saw Gerta behind the counter ringing up a sale on Lazlo's new cash register.

"What happened to Martha?" Mary asked, referring to Lazlo's salesclerk.

"She moved to Manhattan and got a job there," Lazlo replied. "Gerta immediately volunteered to take her place. Took the bother right out of looking for a replacement."

Gerta and Mary waved hello to each other, then Mary smiled at Lazlo, knowing full well Gerta had taken the next step in cementing their relationship whether he realized it or not.

"Yes, very fortunate."

"Oh, Mary, the gentleman over there has been waiting for you." He pointed, and sitting on a bench by the window was Dr. Lawrence. Lazlo had that familiar impish glint in his eye, as if Mary were about to snag yet another client. She decided not to burst his bubble, so she didn't address it and approached Dr. Lawrence.

"Hello, Dr. Lawrence. Why don't you step into my office?"

As soon as they were in her office and the door was closed, Dr. Lawrence began speaking at breakneck speed. "Whatever you think you saw last night, Miss Handley—"

"I know what I saw, Dr. Lawrence," Mary calmly replied, "and I have a photograph to prove it." Mary hadn't developed the photo, nor did she know if there was enough light for the figures to be discernible. It didn't matter. He'd seen her snap the picture, and he was scared.

"What do you want?"

"The truth would be nice."

"You realize that can be a flexible commodity."

"Not in this case. Your study, the title of which should probably read *A Cover for Dr. Lawrence's Unusual Habits*—"

"It was the first time. That nigger convinced me—"

"Please, Dr. Lawrence, I'm trying to afford you a certain amount of respect. I'd appreciate your reciprocation."

He nodded his head, realizing quickly that denigrating Negroes would not sit well with Mary and that she was not naïve enough to accept corruption by the devil as a valid defense.

"Here's what I propose. First, I want you to tell me if there is anyone you know who might want to impersonate you."

"Someone is impersonating me?"

"It's not anything to be concerned about. You're perfectly in the clear."

"In the clear? That implies I was once a suspect in a crime."

"Your behavior is suspect, but not in a crime. At least, not anymore. Think. Someone who may look like you, who knows about your study. Anyone."

"Not anyone I know. Honestly, I do give plenty of speeches. I suppose it is possible any number of people could attempt an impersonation, but why?"

Mary searched his face for any hint of deception. "I believe you."

"It *is* the truth." He looked and waited. "What else do you propose?"

"I propose to do nothing."

"Nothing?" Dr. Lawrence knew there had to be more.

"Nothing. You, on the other hand, will cease your study for whatever reason you want to give: not enough subjects, lack of a control, an emergency at home, I don't care."

"But everyone expects—"

"Like I said, I don't care. What I do care about is a phony

study being published promoting prejudice and racial hatred. Even if it encourages only one person to act upon that hatred, that's one too many."

"I'm dealing in facts."

"Facts involve palpable evidence that is viable, not opinion and innuendo. You forget. I have evidence of one of your data-collecting techniques, possibly your only one."

Dr. Lawrence opted not to contest Mary and got to the point. "If I refuse?"

"Isn't it obvious? You'd force my hand, and that photograph would magically see the light of day."

"You're blackmailing me."

"That hadn't occurred to me, but now that you mention it, yes." Mary smiled at him. He was one of the entitled who viewed America as his exclusive, private club and it felt good to watch him squirm. Dr. Lawrence had no bargaining position and accepted his fate.

"I suppose I only have myself to blame. If I hadn't wanted to amuse Austin by showing him your female feistiness, this never would have happened."

"Yes, misogyny can have some nasty ramifications. Of course being a hypocritical, racist pervert didn't help your cause either."

A slight nod signaled Dr. Lawrence's assent to her deal as he turned and left. Her victory over him gave Mary a certain amount of satisfaction, but there was still major work to be done. She had to find the Carrie Brown killer and free Ameer. From all the eyewitness accounts, it couldn't have been Edgar, but maybe he knew something.

24

Superintendent Campbell had been happy to get Mary's phone call. He was happy whenever he had a chance to get out of the office and feel like he was a detective again. He did his best to mask his excitement when he picked up Mary at Lazlo's Books on the way to Kings County Penitentiary, where Edgar was being held. She hadn't told him about Harper.

"Who's this?"

"Sorry, Chief, I should have warned you. Superintendent Campbell, this is Harper Lloyd." They shook hands as Mary and Harper entered Superintendent Campbell's carriage.

"Warned? Are you consorting with criminals, Mary?"

"No, but I thought you should know that he's an investigative reporter and can be especially annoying."

"Thank you, Mary," said Harper. "I'm flattered."

"I see. You two are dating."

Mary emitted an exasperated sigh. "Why does everyone say that?"

"Because," Harper answered, "it's technically true. We did have a date, and you were very concerned about me last night."

"That was before you forced me to sleep with you on a wet beach."

"I think we should stop right there," Superintendent Campbell said as he raised his right hand. "This is getting a bit too personal for me."

As the carriage took off in the direction of the Kings County Penitentiary, Superintendent Campbell filled Mary in on some of the details she had requested. The woman who was killed by the bathhouses in Coney Island the night before was Lucy Broadhurst, a white prostitute who had been carved up in the same Jack the Ripper manner as Meg Parker and Carrie Brown. Edgar Jefferson was found standing over her, covered in her blood. He was being charged with both the Broadhurst and Parker murders. Mary followed with her information, which clouded what seemed like a very clear case. He listened carefully, and when she was done, he turned to Harper.

"It certainly sounds like opium."

"It felt wonderful, but I have no intention of ever trying it again. I'm a cynic and 'wonderful' clashes severely with my worldview."

"I see," Mary said. "And do you ever feel joy without the aid of alcohol or drugs?"

"Most definitely, every time I prove you wrong."

"Poor, joyless boy."

Superintendent Campbell examined both of their faces. It was obvious they cared for each other, and he wondered when they were both going to realize it.

"I almost forgot," he said. "Thomas Byrnes contacted me. He wanted to know why I unsealed the Margaret Parker file."

"What did you tell him?"

"Only that he had no business sealing a file in my jurisdiction."

"Thanks, Chief."

"He's no dummy. I'm sure it didn't fool him. He knows you're working on the Ameer Ben Ali case, and it's common knowledge that we're close. So, watch your back."

The Kings County Penitentiary was in Crow Hill, one of Brooklyn's early African-American ghettos. It was a prison for both men and women with a section that was a workhouse for less violent offenders. The prison had been a hotbed of scandal since its inception in 1848, known for its mismanagement, deplorable conditions, and abject cruelty to prisoners. Since the prison was always under intense scrutiny, the warden was quick to please Superintendent Campbell and grant his unusual request to allow two citizens to be in the room with him when Edgar was being questioned. Superintendent Campbell neglected to inform the warden that he didn't personally intend to do any of the questioning, but why muddy the waters when he already had the warden's consent?

In shackles and handcuffs, a badly bruised Edgar was escorted by a guard into a bare interrogation room, equipped with only a table and three chairs. His right eye was swollen shut and the marks on his face were ghastly. Mary and Harper both gasped.

"What happened to this prisoner?" Superintendent Campbell demanded.

"He fell," the guard replied.

"He fell, eh? From the looks of it, he must have bounced around a bit."

The guard shrugged as if he knew nothing about it. Superintendent Campbell decided not to press it at that moment but filed it away in his mind for when more atrocities came to light about the prison. He told the guard he could leave and after experiencing some reluctance, he turned his request into an order. When the three of them were alone with Edgar, Superintendent Campbell suggested that Mary, Harper, and Edgar take the chairs while he stood. It wasn't his case, and besides, he thought he might get more out of it standing unobtrusively in a corner and observing. Edgar silently sat across from Mary and Harper, his movement and demeanor indicating a sullenness and mistrust. Harper tried to break the ice.

"Hi, Edgar, Harper from Les Girls." He held up his hand. "See? Still white."

Having taken a number of punches to his cheek and jaw, when Edgar spoke he sounded as if his words were being filtered by cotton. "What do you want?"

"Just some information, Edgar," said Mary.

"I've heard that before," he said as he felt his sore cheek.

"We've been tracking a mass murderer who is guilty of at least eighteen murders that we know of. Miss Broadhurst and Miss Parker are two of them. You'll be happy to know you don't come close to fitting his description."

"That's what I told them. He's a white man, a couple of inches shorter than me, has blond hair and a mustache."

Mary and Harper were completely taken aback. Superintendent Campbell inadvertently leaned toward them, moving a short step forward. Their reactions didn't go unnoticed.

"You're tracking the same man." Edgar allowed this information to sink in, then almost involuntarily, as if his body were rebelling against his efforts to restrain his emotions, he screamed, "Then why don't these idiots let me go?"

Mary remained calm and businesslike. "The police have a different agenda. My name is Mary Handley. I'm a private investigator. My client has spent three years in jail for one of those murders, a murder he didn't commit."

"Then . . . I'm finished."

"That's not so."

"Really? I'm black, I'm in jail for killing a white woman, and the police are ignoring the facts. You tell me what my chances are."

"The truth? They're not good, but if you don't tell me what happened last night, I can't help you and they'll be worse."

Trying to compose himself, Edgar took a deep breath. The lady detective, Mary, made sense. He didn't believe she was trying to railroad him like those bastard policemen.

"When I met Harper, I was looking for him. Him. I don't know his name, and the search was a problem. It's almost impossible for a black man in a white man's bar to be unobtrusive." He stared at them. "Yes, 'unobtrusive.' Amazing, a black man knows a word like that."

"Edgar, we're not your enemies. Please understand that."

Edgar paused. "You're right. I apologize."

"I understand. I'd be insanely furious and panicked if I were in your situation, but we do need you to focus."

"I did enjoy meeting you, Harper. Most white people snub you or go overboard to show how accepting they are. You treated me like a regular person."

"Thanks, Edgar," said Harper. "I enjoyed meeting you, too. I felt we were simpatico, like we could be friends—"

"Harper," Mary interrupted him, "before you two start exchanging phone numbers, I'd like to address the murders. Is that okay?"

"There's nothing wrong with having a human moment. It cuts the tension."

"You're increasing it as we speak."

Edgar looked at them. "Are you two dating?"

Mary's eyes rolled and Harper smirked. She gathered herself and continued, "Did you know the beer you handed Harper was drugged?"

"Drugged?"

Harper nodded. "With opium."

"I had no idea, Harper. Honest. I got it at the other side of the bar. He must have already known I was following him and slipped it into my drink. Damn it!" He pounded his fists on the table. "If I had known that, all this never would have happened!"

"Don't blame yourself, Edgar. If this man is who I think he is, he has brilliantly avoided the authorities for years," said Mary, remaining focused. "Let's hear the rest of the details."

"There's not much to tell."

"Humor me."

"Okay." He took a breath. "Harper knows I was asked to leave Les Girls. On the way out, I saw him, so I ducked behind a curtain and watched."

"How did you know it was him?"

"My friends on the midway helped me narrow it to four men, then I whittled it down. One of the others was there that night, too."

"Dr. Lawrence?"

"Again, I don't know his name, but he was sitting at a table up front with one of the girls."

Harper confirmed it. "Dr. Lawrence."

"I had spoken to some of the prostitutes, and they told me he was just a pervert who liked to play sick games with black girls."

"That is him," said Mary, shaking her head.

"So, he leaves. I follow him to the Bowery, where he picks up a prostitute and heads to the bathhouses. I stay back, playing it smart, thinking I'm a big-time detective. And like that, they're gone, vanished, nowhere. Then, whack! I'm hit on the head and wake up to every black man's nightmare: a dead white woman." Edgar's face was full of incredulity.

"Did you know her?"

"No. . . . How could one human being do that to another? How?"

Edgar's energy level ebbed, as if retelling the events had drained him. He became depressed, almost despondent. Mary didn't want to push, but there was still a huge hole in his story that had to be filled.

"What I don't understand," she said softly, "is why you were following this killer."

"Because I promised myself I'd protect her and I didn't," he replied, a lump forming in his throat.

"You just said you didn't know Lucy Broadhurst."

"Not her. Meg."

"Meg Parker? Did you know her?"

"I guess you could say that," he said, his face tensing, fighting back pain. "She was my mother."

25

There were certainly reasons why a person whose mother was a prostitute might form a hatred for all those in the profession and want to kill as many as he could. In Edgar Jefferson's case, there were too many other factors that pointed in the opposite direction, the most compelling to Mary being the man with blond hair and a mustache. Edgar's description fit the ones given by Horace Mitchell and Klaus Kastner. Was it possible that there were two Jack the Ripper impersonators or one real Jack the Ripper and one impersonator? Yes, but highly unlikely.

"The first time I met my mother," he recounted, melancholy having seized hold of him, "she offered herself to me for five dollars." He shook his head. "Difficult to follow that with 'Hi, Mom.' "

Edgar told them his story, not because they needed to hear it, which they didn't, but because he had hidden it from the world for too long and he needed to finally tell someone. They saw no reason to deny him.

Meg had been repeatedly raped by her father, and when

she was fifteen, she ran away from home. "If you could call it that," said Edgar. It was not surprising that a young black girl on the streets turned to prostitution. Inexperienced, she got pregnant pretty quickly and had Edgar shortly after her sixteenth birthday. She knew she couldn't care for her baby and gave him to her older, married sister with one caveat. She made her swear to tell Edgar she was dead. Meg was barely literate, but she could write enough to ask the simple question "How is he?" Her letters were rare, but her sister's answers—she'd corral anyone who could read into telling her what they said—confirmed that she'd done the right thing. Edgar was healthy and blossoming.

Edgar's aunt was a wonderful mother. She treated him as if he were her own and saw to it that he got the best in life that a poor black family in Brooklyn could give him. He was educated at a black church school, and she did everything she could to feed his thirst for knowledge. When he announced his desire to become an actor, she didn't discourage him by telling him that a black man's best hope of finding acting work was in degrading black minstrel shows. She filled him with stories of Ira Aldridge, the American black actor who achieved fame in England and all of Europe for his brilliant portrayals of Shakespearean characters. Edgar was loved by his aunt and was never made to feel like an outsider, even though she had three of her own children.

Two years ago, on her deathbed after catching a fatal case of pneumonia, his aunt had told him about his mother and that her last letter indicated she lived somewhere near the Gut. Edgar's world was thrown out of control, but it was only temporary. His anger and confusion soon turned into sympathy for the woman who gave him up. His dream was to save up enough money to go to England and accomplish what Ira Aldridge did. He would just save more and bring his mother along so she could start a new life. That made perfect sense . . . until he met her.

"I took a job on the midway, but she wanted no part of me." Edgar shrugged, exasperated. "I kept at it, though, chipping away at that tough shield she had. . . ." His voice trailed off, then he looked up at Mary. "All I wanted was to make her life better. That's all."

"You had done so well without her. She probably thought she'd mess it up for you."

"My big success: the main attraction in Kill the Coon."

"Stop it. That kind of thinking is the last thing your mother or your aunt would want."

"You're right. Besides, my boss, Arthur, is a good man. He made it bearable." Edgar grew sad in a nostalgic sense. "I have some money put away. I'm going to use it to bury her next to my aunt. I think they'd both like that. That is, if I ever get out of here."

"You will," said Harper. "You've got Mary, me, and that man over there in the corner." He pointed to Superintendent Campbell. "He's the Brooklyn superintendent of police. With the three of us working for you, we'll get you out of here."

"Speaking of that," said Superintendent Campbell, "let's wrap this up. I need to go."

They said their good-byes on a much friendlier basis than their hellos, called for the guard, and before he left with Edgar, Superintendent Campbell issued his warning. "I'll be coming back. I'm telling you the same thing I will tell the warden. I better not see any more marks on this prisoner or I'll have your job and his. Good day." The guard's nonchalant attitude melted into fear as Superintendent Campbell gave him a perfunctory nod and they left.

Outside the prison and in Superintendent Campbell's carriage, he gave Harper a strict dressing-down. "Don't ever tell a prisoner that I'm in his corner unless I've already said so."

"But you heard the same thing we did. Edgar clearly had nothing to do with this murder, from the description of the real killer to his life story."

"It could just be a story, and he might be a very good storyteller. Besides, a lot of men have blond hair and a mustache. Maybe he got lucky describing a killer who looked as different from him as possible. But what stands out is that he conveniently omitted one very crucial detail. When he was discovered on the beach, he had a bloody scalpel in his hand."

Mary and Harper were both shocked. "It would have been nice if we had that information beforehand, Chief," said Mary.

"Isn't it possible," added Harper, "that he forgot? He has suffered a great deal."

"Yes, it is possible. It's also possible he didn't bring it up because any excuse seems manufactured, phony, or just plain stupid."

"That doesn't mean it isn't true."

"Convince a jury of that." A moment of silence passed as they considered his words. "Edgar seems like a nice enough fellow and he tells a convincing tale. Remember though that psychopaths can be very likable. That's what makes them so deadly."

"All right, Chief," said Mary, "out with it. What does your instinct tell you?"

"My instinct and my police experience both tell me that

regardless of whether Edgar is guilty or not, he better get a good lawyer. People have been convicted on much less evidence than they have against him. The blond-man defense probably won't work since Edgar was the only one alive who saw him and you haven't proved that a blond man killed Carrie Brown."

"Then I have no choice but to prove it. Two lives are depending on me."

"You better do it soon. The evidence against Edgar is even stronger than what they had on Ameer. He'll be facing the death penalty, and there's no coming back from that."

26

Mary asked Superintendent Campbell to drop her off in Williamsburg at Sarah and Walter's house. She didn't really know whether Walter did criminal work, but even if he didn't, he might know a good lawyer who did and was willing to donate his services for a good cause. It wasn't an easy task and Edgar wasn't her client, but he seemed like a decent man and she didn't want him to become yet another victim of this maniac killer.

When they had arrived and Mary had alighted, Superintendent Campbell spoke to her through the carriage window. "Mary, I've been a policeman for quite a few decades now, and the human garbage I've seen tends to make me pessimistic. Please know that I hope you're right about both Edgar and Ameer. I just can't commit to a person's innocence until solid evidence is in my hands."

"I know, Chief. Being a curmudgeon is part of your charm."

"It's the curse of being a public servant."

"Then I'm glad I'm out on my own."

Harper opened the carriage door and joined Mary. He cut her off before she could speak. "I know that you are closer friends with Walter than I and you think you can handle this best alone. That's not necessarily so. The last time Walter saw us together we were decidedly on opposite sides of the fence."

"You were irrationally antagonistic."

"Let's argue the merits of that disagreement another time. The point is, if Walter sees both of us passionately vouching for Edgar, it might help sway him in our favor."

"That's incredibly perceptive, Harper. Why can't you be like that all the time?"

"Because I leave that to you."

"Wise man."

As they headed for the house, Mary turned back to Superintendent Campbell to say good-bye and saw him mouth the words *I like him* before his carriage drove off.

Shortly afterward, when Mary and Harper were let into the Cooper house by their maid, Sophie, Mary could tell that something was wrong. Sarah was always in the backyard when the children were playing, and she could see they were alone. She turned and spotted Sarah and Walter in his office, engaged in what seemed like a very serious conversation. When Sophie alerted Sarah and Walter to their presence, Sarah marched out of the office to greet them. Her behavior was unnaturally reserved.

"Sorry, Mary and . . ."

"Harper, Sarah. This is Harper Lloyd."

"Pleased to meet you, Mr. Lloyd. I don't mean to be rude, but unfortunately now is not a good time. We are dealing with a family crisis and need our privacy."

"My God, Sarah, are you okay?"

Sarah was never good at hiding her emotions and could no longer hold in what was distressing her. "Apparently, Walter, without my knowledge, took on a case that could endanger his whole career, and it has done just that."

At that point, Walter came out of his office. "Hello, Mary, Harper."

After they returned his greeting, Sarah indicated Harper. "You know him?"

"He's been helping us out on the Laidlaw case."

"That case, the one that's ruining us." Suddenly, it dawned on Sarah. "Mary, did you know about this?"

"I found out about it a few days ago."

"Why didn't you tell me? I could have stopped it."

"They said to keep it confidential for Walter's sake."

"That certainly turned out well."

"Sarah—"

"You're my best friend, Mary. Don't you think it was important enough to tell me when my husband was risking everything?"

"Honestly, I didn't know you didn't know and—"

"Go to hell, all of you!" She stomped off to the back of the house. Mary took a few seconds to process what had just happened and ran after her.

"Welcome to married bliss, Harper," said Walter. "Bet it makes you want to run out and tie the knot."

"I can't decide between that and stabbing myself in the eye. Now, what the hell happened, Walter?"

Mary found Sarah in her sewing room, sitting in a club chair with a piece of knitting on her lap. It was a work in progress, so much so that it was impossible to determine what it would eventually be.

"I don't care how mad you are at me. We have to talk."

"What if I don't want to?"

"You don't get that choice. We've been close for too long. Yell at me, berate me, accuse me, but you have to speak."

"Okay. I hate you and you're a shit, Mary Handley!"

"That's a start. Now tell me what happened."

"Figure out for yourself how you destroyed us."

"Here's how it's going to work. You tell me everything you know, then I tell you everything I know. Afterward, if you're still mad at me, we can choose seconds and have a duel, box, cross swords, arm-wrestle, your option, but we're going to work this out."

"I used to always beat you and Sean at arm-wrestling."

"Apparently, you've already chosen." Mary waited patiently for Sarah to start. They could both be stubborn, but after a while Sarah relented.

"The telephone rang, I answered it, and it was a woman who wanted to speak with Walter."

"Colleen Murphy?"

"Who's that?"

"She's the daughter-in-law of my mother's friend. I'll tell you all about that later. Go on."

"The woman was a wealthy client, and she had decided to fire Walter. They discussed it for a while, but she was resolute."

"I'm sure that's happened before."

"Not that often, but you're right. It had. Still, Walter was upset. I told him not to let it bother him, that even great lawyers like him lose clients once in a while. Nothing soothed him. He started pacing, working himself into a frenzy. I couldn't understand why he was bothered so. Then phone calls started coming in. One by one, clients, good-paying clients, began firing him. In the space of a few hours his whole practice disappeared."

"All his clients?"

"Every single case except one."

"The Laidlaw case?"

"You know that, too. Did everyone know except me? Was Sophie in on it?"

"Russell Sage is behind this. The man's a sour, vindictive—"

"Maybe Walter should have considered that before he decided to sue one of the most powerful men in America."

"He was trying to help someone. Walter's a wonderful, generous man, Sarah, and I know that's a large part of why you love him."

Mary then told Sarah every detail of what she knew and how she got involved. "Can you believe it?" she exclaimed. "I wanted to kill him because I thought he was cheating on you, then I find out he's just trying to help a poor, crippled man."

Sarah's anger had subsided, softening a bit. She shook her head and grimaced. "That's my husband. Kind to a fault."

"Sarah, you have my word that I will do everything in my power to correct this, and you know what happens when I get determined."

"You're as stubborn as your mother."

"Believe me. Russell Sage has never gone face-to-face

with anyone like my mother." The mood finally lightened. "I will find a way."

"Here's hoping."

"Take it easy on Walter. You know he has a good heart."

"I will . . . later. I want to keep the upper hand for a while."

Mary smiled, then pointed to the knitting. "What are you making?"

Sarah held it up. "It was going to be a sweater, but maybe I'll make it a tent in case we have to live on the streets."

Mary left Sarah knowing that for now her friend was still her friend and her marriage was intact. Walter and Harper were still in the entry hallway.

"She's calmed considerably, Walter," said Mary, "though the days ahead may be a bit bumpy for you."

"I can handle bumpy. It's the catastrophic explosions that worry me."

"Are you talking about Sarah or Russell Sage?"

"Both."

"I guess that's a form of equality we women have attained. I assume you've told Harper."

"I've heard all the gory details," Harper said. "By the way, Walter does have some criminal experience, and he has agreed to take on Edgar's case."

"That's so generous of you, Walter."

Walter shrugged. "I have nothing else to do."

"Harper and I are going to find out how this happened and what we have to do to turn it around."

"You may not have much luck," Walter said. "In my experience, fired is final."

"Not when Russell Sage is involved."

Outside the Cooper house, Mary turned to Harper. "I'm going to visit Colleen Murphy, and I think it's best if I do it alone. Her husband's family has been friends of mine for many years, and I'll get more out of her without a relative stranger there."

"I'll see Choate, find out what he knows about this, and even more important, if he has any suggestions."

"Good idea."

They took off in opposite directions. After a few steps, Mary turned back toward him. "Harper," she called. He stopped and looked at her. "I'm glad we're on the same side."

He smiled. "So am I."

It was more than just an apology for all the scolding she had given him, and he knew it.

27

The Murphy family owed Mary a favor. She had given Brian free investigative services and Colleen sound advice about the Laidlaw case. Besides, as her mother had pointed out, she and Brian's mother had been friends ever since the day she "first set foot on these shores from good ol' Ireland." She expected that some or all of this gave her enough cachet that if they knew something, they would tell her. Of course, she had to tread lightly. She didn't know whether Colleen knew about Brian's hiring her or whether she had told him about testifying. Mary figured she would judge how to navigate those waters when she saw who was home.

A Conestoga wagon was on the street outside their apartment house, along with numerous pieces of furniture, which two men were loading onto the already half-full wagon. Mary didn't realize it was Colleen and Brian who were moving until she entered their apartment and saw that it was almost empty. They were both scurrying around, checking closets and drawers, making sure they weren't leaving anything of worth behind. Brian came out of the kitchen.

"Colleen, you left your grandmother's pot under the kitchen sink." He saw they had a visitor. "Hi, Mary."

"Hello, Brian." Before she had a chance to speak another word, Colleen came out of one of the bedrooms.

"I can't believe I almost forgot—" She stopped once she saw Mary. The guilt on her face was unmistakable. "Mary, hello. What brings you here?"

"It's lucky I did stop by or I may not have found you."

"We bought a house in Clinton Hill," said Brian. "Three bedrooms, a big backyard for the children—" He suddenly stopped, having noticed that Colleen was staring daggers at him. "She's going to find out eventually, Colleen. We might as well tell her now."

"The expression you see on Colleen's face, Brian, is the remnant of what little conscience she has left. Clinton Hill is expensive, and I'm sure you didn't get there from your savings as a merchant marine. This reeks of Russell Sage."

"She did what she had to do for the sake of her family."

"I don't know how he found out about me. I swear. When Mr. Byrnes stopped by—"

"Thomas Byrnes, Inspector Thomas Byrnes?"

"Yes. I was scared. I thought Mr. Sage was going to have me arrested. Powerful men like him can do that, you know. It turned out—" She pointed to her surroundings, indicating the move, obviously meaning it was a bonanza.

"I suppose I can safely assume you're not testifying?"

"Would you?"

"I'm not a good person to ask. I've never taken blood money and I never will."

Brian stepped forward. "Now, wait one minute. If you think—"

"Reserve your indignation for someone else, Brian. I was honest with you when you hired me, and I'm not going to change in order to ease your guilt."

"Brian told me all about that, Mary. Thank you for helping out."

"Maybe you're upset I didn't pay you," said Brian. "I can now."

"My offer was genuine, and like I said before, I don't take blood money."

"You can't seriously be likening us to Judas."

"Because you've allowed yourselves to be bought, a poor man will live in poverty and agonizing pain for the rest of his life. A lawyer, a good man also with a family, has been stripped of his livelihood."

"Mr. Choate?" Colleen asked.

"Not him. He's too big to be affected: Walter Cooper, but who cares? You get to move to Clinton Hill."

Brian held steadfast. "Walter Cooper was not part of our deal, and we're not changing our minds." Colleen suddenly turned pale. Brian noticed. "What is it, Colleen?"

"I may have accidentally mentioned his name to Mr. Byrnes. I feel awful."

Brian quickly jumped in. "Not awful enough to give the money back. Not now, not ever."

Mary ignored Brian. "Colleen, do you honestly want to be the cause of so much misery?"

Colleen didn't answer right away and Brian became concerned. "Colleen. Colleen, tell her. Tell her that we're keeping it."

Colleen straightened, seeming resolute. "I have been poor all my life, and I'm not going to pass up my one chance of bettering myself."

"I guess we have different definitions of 'bettering.' "

"That's enough, Mary," said Brian. "You can go now."

"I'd be happy to. This conversation is making me ill." Mary headed for the door, then stopped and turned. "By the way, might I ask how much he paid you?"

"It's none of your business," Brian quickly answered.

"It's okay," Colleen said. "I don't mind telling you. Eight thousand dollars."

Mary smiled, shaking her head.

"It's a lot of money," Colleen insisted.

"Russell Sage stood to lose hundreds of thousands on that lawsuit. I'm sure he was thrilled to find a couple of fools he could buy so cheaply."

Brian immediately turned on Colleen. "I told you we should have held out for more!"

As the two of them argued, Mary made her exit. She had discovered the source of the leak. Doing something about it would be more difficult.

28

Theodore "Teddy" Roosevelt was on his way back from his ranch in the Dakotas to Washington, D.C., when he was induced to make a detour to New York City. His second wife, Edith, was with him, along with his five children, whose ages ranged from just a few months to ten years. The oldest, Alice, was his only child from his first wife, who had died shortly after Alice was born. They were staying in a luxurious suite of rooms at the Waldorf Hotel, which had been built the year before by William Astor. Astor and his aunt Caroline were feuding, and he had built it right next to her home for the express purpose of annoying her. In that respect and also financially, it was very successful.

It was after dinner on Sunday and their nanny had the night off. Edith was busy with the children: putting some of them to sleep, seeing that others were reading or playing quietly, and eventually getting some alone time nursing the baby. In the main living room, Roosevelt was entertaining his good friend and confidant Henry Cabot Lodge, the

Republican senator from Massachusetts; Jacob Riis, whom Roosevelt greatly admired for his journalistic and photographic exposure of societal inequities; Harper Lloyd; and Mary Handley. They were all seated, Roosevelt on the edge of a desk. The day before a group of influential New York reformers, including Republican mayoral candidate William Strong, had met with him.

"Can you believe Strong offered me head of sanitation?" said an incredulous Roosevelt. "I may be a lot of things, but I'm not a garbage collector."

"That was a couple of weeks ago, and he corrected it yesterday, TR," said Lodge. "President of the New York Police Commission is a completely different matter."

"It's a lovely offer, Henry," said Roosevelt, "but I must think of my family. Edith loves our life in D.C., and the children are very happy there." Roosevelt was currently head of the Civil Service Commission. The job had lasted through two administrations; he'd been appointed by the Republicans and asked to stay on by the Democrats.

"You conveniently left out one very important element, TR. You."

"I'm fine. The Civil Service Commission isn't the most exciting place to be. In fact, it's downright boring, but it's steady, and that's been good for all of us."

"And since when does Teddy Roosevelt settle for boring?"

"Experience has told me that boring is the desired state. Whenever I've stirred the pot, the party hacks run around as if they were chickens and I was about to cut off their heads."

"Those were crooked politicians, and they had every right to be afraid of you. You would have had their heads."

"They do rule the roost though."

"I know you had a bad experience when you ran for mayor." Roosevelt had been the Republican nominee for mayor of New York City in 1886. It was a three-way race, and the party was afraid he and the Democratic candidate, Abram Hewitt, would split the vote and give the election to Henry George, the independent candidate. Their fear of George's radical views on taxes and property ownership was stronger than their belief in Roosevelt. Many of them voted for Hewitt, who won the election. Roosevelt came in third.

"But this is different," Lodge continued. "There's nothing between you and the job. You will be anointed, TR, and the politicians can't stop you. Your power will be absolute."

"I must admit that does sound enticing."

"And mark my words. This is New York, the largest city in our great country. If you become the man who cleans up the cesspool that currently calls itself the New York City Police Department, it will be noticed. Who knows where it might take you?"

"Maybe Strong was confused about what garbage he wanted me to sweep away."

They all laughed. Roosevelt walked around the desk and sat in a chair. Serious again, he turned to Riis. "You've been silent, Jacob. What's your opinion here?"

"I can't speak to your family's welfare. Only you and Edith can do that. I can say that there is an unrest in this country that is unprecedented. Go to any workingman's neighborhood and you can see the despair on their faces. I fear more anarchist violence like the Berkman attack on Henry Frick and the Norcross bombing is not far off."

"It's never been proved that Norcross was an anarchist."

"I've brought my friend Harper Lloyd with me. He's a

very talented and devoted journalist who has been investigating the Norcross case." Riis gestured to Harper.

"You're right, Mr. Roosevelt. It's never been definitively proven that Henry L. Norcross was an anarchist. But let's just look at the action. He decided to blow himself up with the hope of taking Russell Sage with him. To the best of my knowledge, it is the first suicide of its kind in the United States, clearly an act of desperation."

"And more likely the act of a lunatic."

"Agreed, but when does anarchism turn to lunacy? An anarchist in Russia killed himself and the czar."

"I heard there are conflicting reports. Some say he just wanted the money and the explosion was an accident. The satchel with the bomb slipped off of his shoulder."

"Even so. Think about who Norcross chose. It wasn't a doctor or a random wealthy person who might have been an easier victim. It was Russell Sage, who epitomizes capitalistic greed."

"Excuse me, everyone," said Mary, "but no matter how much I might agree with all of you, we have wandered off topic."

"Leave it to a woman to bring us males down to earth. Edith does that for me, and I'm forever grateful she does. Bully for you, Miss Handley."

"Thank you, sir. We should be concentrating on what you can personally accomplish as president of the New York Police Commission, and the answer is plenty. Most important of all is to restore the people's trust in their own police force. Clubber Williams has openly bragged about taking bribes, and it is widely known that Thomas Byrnes has acquired great wealth doing the bidding of Andrew Carnegie, Russell Sage, Jay Gould, and others. Because of their influential friends, the Lexow Committee investigation into their activities will be proven fruitless. We need someone to clean house, say 'you're gone' and mean it."

"And you think I'm the man to do this?"

"I can't think of anyone better. As a New York assemblyman, you put Jay Gould in his place when he tried to lower his taxes, and by doing so, exposed the corruption in Albany. New York City needs a man like you."

"That was back in '82. How old were you then, twelve?"

"I was eighteen, but I had been reading about politics and civic matters since I was ten."

Roosevelt emitted a bellowing laugh. "So when other little girls were playing with dolls you were weighing the world's problems."

"Dolls never interested me, much to my mother's chagrin."

"I admire your spunk. Keep at it, never let it die." He turned to the others. "You've got the wrong person, boys. Miss Handley should be your choice for police commissioner."

"I'm flattered, Mr. Roosevelt, but unfortunately that option is not available."

Roosevelt looked Mary in the eye. "If I have anything to do with it, it will be someday."

"Thank you, but for now I'm dealing with the present realities. I have a client in jail for life merely because Inspector Byrnes needed a scapegoat to protect his ego. I'm working on another case in which he literally acted as an agent for Russell Sage. How can the ordinary man have faith that the police are on his side when the department stinks from the top down?"

"You present a very persuasive argument."

"She most definitely does," Lodge said. "And you are the only man for the job."

"It's time to stop selling, Henry. You're beginning to sound like a Western medicine man peddling his bottle of cure-all."

Lodge began to laugh. "Oh no, was I that bad?" Off Roosevelt's definitive nod, Lodge continued, "Well, it's for a good cause, and you know it comes from the heart, TR."

"I do know that. Anyhow, gentlemen and lady, I appreciate your advice. After we get back to Washington, Edith and I will mull it over."

"Whatever happened to the TR who when asked to solve a problem would jump in willy-nilly?"

"Five children are what happened, Henry."

Lodge chuckled. "Good answer. There's no need to rush. As they informed us yesterday, the job won't be available for months. First, Strong has to win."

Roosevelt shook hands with all of them before they left, then went into the next room, where Edith was nursing the baby.

"How's Archie?" he asked.

"He's a hungry little fellow." She looked down at the baby. "Aren't you, Archibald?"

"Good. He'll grow up big and strong."

"I couldn't help hearing some of the conversation. Henry's urging you to back up the wagon and take out the trash."

"Human trash. And one wagon would hardly be enough. This job would involve a very long wagon train."

"Sounds like something you'd enjoy."

"I also enjoy our life in D.C."

"Don't try to pull the wool over my eyes, darling. You're a fighter. You like to get in there and mix it up, and the Civil Service Commission is annoyingly quiet."

"Those meetings can get tedious. Sometimes I have to kick myself to stay awake."

"I feel terrible. When they came to you last year to run for mayor again, I selfishly thought of my own happiness. It was a mistake to talk you out of it."

"That's never a mistake. Your happiness is important to me."

"It's no fun watching you mope around the house waiting for a mountain to magically appear for you to climb. I do know that's not going to happen on the Civil Service Commission."

"Hardly." Roosevelt chuckled, then became pensive. "Still, of all the jobs in the world, me . . . a policeman. I'm not sure."

"Whatever you decide, I'm behind you ninety-nine percent."

"What about the remaining one percent?"

"Please, Teddy, a woman must have some mystery about her."

Roosevelt gave her a loving peck on the cheek and patted little Archie. He then returned to the living room, sat in a cushy club chair, and resumed reading his copy of *Moby-Dick*. He was plowing through it for a second time. An avid reader, Roosevelt didn't expect to find the answer to his dilemma in the tortured soul of Captain Ahab, but it was a good diversion, and when the mind is being entertained, one never knows what ideas might pop in. Roosevelt hoped for one that was decisive. He despised being wishy-washy.

It was exciting to imagine Theodore Roosevelt cleaning house, but Mary couldn't count on his decision to help solve her cases. Harper had told her that Choate was upset but had no helpful suggestion about Walter's situation. Choate did find out in a quick visit to Laidlaw that he had fallen in love with his nurse Emily and had trusted her with Colleen's name. He was upset that Emily might have betrayed him, but even more distraught that she had been transferred to another nursing facility. It didn't take long for Choate to discover that Byrnes had orchestrated the transfer, thus making Emily the obvious source of the leak. His case was made significantly weaker by the loss of Colleen, but he still thought he had a good chance of winning.

It was Monday morning, and Mary felt it was time to give Basem an update on his brother's case. She had hoped to tell him by now that they had the real killer in custody and Ameer would soon go free. Unfortunately, Dr. Lawrence was no longer a suspect, and after all this time, she essentially had nothing except for a vague description that fit many men.

When Mary entered Leo's Meats, she didn't see Basem. A person she had never seen before, a round man, fortyish, with gray hair, was behind the counter.

"How may I help you, miss?"

"I'm looking for Basem Ben Ali. Is he in the back?"

"Basem isn't here today. I'm filling in for him. I'm sure I—"

"I don't want to buy meat. I need to speak with Basem."

"Basem had a family emergency."

"A family emergency? Did something happen to his brother Ameer?"

The round man was hesitant to give out information. "Do you know Ameer?"

"Ameer's my client. What happened?"

"I don't know if I should tell you. It's personal."

"Basem told you. Are you close with him?"

"I've never met Basem. Leo told me when he asked me to fill in."

"You know, Leo knows, God knows how many others. It's not a big secret. Tell me, please."

He considered her words. "Okay, but you didn't hear it from me. Ameer was stabbed by another inmate. His chances of living are not good."

Mary froze, momentarily in shock. Though she logically knew there was always a chance of being attacked in a place like Matteawan, she'd never really considered the possibility. She had to call and find out how Ameer was, and she couldn't wait.

"Can I use your phone?"

"Gee, I don't know—"

"It's urgent. I need to call Matteawan."

"Long distance is expensive. Leo could fire me."

Mary took several bills out of her pocketbook and threw them at him. "This ought to cover it and more."

She ran to the phone and got the operator to connect her to Matteawan. It didn't do her any good. Mary was not a relative, and the officious receptionist refused to give her personal information. Her frustration was tangible.

"Can you at least tell me if he's alive?" an exasperated Mary asked.

The receptionist was hesitant to answer and spoke very slowly, drawing out the word: "Ye-e-e-s-s-s."

"Thank goodness he's alive!"

"I didn't say that."

Mary tensed. "You mean he's dead?"

"I didn't say that either."

Mary was flustered. "I don't understand."

"You asked if I could tell you if he was alive. If you had waited for me to finish and not rudely cut me off, you would have heard me reply, 'Yes, I can tell you that.' "

Mary gathered what little patience she had left in order to extract the information she needed. "Thank you. So, is he alive?"

"Yes. I can't tell you any more than that. There are procedures I—"

Mary hung up. She had gotten the information she needed and didn't feel like staying for a lecture on Matteawan bureaucratic procedure. Besides, the round man was eyeing her very closely to make sure she didn't exceed the amount of money she had given him.

She waved to him and shouted, "Thank you," as she

rushed out of the butcher shop on her way to Grand Central Depot.

On the train up to Matteawan, Mary reviewed the events of the weekend: the Dr. Lawrence fiasco, Harper's being drugged, Edgar's getting framed for murder, Colleen's refusing to testify, Walter's law practice being destroyed, and now Ameer. How could so many things go wrong in such a short period of time? She felt like she was a curse to everyone she had come in contact with.

She hired a carriage at the Fishkill Landing train station, and just a few hours after hearing the news about Ameer, she found herself standing in the entrance lobby at Matteawan. Luckily, Wendy, the nurse Mary had met on her last visit, the one with whom she had discussed Lizzie, recognized her.

"I thought you might come," she said.

"I was on the first train the second I heard," said Mary.

"It's been hard. No one has shown up, not even her mother."

"Her?"

"Your friend Lizzie. I don't know what possessed her to do a thing like that."

"I'm here to see my client, Ameer Ben Ali."

"Then you don't know. Lizzie is the one who stabbed Ameer. It may not be too awful for her. It looks like Ameer is going to pull through, thank God."

Mary had trouble processing the information. She was happy Ameer was going to be okay, but Lizzie had stabbed him. Could it be that Mary was responsible for this? Did Lizzie find out that Ameer was her client and stab him out of some sick attempt to hurt Mary? Mary was beginning to think she really was cursed.

"I'd like to visit with Lizzie. Would that be okay?"

"Of course. I'm sure she would love to see you."

Lizzie was in solitary confinement, locked in a padded cell and restrained with a straitjacket. Wendy told Mary that Lizzie had stabbed Ameer with her knitting needles, which she had been slowly sharpening for days. The Matteawan brass were taking no more chances with her until they were absolutely sure she wouldn't hurt anyone else. Of course, how they could determine that with someone so far gone was beyond Mary. Wendy saw no harm in letting Mary into her cell. Between Lizzie's straitjacket and the sedatives they had given her, she saw little risk of danger. Lizzie was lying on her right side, her back pressed against the padded wall. Groggy but conscious and somewhat giddy, she often talked in a singsong way, her voice rising and lowering within one word.

"Ma-a-a-r-y-y-y-y."

"Hello, Lizzie. How are you?"

"Terrible, just te-e-er-i-i-i-ble. Never getting out. Never."

"What did you expect? You've got to stop hurting people."

Lizzie burst into insane laughter as she sat up, her back still against the wall. "You think . . . oh no, not them. You think they were going to let me out?" Lizzie's laughter continued.

"How were you going to get out?"

"All I had to do was kill him. Simple. And I'm free."

"How is that? Who would free you?"

"I never had a trial, Mary. I can go to another state and they can't bring me back. Free. Completely free. But he's alive, damn it! I messed up!" Lizzie's laughter quickly turned to tears. She was sobbing uncontrollably.

Lizzie may have been completely unstable but Mary knew she was right. There was a prevailing policy in most states where if a person never had a trial and was sent straight to an institution like Lizzie had been, they couldn't be extradited. The possibility of that happening for Lizzie at that point was remote. Someone had promised to help Lizzie escape if she killed Ameer, and Mary needed to find out who that person was.

"That's terrible, Lizzie." Mary spoke gently as she inched closer to her. "Maybe I can talk to him, tell him how hard you tried. I'll make him understand, and you can be free."

Lizzie stopped bawling, lifted her head up, and stared at Mary. "You think I'm stupid."

"Of course not, Lizzie, I'm your friend. I want to help."

"Well, you can't, 'cause she hates you more than I do."

"She does? It must be a misunderstanding. What's her name?"

Lizzie got up on her knees and started screaming, "I hate you, Mary Handley! I want you dead! Dead!" Wendy opened the cell. A couple of attendants rushed in to calm Lizzie down. She struggled, but one of them already had a syringe in hand, and she was soon asleep.

Mary was shaken, in part by Lizzie's outburst but mostly because there was an unknown woman out there who hated her and wanted Ameer dead. As she and Wendy walked to the hospital ward, she tried to piece it together.

"I thought she'd be happy to see you," Wendy said. "I don't know what got into her."

"Do you by any chance keep the mail Lizzie gets?"

"We often keep patients' mail, especially the violent ones, but I've been here ever since Lizzie was transferred and she hasn't gotten any to my knowledge."

"You had told me that her mother visits her. Who else has?"

"Just her mother. Lovely woman, always dressed well, with the most beautiful red hair."

Mary had met Lizzie's mother. She was plain and simple country, and her hair was a mousy brown. In short, she wasn't anything like Wendy's description. The redheaded woman at the luncheon where Dr. Lawrence had spoken popped into Mary's head. It was a hunch, but what else did she have?

"Did she by any chance wear a necklace with a large diamond and gold heart locket?"

"Why, yes, it's beautiful. It must be very expensive."

"Wendy, that isn't Lizzie's mother. If that woman ever shows up again, have her held and call the police. She was the one who convinced Lizzie to stab Ameer."

"No!"

"I'm afraid so."

"Oh my goodness!"

"What?"

"There were times she'd ask me about Ameer. I never thought anything of it then, but now . . ." Wendy was aghast that she had been so fooled by this woman. Mary questioned her further, and she really knew nothing else about her. She was at the Dr. Lawrence luncheon, so he might know something, if he would speak to her.

Wendy gave Mary directions to the hospital wing. Mary thanked her and Wendy left, still shaken by Lizzie's explosion and all the deception. The wing was a long, large room with rows of beds on opposing walls, twenty in all, with a spacious pathway between the two rows. Five of the beds were empty. As Mary entered, she saw a doctor and nurse loading a man onto a gurney. When she realized it was Ameer, she rushed over.

"I thought he was okay. What happened?"

"A collapsed lung," said the doctor. "It often happens in these cases."

"Mary," Ameer said, his voice weak and raspy.

"Save your strength, Ameer."

"You have to stop Basem."

"Basem? Why?"

"Wants revenge. Going to kill Byrnes and Carnegie."

"Carnegie? Andrew Carnegie?"

Ameer nodded. "My fault. I brought him back to America."

The doctor interrupted. "No more. We have to get him to surgery or he will die." Mary quickly handed the doctor her card and asked him to call her after the surgery. As they wheeled him out of the room, she called out, "Was his brother here?"

The nurse replied, "He left two hours ago." And they were gone.

Mary took a moment to process what had just occurred. It could have been the delirious rant of a sick man, but with Byrnes in the mix, it certainly sounded real. She couldn't afford not to act. She had two murders to stop.

30

The next train heading to New York would arrive in twenty minutes. Mary needed to warn Carnegie and Byrnes. Seeing a telephone at the receptionist desk, she asked if she could use it, quickly adding she was willing to pay. It turned out the receptionist was the same officious bureaucrat to whom Mary had spoken on the phone earlier. As she was being denied access and Matteawan procedural policy was being recited to her, Mary remembered having seen a coin telephone at the train station. Rather than waste time arguing with the receptionist, she left. The carriage she hired arrived at the station with ten minutes to spare. Unfortunately, the coin telephone was broken.

Her ride back to New York was filled with anxiety, but it did give her a chance to review the information, which was getting worse with each new piece. Who was this redheaded woman and why did she want Ameer dead? Did it have anything to do with the Immigration Restriction League luncheon or was it just a coincidence? She concluded that it would have been too random for her presence at the luncheon to be a coincidence. The woman was either following her or was acting as an agent for someone there. But who was that person and why would he or she want to kill Ameer? Mary kept on coming back to herself. It must somehow be related to her, but she didn't know how.

Frustrated in her thinking about the redheaded woman, she turned her attention to Basem, Byrnes, and Carnegie. As much as she liked Basem and was sympathetic to his circumstances, she had to warn Byrnes and Carnegie. She couldn't idly stand by when she knew murders were about to be committed. She hoped to somehow stop Basem, maybe talk him out of it, but warning the victims was paramount.

When she arrived at Grand Central, she went straight to a coin telephone. This one was working. She got some change and called Leo's Meats. Basem wasn't there. Then she called Byrnes's office. He wasn't there either, and they had no idea where he was. Carnegie's office was next. He also wasn't in. She asked where he was, and his secretary refused to give his whereabouts.

"My name is Mary Handley. I used to be engaged to George Vanderbilt, and I have met Mr. Carnegie several times. I'm not joking when I say this is a matter of life and death. Now please tell me where Mr. Carnegie is."

"Ah yes, Miss Handley. Mr. Carnegie has mentioned you. Of course, I'll tell you. He left a little while ago for a meeting with Russell Sage at his office."

"Thank you." Mary immediately hung up and called Russell Sage's office. It rang many times without an answer.

"No one is there," said the operator.

"Please keep trying."

The operator dutifully granted Mary's request. Finally,

Mary realized no one was going to answer and hung up. Only one course of action was left: rush down to Russell Sage's office as fast as she could. To do that, she headed for the elevated train. They had been built all over Manhattan in the last twenty-four years, and it was the fastest mode of transportation.

A half an hour later, Mary found herself in the Arcade Building on Broadway, running up the stairs to Russell Sage's office. When she got there, it was very quiet, and no one was in the outer office. With it being a few minutes past six o'clock, it was entirely possible his employees had left for the day. Then she smelled the distinct odor of Turkish tobacco.

"Basem," she called out. "Are you here?"

Basem answered, his voice emanating from Russell Sage's office. "Leave, Mary. You don't want to be here."

Mary slowly made her way to the office as she spoke. "I do, Basem. You're a good man. I don't want you to make a mistake."

Mary now stood in the doorway. Basem, Carnegie, Byrnes, and Sage were all standing. Basem was a few steps to her right, a bulky satchel slung over his shoulder. Carnegie and Byrnes were in the middle of the room, and Russell Sage was behind his desk.

"I just came from seeing Ameer. He's going to be okay, and he's afraid for you. He doesn't want you to do this." Mary started walking toward him.

Basem tensed. "Don't come any closer, Mary. Back away."

She stopped.

"He has a bomb in that satchel," said Carnegie. "He's threatening to blow us all to pieces."

As Mary slowly stepped backward into the room, she glanced at Sage. He had a look of horror on his face, as if that déjà vu nightmare he had been having since the Norcross incident was coming true.

"Nothin's gonna happen," Byrnes said. "He's a scared little weasel with no guts."

"Though that approach may work with some, Inspector Byrnes," said Mary, "I should inform you that the man you're attempting to rattle is a seasoned veteran who served four years in the French Foreign Legion and is probably quite skilled in the use of explosives."

"A real man would fight me straight on, not take the spineless way out."

"You frame an innocent man to cover your incompetence and I'm spineless?" Basem asked as he put out his cigarette in a nearby ashtray. "No, Inspector, you're a bully, and bullies need to be punished."

"Come on, punish me. I enjoy stickin' it to ya Arab trash."

Byrnes's ploy wasn't working. Basem trembled, not with fear but with anger. As he moved to block the doorway, the satchel slipped off his shoulders, but he caught it before it hit the floor.

Carnegie swiveled toward Byrnes. "Tom, shut the hell up!" He then turned to Basem. "Look, Basem, that is your name?" Basem didn't reply. He just stared. "Let's reason this out. You tricked us with this phony meeting to get Tom over here. You have a grievance with him. Russell and I have nothing to do with it. We've never even met."

"I was in the elevator the other day with you and the inspector."

"You were? I didn't—"

"Why would you notice? I'm unimportant, merely one of the faceless thousands whose lives you destroyed."

"What are you talking about?"

"Johnstown, Mr. Carnegie. I lost my wife, my son, my business, everything."

Mary remembered that Basem had told her he had lived in Pennsylvania before he returned to Algeria. But he had never mentioned Johnstown.

On May 31, 1889, after several days of heavy rains, the South Fork Dam above Johnstown, Pennsylvania, burst and the waters of Lake Conemaugh emptied, rushing downhill and devastating the town. Over twenty-two hundred people were killed. The South Fork Fishing and Hunting Club had made adjustments to the dam in order to aid their pursuits, adjustments that weakened it. The club's members were some of the wealthiest Americans, Andrew Carnegie the most prominent among them. The people of Johnstown sued, but the club also had top-echelon lawyers as members and its financial structure was devised so none of its elite members' fortunes could be touched. Needless to say, the lawsuit netted nothing.

Carnegie was surprised and his confidence shaken. "I am so, so sorry for your wife and son, and all of the misfortunes you suffered. But I was just a member of a club. That's all. Surely you can't blame me for that?"

"You knew the dangers of adjusting a dam. You could have stopped them, but your hunting and fishing were more important."

"I felt terrible about what happened. I tried to help."

"You built a library. Thousands die and a few books make it okay?"

"What about me, damn it?" Sage said, interrupting. "I

don't know your brother, I don't fish, and I've definitely never been in Johnstown."

"You were the only person I knew who could bring them together. Unlucky for you, like the many people who have been hurt in your stock market manipulations."

"You can't do this. I'm innocent!"

"There are no innocent bourgeois."

Mary recognized his words. "Émile Henry. Now I understand."

"Who the hell is Émile Henry?" Sage demanded.

Émile Henry was a French anarchist who had bombed a café in Paris that year. They caught him, and he was sent to the guillotine. Mary wasn't going to waste precious time explaining it to Sage.

"When did you become an anarchist, Basem?"

"I finally reached my—how you say it—saturation point. Yes?"

"Your English has never been a problem. It's your logic that's faulty."

He gestured toward the other three. "These pigs abuse their power and do what they want without any consequences while millions suffer. It's time for them to suffer."

"And what will it accomplish besides killing all of us?"

"Others will see. Capitalist greed must be punished."

"All people will see is that the brother of notorious killer Ameer Ben Ali is also a killer. They'll say it runs in the family, and all Arabs are criminals. Ameer will lose any hope of ever being set free. Is that what you want?"

"You need to leave, Mary."

She started slowly edging toward him. "Why? Am I making too much sense?"

He moved to the side, clearing the doorway. "Go, Mary!"

She kept heading for him. "Please don't do this, Basem."

Out of the corner of his eye, Basem saw Byrnes reach inside his coat. "Stop it, Inspector, or we all die right now!"

"A gun, Tom!" shouted Carnegie. "Are you out of your mind?"

"I'm not waiting around for this scum to kill us all!"

Sage jumped in. "So you want to die sooner?" Byrnes looked confused. "Think, moron. If you shoot him, he falls and so does the bomb. I've been around this block before."

"The voice of experience," Carnegie declared. "What's your plan, Russell? Shall we short his stock and watch him go bankrupt?"

"Shut up, Andy! If it weren't for you, I wouldn't be in this situation."

"You're the one who's been trying to drag me in on one of your schemes."

Carnegie, Sage, and Byrnes continued arguing between themselves as if Basem and Mary weren't there. Mary and Basem's eyes met as they shared a brief moment of disgust for the three men. Then Basem's expression changed to one of sorrow. He was asking forgiveness, and she knew what that meant.

Mary was a little more than a body's length away from him. She dove right before he dropped the satchel, slid underneath it, and caught it in the air before it hit the floor. Oddly, her first thought was that if she had been wearing a corset and hoop skirt, they'd all be dead.

She hadn't yet heaved a sigh of relief when the first shot rang out. "No!" Then two more in rapid succession.

Basem slumped to the floor. The satchel safely sitting

in her lap, Mary leaned over and felt his pulse. "You killed him!"

Byrnes returned his pistol to its holster and announced smugly, "I always get my man."

"You didn't have to do that. I already had the bomb!"

"That crazy Arab coulda done anything."

As much as she hated Byrnes and what he stood for, she had to admit he did have a point. It was possible Basem might have tried to pry the bomb out of Mary's hands or done any number of things that would have meant disaster. Byrnes indicated the satchel.

"I'll take that off yer hands." Mary let him have the satchel. "Russell, mind if I leave it on yer desk for a bit?" Sage's knee-jerk reaction of horror was what he had wanted. "Just jokin'. I'll get one of our bomb experts down here to defuse this."

"While you're at it . . ." Mary motioned toward Basem's corpse.

"Right, almost forgot about him. I'll call a hearse." Byrnes emitted a chuckle as he walked out carefully carrying the satchel.

Carnegie and Sage had already recovered from the trauma of their near-death experience when Mary rose to her feet. Carnegie approached.

"Miss Handley, I can't thank you enough."

Still glum, Mary stared at Basem's dead body. "I didn't want anyone to die."

"You're a remarkable woman. George Vanderbilt is a fool to have let you go."

"I don't think that was your opinion at the time."

"Well, we all grow and change, don't we?" He turned to

Sage and tipped his head. "Good night, Russell." Completely recovered, Carnegie straightened and marched out. Mary was about to follow when Sage spoke.

"Miss Handley, I would be remiss if I let you go before thanking you from the bottom of my heart. Most people think I don't have one, but I assure you it's in place and I do."

"You're welcome, Mr. Sage, and if you would please indulge me, I have a favor to ask. Two, really." It was an odd time for such a request and, considering what had just occurred, probably inappropriate. But Mary didn't know if she'd have this opportunity again.

"I do not entertain many favors, but after your heroic efforts, of course."

"I am close with Walter Cooper and his family. His wife and I have been friends since we were little girls. Walter is a lawyer, and he recently had a setback in his career. Inexplicably, all his clients fired him in one day. I was hoping you could rectify that."

"You're not implying that I'm responsible?"

"No, of course not. I would never suggest that." His very question convinced Mary that he indeed was responsible, but pointing that out would have been counterproductive. "You're a very influential man, and I was hoping you could speak with these people. Convince them to change their minds."

"I have no problem with that. Get me a list of who to contact."

He knew who they were, but she played along. "It will be done posthaste. Thank you, Mr. Sage. You're a very compassionate man." Mary started to leave.

"What about the second favor?" he asked. "You said you had two."

Halfway to the door, Mary turned. "You've been more than generous. I don't want to put you out." She had secured Sarah's happiness and had decided not to risk it.

"Nonsense. You saved my life. What else can I do for you?"

He was not going to let her drop it. "Well, not me," she said, then continued with some trepidation, "William Laidlaw." Sage's pleasant expression faded into a scowl. At this point though, she had no choice but to continue. "The man is now doomed to live in constant pain and dire poverty for the rest of his life. If you could see it in your heart to give him what you deem to be a fair amount, just enough to make his sorrowful existence a bit more bearable—"

"William Laidlaw has ruined my reputation. I can't walk down the street without people whispering behind my back. Every day I am forced to live with the labels of 'skinflint,' 'coward,' and 'heartless.' I am not a social being and can live with it, but it has caused my wife a great deal of upset. Under no circumstances will I give credence to this man's claims by paying him. I don't care how much it costs me in lawyer fees. I will see that he never gets a penny from me."

"I apologize for asking. I didn't know how strongly you felt."

"Now you do."

"Yes, and I apologize again," Mary replied, then quickly added, "I will get you that contact list of Walter Cooper's clients."

"Please do."

Mary was happy Sage was still going to help Walter and decided to get out of there as fast as she could. As she left, she glanced at the tangled mess on the floor that was Basem's dead body and wondered if there was anything she could have done differently that would have spared his life. She was sure that thought was going to torture her for a long time.

31

Mary didn't feel like going home. She went to Harper's apartment to tell him the events of the day and relax. Having been given a last-minute assignment by the *Brooklyn Daily Eagle,* he was rushing to meet a deadline.

"I'll be finished in about an hour."

"Okay, I'll be at Lazlo's."

He could see something was bothering her. "I'm sorry. Every once in a while I have to take an assignment that actually pays the bills. Are you all right?"

She put on her brightest face and lied. "I'm fine. What's it about?"

"The new baby lion at the zoo."

"Sounds fascinating."

"Like I said, pays the bills. Mary—"

"I'm absolutely fine. Really. I'll see you later."

The fact that she repeated she was fine convinced him she wasn't, but he had to let her leave. He had a strict deadline. He would be finished with his article in a few minutes, then he had to run it down to the *Brooklyn Daily Eagle* offices. It might be sooner, but an hour gave him some leeway.

When Mary got to Lazlo's Books, it was almost eight o'clock, which was closing time. Lazlo was alone.

"Where's Gerta?"

"She's having dinner with her daughter and grandchildren."

"She didn't invite you?"

"She knows children and I are not a good combination. I don't consider them human beings until they can recite the Shakespearean sonnets."

"There are many people in their fifties who can't do that."

"Which explains why our world is in shambles. Now come sit down. We've both been occupied this past week and haven't had a chance to have a proper chat."

About forty-five minutes later, Mary was practically finished telling Lazlo everything when the phone rang. Lazlo rose to answer it.

"That could be for me, Lazlo. I'm expecting a call from Ameer's doctor."

Lazlo spoke into the telephone. "Hello, Lazlo's Books . . . Yes, she's here." He pointed the phone toward Mary. "For you."

Mary took the phone from him. "How is Ameer, doctor?"

"Doctor, is it? Well, it's nice to know I've been promoted."

"Who is this?"

"Mary, this is Harper's friend Ivan Nowak. I was able to examine the fingerprints sooner than I had anticipated."

"Oh, Ivan, I'm sorry. If I had your number, I would have called you. I found out the man whose thumbprint I asked you to examine is not the killer. I apologize for troubling you."

"That's exactly why I called. You're right. The thumbprint you asked me to examine was not a match, but the other thumbprint on the paper was spot-on."

Mary was puzzled. "The other thumbprint?"

"There were two distinctly different thumbprints on that paper. Did you not know that?"

Mary's mind was racing, poring over the events of the past four days, until she finally realized who the thumbprint belonged to. She was stunned.

~

Leo's Meats had just closed. Jeffrey Handley had locked the door and was doing some last-minute cleaning up as Leo was on the phone. He was speaking in a low, intense whisper.

"Friday is the soonest time? . . . Yes, all of them, all my shops. You've got my instructions about what to do with the proceeds? . . . I know I won't get a premium price. . . . Yes, I know I'll be taking a beating. Just do it!"

Leo hung up and walked into the back, where Jeffrey had just finished putting away the meat cleavers and knives after cleaning them. He had been trying very hard to make a good impression on his new boss and had just grabbed a broom when Leo stopped him.

"Go home, Jeffrey. You can take care of that tomorrow morning."

"It's okay, Mr. Cosgrove. I don't mind."

"Jeffrey, how many times do I have to tell you to call me Leo? You're almost old enough to be my father."

"Sorry, Mr.—Leo. That's how I'm used to addressing my boss."

Leo smiled. "Go on home. I insist."

"It's okay, I can finish." Jeffrey started sweeping, and Leo reached over to pull the broom out of his hands. Jeffrey tripped and knocked over a large suitcase that was in the corner. It popped open, and among other things, a man's blond-haired wig fell out.

"Oh, Jeffrey, what am I to do now?"

Jeffrey quickly began repacking the suitcase. "I'll get that. It's not a problem."

"But it is. You just accelerated my plans."

Jeffrey had no idea what that meant as Leo stepped toward him.

~

Elizabeth Handley was upset that Jeffrey was late getting home. "My dinner is going to be ice cold," she complained to Mary, "and your father will be the first one to point that out."

Knowing that the butcher shop would be closed, Mary had come straight home to speak with her father. She needed to find out where Leo lived, and her mother kept going off on tangents.

"Mother, I can't wait until Dad gets home. Do you know where his boss, Leo, lives?"

"Yes, you've asked me that before, and I told you he has numerous homes."

"I need you to be more specific."

"Oh, let me see. There's an apartment in Manhattan—"

"Where?"

"The Stuyvesant Apartments. Very ritzy . . . He rents a summer home on Long Island."

"That's for vacations. He wouldn't be traveling back and forth to work from there every day. So, the Stuyvesant Apartments. Thanks." Mary headed for the door.

"Wait. He's also renting a house by the beach."

Mary stopped. "Which beach?"

"Stop badgering me and give me a second to think."

"I'm not badgering you."

"Yes, you are. Believe me, I know what badgering is."

"Mother, this is important."

"I know. Everything you do is important. Everything I do isn't." Suddenly it hit her. "Brighton Beach!"

"Brighton Beach. Are you sure?"

"Well, close to it. It's really in Coney Island. You know, your father and I used to love taking you and Sean there when you were children—"

"Where, Mother, where in Coney Island?" Mary was sure that was where she could find him as she stood there, waiting for her mother to remember.

~

Because of what was at stake, Mary's ride out to Coney Island on the train seemed excruciatingly longer than usual. The last stop felt like it was in London and not Brooklyn. There was one positive. It gave her a chance to review the mounds of information she had and put some of the pieces together. Working from the premise that Leo had killed all those women starting with Carrie Brown, Ameer was the only person convicted of one of his murders. The others were shoved under the mat by Byrnes to protect his reputation. By keeping tabs on Ameer at Matteawan, Leo found out his brother Basem was coming to New York to help prove his innocence. He obviously tracked down Basem and offered him a job, so he could have firsthand knowledge of the investigation. That was probably also the reason why he bought Flanagan's Butcher Shop and kept Mary's father employed there. Questions still remained. Who were the blond man with the mustache and the redheaded woman? Were they all in it together? The blond man's thumbprint was on Carrie Brown's key and that thumbprint was a perfect match for Leo. The only conclusion that Mary could draw from that was that Leo disguised himself to throw suspicion off of him and possibly direct it toward Dr. Lawrence. That appeared simple enough, but who was that redheaded woman? These weren't the type of crimes where one had an accomplice, though at this point almost anything was possible. Then Mary remembered something. In the few dealings she'd had with Leo he'd repeatedly mentioned how much he loved the theater and that he was especially enamored with Shakespeare. In Shakespeare's time, there were no actresses. Boys played the female roles, and cross-dressing was a recurrent theme in his plays.

Could it be?

32

Jeffrey was passed out on the bed in Leo's bedroom. Emanating from the bathroom was a female's voice singing one of the most popular songs of that decade, "After the Ball."

After the ball is over, after the break of morn,
After the dancers' leaving, after the stars are gone,
Many a heart is aching, if you could read them all—

Leo, dressed as the redheaded woman, danced out of the bathroom with a flourish, wearing a black silk dress with long sleeves, black leather buckle shoes, and the necklace with the diamond and gold heart locket. He looked incredibly feminine as he modeled, striking various poses.

"So, how do I look, Jeffrey?" he said, maintaining his feminine voice. "Oh, I know silk shoes are more in style, but I find the leather ones give me more support. We large girls can't be too careful." Jeffrey was silent, still passed out. "What's that, Jeffrey? What's my secret? Well, a girl should never tell, but you're special."

Leo whispered, "Alopecia universalis." He abandoned the whisper and returned to his masculine Leo voice. "Well, not completely universalis. I was spared some hair. My eyebrows. You know how important they are to us girls." He walked closer to Jeffrey, as if he were confiding in him. "I thought I was cursed. I mean, small unnoticeable features and no hair. How was I to stand out? Then I went to the theater, and I realized what a blessing it was. With the help of makeup and some minor prosthetics, very minor, I can be anyone." He curtsied, stuck his arms out, and once again spoke as a woman. "Voilà! I have dubbed myself Leticia. That name has an exotic feel to it, don't you think?"

Leo paced around the room, returning to his male voice once again. "I must admit your daughter has caused me some trouble. I have to sell my butcher shops for much less than they're worth, but making money has never been a problem for me and there are positives. I was getting bored with imitating Jack the Ripper. It's time to move on. Leticia is a true original and tonight she will burst onto the scene. There is an abundance of male degenerates out there, and when they reach down for Leticia's goodies, boy, will they be in for a surprise!"

Leo burst into laughter, then looked at Jeffrey, who was beginning to stir, mumbling incoherently. He disappeared into the bathroom and returned with a rag. "I apologize. I hate seeing you miss out on all the fun."

He covered Jeffrey's mouth and nose with the rag, and he once again became still.

~

After Mary got off the train, she made her way to Surf Avenue and West Tenth Street. Her mother had told her Leo's house was across the street from Feltman's Restaurant. Anyone who had been to Coney Island knew Feltman's. Charles Feltman had invented a new food by simply putting a hot sausage on a bun. Hot dogs had quickly become a Coney Island staple, and his business had grown from being a little cart on the street to a large restaurant.

The area had become very commercial, and there were no residential structures on the four corners. Mary was concerned that her mother had been mistaken until she saw a house on West Tenth Street nestled behind a novelty store. One of the many things she had contemplated on the train was how she would handle this meeting. Leo had been privy to so much of her investigation. Should she assume he knew she was aware of his guilt or invent some reason for her traveling out there, possibly to tell him about what happened to Basem? There was no real answer, and she decided to see how he reacted to her showing up.

As it turned out, there was no mystery. Leo answered the door in full dress as Leticia.

"You're early, Mary. I was expecting you tomorrow." She entered, keeping a close eye on him as he closed the door. "Ivan Nowak must have gotten to the thumbprints sooner than he had thought."

"Were you aware of every move I made?"

"Most every one. You did fool me with the chopped meat."

"You'll be happy to know it was an accident."

"I wouldn't say happy. It forced me to make some changes."

Mary indicated his female persona. "I see."

He temporarily went into his female voice. "We've never been formally introduced. Meet Leticia. She is an enchantress."

"Is that what they're calling a deranged killer nowadays?"

Leo returned to his male voice as he started pacing. "All this could have been avoided. You never would have had a client if it weren't for your friend Lizzie. She took two months to convince, and then she bungled the job."

"It's hard to predict the insane," Mary said pointedly.

"Touché. I must admit though, radicalizing Basem was fun. It's amazing how easily the right literature with the right lies can influence a troubled man."

"Basem is dead."

"He didn't do anything that he didn't want to do. I just showed him the way."

"Like you showed Carrie Brown and all the other women you killed?"

"Carrie Brown was a mistake. August thirty-first was my plan. She was my dress rehearsal, but that infernal woman started butchering Shakespeare and, well, you know how much I love Shakespeare."

"And how much you hate women."

"You think I hate women?" Leo laughed as he extended his arms to assume a model's pose. "I have plans, a list that will keep me busy for years—grandfathers, baseball players. Wouldn't it be fun to see how truly religious a priest is as the light goes out in his eyes?"

"My, my, the little orphan is branching out."

"Orphan by choice."

"So we must add parricide to your illustrious résumé . . . something you don't include in that boring life story you spout to everyone you meet."

"They were stifling, insufferable people, and the story worked. You didn't suspect me."

"You did make some costly mistakes. Next time you'll need to find a better sucker than Dr. Lawrence."

Leo's delight turned to disgust. "The police are idiots. When I first saw Lawrence speak a few years back, it was a magical moment. I couldn't have devised a better target."

Mary pulled a gun out of her pocketbook. "This time the police will believe me."

"You may want to wait a tad on that, Mary." He walked toward the back of the house.

"Don't underestimate me because I'm a woman."

"Never. We ladies can be a deadly lot." He pointed to a lever on a wall. "I've spoken about my affinity for the theater. What I haven't mentioned is I'm also a fan of the macabre."

"Not really a surprise."

"I'm an avid reader of Edgar Allan Poe. Are you familiar with his work?"

"Every piece."

"Then you know what happened in 'The Pit and the Pendulum.' I've rigged my own little version of it. It's a bit primitive. No pit, but you can't have everything." He pulled the lever. "The pendulum is now swinging back and forth, propelling downward each time it passes over." He waved his hand from side to side, imitating the pendulum. "By the way, this one is faster than the one in the story. The victim has maybe two minutes."

"So?"

"So, I'm presenting you with a choice. You can arrest me or you can save your father's life." He opened the door next to him, revealing a well-lit basement below. Keeping an eye on Leo, Mary cautiously walked down a couple of steps to see if he was bluffing. He wasn't. Jeffrey was tied to a table with a pendulum swinging slightly above him, a huge, razor-sharp blade at the end of it.

Mary cried out, "Daddy!" Jeffrey wasn't moving, and she quickly turned to Leo, filled with rage. "He better be alive."

"I knew you had that fear in you. I just had to probe a bit."

"Did you also know I had this in me?"

Mary shot Leo in his right leg. A combination of surprise and pain filled his voice as he cried out, "Damn it!" and collapsed to the floor. By that time, Mary was already halfway down the stairs to the basement.

Leo took a breath, then, balancing himself on a nearby table, he pulled himself up. His red wig was askew and his first step hurt beyond description, but as he limped toward the door, it became more bearable. When he opened it, he saw Harper standing before him. He was about to knock when he froze at the sight of Leo dressed as Leticia.

"What the hell!" Harper exclaimed. It gave Leo just enough time to deliver a crushing blow to Harper's jaw, sending him to the pavement. Then Leo limped off into the night.

The pendulum Leo had rigged up was indeed primitive but also effective and deadly. As the razor-sharp blade swung over Jeffrey, getting closer with every passing, Mary had to decide how to stop it without injuring him or herself. Grabbing the pendulum was too dangerous and shoving it was unpredictable. It could fall away from Jeffrey or onto him.

She finally had to take action or face disaster. She kicked the table as hard as she could, knocking it over and sending him out of the range of the pendulum. The pendulum then crashed to the floor, its blade slicing through the legs of the table and splintering them in many directions.

Mary quickly circled around to her father. She felt his pulse and was relieved that he was alive. "Daddy, Dad." He was starting to come to. Mary looked around for tools. She found a knife on a workbench and used it to cut the ropes around Jeffrey, freeing him.

Disoriented, in a cloudy haze, Jeffrey opened his eyes. "Mary?"

"Daddy, are you in pain, are you okay?"

Taking inventory, Jeffrey paused. "I'm . . . fine. Woozy but . . . where are we?"

"Leo's basement. I'm going to help you up now. Are you ready?"

He nodded. She put his right arm around the back of her neck and over her right shoulder, then slowly helped him to his feet. He saw the pendulum for the first time, and it shocked him further into consciousness.

"What is that?"

"It doesn't matter. It can't hurt you now."

"The last thing I remember Leo shoved a rag in my face. It had a strong sweet smell."

A voice came from the stairs. "It was probably ether."

Mary looked up to see Harper. "What are you doing here?"

"Thanks for the welcome," Harper said as he descended the stairs. "Next time I'll know not to run all over Brooklyn from Lazlo's to your mother's to here."

“Did you see Leo upstairs?”

“I think so, on his way out as his fist came down on my face.”

“From now on, Harper, stick to your typewriter.”

“Sound advice. Leo shouldn’t be hard to find. He was wearing a dress and sporting a bizarre red wig.”

“A wig,” said Jeffrey. “That’s how it started. I saw a blond wig.”

“Dad, this is Harper Lloyd. He’s going to take you home.” Jeffrey nodded that he understood. She removed his arm from around her neck, saw that he remained standing, then headed for the stairs.

“Mary,” said Harper, “you can’t go after this man by yourself.”

“I can’t if I have to worry about you and my father. See that he gets home safely.” She continued up the stairs and was soon gone.

Harper turned to Jeffrey. “Can you walk on your own, Mr. Handley?”

“I think so.” Jeffrey headed for the stairs with Harper close by, making sure he didn’t fall. “Harper Lloyd,” said Jeffrey, musing out loud. “Sounds made up. What’s your real name?”

Harper shook his head. “I see it runs in the family.”

33

Mary was faced with the task of figuring out where Leo had gone. Outside the house, she found drops of blood that she was able to follow until she got close to Feltman's. It was September tenth, and the balmy summer weather filled the air. Warm nights and Coney Island went together, and the crowds were out in force even during a weekday. Mary tried to push through, but it was impossible to follow a blood trail with mobs of people covering the streets. She had to stop and try to reason where Leo might have gone.

He needed medical help. There was a first aid station at West Third Street and the beach that had recently been converted to the Coney Island Reception Hospital. It made sense that he would go there for treatment.

As she hurried to the hospital, Mary couldn't help noting the incongruence before her. People were laughing, taking in the amusements. Young lovers were strolling, holding hands. And there she was, stalking an insane mass murderer.

Mary had always been confounded by how people who are merely out to have a good time wind up getting into bizarre accidents. There were a decent amount of those cases that night at the Reception Hospital, including a sideshow barker who had been hit in the eye by an errantly thrown dart meant for a balloon. Added to that group was the normal traffic from the Gut, ranging from drunks who had fallen down to participants in a particularly mean knife fight.

After a quick inventory of the room, Mary saw that Leo was not one of the many patients waiting to be treated. Repeatedly uttering, “Excuse me,” she pushed her way through the dozen or so people in line to check in with the nurse at the admissions desk.

“Has a redheaded woman with a gunshot wound come in this evening?”

“No,” the nurse answered curtly before turning to the next person in line.

“Are you sure?”

The nurse was overworked and impatient. “I wouldn’t have said it if I wasn’t sure.”

“Okay, thank you.” Mary began walking away, trying to devise another plan, but the nurse wasn’t finished.

“The only gunshot wound we’ve had tonight was a man and he’s sitting right over—” The nurse pointed to a chair currently filled by a midget with a towel pressed against his bruised head, the result of an unfortunate run-in with a door. “He was there. Maybe he left.”

“Was he bald?”

“Yes, very.” The nurse returned to the line of people.

It made sense. Leo was much too smart to wait endlessly in a hospital for treatment. Mary was also confident he would first seek treatment before venturing anyplace else.

She began searching the hospital room by room. The staff was swamped and too overwhelmed to notice. She finally came to a narrow door that looked like it might be a supply room. An opened combination lock hung on the outside latch. The door was slightly ajar and Mary heard Leo's voice emanating from inside. She took the pistol out of her pocketbook and slowly opened the door.

Now dressed in men's clothes with his right pant leg rolled up, Leo was sitting on a stool with a hypodermic needle aimed at the jugular vein of a nurse who was dressing his wound. She was rigid with fear as she worked on him.

"Ah, Mary, come right in. Hilda here is doing a marvelous job. She kindly removed my makeup, then used carbolic spray to ward off any infection to my leg, and applied just the right pressure to the tourniquet in order to stop the bleeding. Lucky for me, your bullet went in one side and out the other without causing much damage . . . except to that dress. I really liked that dress, Mary."

"Then you'll also be upset your attempt on my father's life failed. On the plus side, it gave you time to go shopping."

"Actually, shoplifting." He shrugged. "That's what happens when you rush out without your pocketbook. And just between you, me, and Hilda here, it didn't matter to me whether your father lived or died."

"Let Hilda go, Leo. She has nothing to do with this."

"She does now. Did you know that Hilda is German?" Leo saw that Hilda had stopped working on his leg. "*Bist du fertig?*" Hilda didn't respond. "You don't understand German? That's a shame. People come here and don't bother to teach their children about their heritage. When I was with

Barnum and Bailey, I traveled the world and became fascinated with the different cultures. I'm fluent in many languages, including—"

"Leo, no one gives a shit."

"Mary, language! And in front of Hilda." He glanced at the tense Hilda. "Okay, I'll ask you in English. Are you finished?" She tensed up even more. "Oh, I forgot. You're afraid to talk because . . . well, because. Tell you what. Roll down my pant leg if you're through." Hilda did just that. "Excellent. Now the trickier part. Let's stand at the same time. Careful now. We don't want any accidents, do we?"

They slowly rose together, Leo keeping the hypodermic needle next to her jugular. He quickly glanced down at his leg. "Good job, Hilda."

"Let her go. We can settle this between us."

"When you have a pistol and I have a hypodermic needle. Not exactly a fair match. Move away from the door, Mary." He waved his free hand to indicate the direction. Mary obeyed and he edged toward the door with Hilda in tow.

"Hilda, be a darling and open the door." She complied. "You're a dear. Thank you."

Leo then stabbed Hilda in the jugular and ran off, slamming the door shut. Mary caught her as she fell toward the floor, gasping for air with blood gushing out of her neck. She gently laid her down, then bolted into the hallway screaming for help. No one came immediately.

"The supply room, hurry! Nurse Hilda's bleeding to death!" Mary had started running toward the nurses' station when a doctor and two nurses came charging down the hall. Mary pointed. "She's in there!"

They rushed in and immediately started working on

Hilda. Once Mary knew she was in good hands, she took off after Leo.

Outside of the hospital, she stopped and whipped her head around, looking in all directions. Leo was nowhere in sight. She didn't have time for despair. She had to pick a direction and go. She chose the park. That was where she'd have gone if someone were following her.

The moon would be full in a few days, and it was shining brightly in the sky, casting a good amount of light. She spotted the moonlight illuminating a man's bald head a good distance up the beach on the sidewalk. She had no idea who it was, but she had nothing to lose and began running as fast as she could. Unlike her earlier experience at the Oriental Hotel, she was wearing dress more suitable for her detective work, dress that didn't hamper her movement.

The bald man was startled when she jumped in front of him. Unfortunately, he wasn't Leo, and after apologizing, she crossed the street and entered the amusement park.

~

Mary was right. Leo was trying to lose himself in the crowds at the amusement park, so he could eventually leave safely and find someplace to recuperate.

He stopped at a souvenir stand. The vendor was occupied by a family of four from Pennsylvania who were very much interested in any object that had Coney Island emblazoned on it. It was simple for Leo to swipe a hat and T-shirt. It wasn't until later, when he ducked into an alley to change his shirt, that he noticed the hat had ELEPHANTINE COLOSSUS written on it and the shirt GRAVITY PLEASURE SWITCHBACK RAILWAY.

He chuckled with delight, figuring he'd blend in perfectly with all the tourists.

~

Not wanting to waste time, Mary had made a beeline for the Kill the Coon booth. Arthur was out front doing his sales pitch, but it wasn't like before. There were no lines and no customers.

"Step right up, ladies and gentlemen, and take a shot at this savage from the wilds of Africa. You, lovely lady. A nickel will get you three balls."

"You do realize," said Mary, pointing to the man who had replaced Edgar, "how obvious it is that he's a white man wearing blackface?"

Arthur turned to look. "You're costing me a fortune, Carl! Check your makeup. You've got white blotches on your face again."

"I can't help it, Uncle Arthur. Every time they hit me, some of the black stuff rubs off."

Arthur looked skyward. "Damn it, Edgar. Why'd you do this to me?"

"He didn't. He's innocent." Mary quickly introduced herself, then returned to what was important. "The man who killed that woman and framed Edgar is here in the park, and I need your help."

"Why didn't you say that in the first place? Anything for Edgar . . . and my business."

He started to lower the flaps, closing his booth. Mary followed him to each one. "He's bald, about five foot seven, and he walks with a limp, favoring his right leg."

"Polio?"

"I shot him."

"That could do it."

Carl came out from behind the curtain. He was a tall gangly kid of about nineteen. "Are we shutting down early?"

Arthur tossed Carl a towel. "Wipe that crap off your face. We've got a real job to do."

It didn't take long for Arthur to spread the word. Not many booths or rides closed but there were quite a few that were two- or three-man operations and were willing to spare one. They spread out all over the park in search of the bald man with the limp.

Leo was getting bolder. There was no sign of Mary, and as he headed for one of the park's exits not far from the Elephant Hotel, he was making plans for his future. He obviously needed to change identities. That was a simple matter. He'd done it many times before. Sadly, Leticia would have to disappear along with Leo. Keeping her would be much too brazen. Of course, in the future, when things settled down, Leticia could be reborn. He was looking forward to starting his new life. If a man didn't mix things up once in a while, he could stagnate.

He spotted two men by the exit who were carefully looking over every person who left. One of them pointed to a man about Leo's size.

"What about him?" he said.

"He has a full head of hair," the other man replied. "Do you not know what bald is?"

Leo made a fast about-face and joined the long line for the toboggan ride. He pulled his hat further down and turned toward the ride with his back to the rest of the park as the people inched toward the front. Two more men showed up and began searching through the people in line for the ride across from the toboggan. Leo remained remarkably calm.

"Where's your ticket, sir?" said Lois, the woman at the entrance who collected them.

"Ticket?" he asked, feigning ignorance.

"It's a nickel a ride. You can buy your ticket over there." She pointed.

Leo dug his hands into his pockets and acted shocked when he didn't come up with any money. "I must have lost my wallet."

"That's terrible. Go look. You may have dropped it while you were in line."

"Wait a second. Now I remember. I gave it to my wife to hold for me."

"Glad you didn't lose it. Next."

The line started moving, with the people behind Leo entering.

"My daughter's up there waiting for me. She's afraid to go on the ride by herself. Could you just let me in? I'll get the wallet from my wife later and buy two tickets, even three."

"Sorry, can't do that, sir. I need a ticket or I lose my job."

Leo feared he would call too much attention to himself if this discussion continued. He reluctantly reached into his pocket and took out the diamond and gold heart locket. "This should cover it." And he dropped it in her hands.

Lois looked at the locket. "Is this real?"

"Yes, it's real. Can I go in now?"

She bit it. "Wow, it is real. Go ahead, mister. Ride as many times as you like. You and your daughter."

Leo entered the toboggan ride just as the two men started inspecting its line.

The toboggan ride was tamer than the Gravity Pleasure Switchback Railway, but like it, it was also pulled by gravity. He had to climb up many stairs to get to the top of the track and board the toboggan. The toboggan slowly went down the track until there was a deep dip, which gave it enough momentum to make it up another incline. It stopped at that point, the workers moved it to the return track, and it went back where it came from. Leo took Lois at her word and kept riding it, hoping that in time he would be able to sneak out of the park undetected.

Mary had been around the park a couple of times and had come up with nothing. As she was about to start her third go-around, she bumped into Arthur.

"Have you seen anything?" she asked.

He shrugged and shook his head. "Do you think he snuck by us and got out?"

"I don't know. Maybe I was wrong. Maybe he was never here at all."

"This is no time to doubt yourself. Edgar never did. He was going to get to England if he had to take a million balls in the face."

"If he did, he would definitely have to play character roles."

Arthur laughed. "I like you."

Mary joined him. "I like you, too, Arthur. Edgar is lucky—" Mary stopped. She had turned her head while talking and spotted something.

"What is it?"

"Maybe I wasn't wrong."

Arthur followed as Mary headed straight for Lois and pointed to the necklace with the diamond and gold heart locket that she was wearing. "Where did you get that?"

Lois smiled with pride. "It's pretty, isn't it?"

"Where did you get it?"

"I don't appreciate your tone."

"Answer her," Arthur demanded.

"Who are you?" Lois said. She was a new employee who didn't know Arthur.

"The only thing you need to know about us," said Mary, trying to control her frustration, "is that I have a black belt in jujitsu." Mary stared at the woman and she broke.

"I didn't steal it. Some man gave it to me."

"Where is he?"

"Inside, on the ride."

Mary turned to Arthur. "You stay here in case he sneaks by me." Before Mary entered, Lois stopped her.

"A ticket." She shrugged. "It's my job."

Mary quickly opened her pocketbook and tossed a nickel to Arthur. "Go buy a ticket." She then charged up the stairs to the toboggan as fast as she could. Lois turned to Arthur, indicating her necklace.

"Does that mean I get to keep this?"

Meanwhile, Leo had taken a breather from riding the toboggan and had been peeking over the wooden railing to see if it was safe to leave. He saw Mary and knew she would soon be upon him. He looked around for an escape route, but everything he saw would lead him straight to her.

When she made it to the top, Mary didn't see Leo anywhere. He wasn't on the platform, and he wasn't in the toboggan that was about to take off. She immediately leaned over the railing to signal Arthur that she hadn't found Leo and to look for him coming out. She crossed the tracks to the other wall, the one that faced outside the park and hovered over the Elephant Hotel. It was the highest point of the ride and a considerable distance to the street below. When Mary peered over it, she was astounded at what she saw.

Leo was climbing down the toboggan structure, barely making it through the large spaces between the wooden slats.

As Mary flipped the clasp on her pocketbook and pulled out her pistol, she shouted, "Leo!" He ignored her. "I will shoot you, Leo. This time it won't be a leg."

Leo looked up at Mary, then at how much further he had to go. He was about halfway down. Jumping was not an option. He stood straight up on one of the wooden slats and turned around to face the street below.

"I warned you, Leo!"

Before she could shoot, Leo dove off the toboggan structure, flew through the air, and latched onto the left tusk of the Elephant Hotel. It was an amazing feat, worthy of any circus act, and Mary was stunned. Leo quickly flipped his body around until he was lying on top of the tusk, hugging it. She couldn't risk taking a shot at him. There were too many innocent people on the street below.

A ragpicker's wagon passed below, pulled by a horse. It was actually an old, broken-down delivery wagon that the owner had found abandoned and had fixed. The roof had been missing, so he'd replaced it with a canvas canopy. Leo glanced at Mary, a wide smirk on his face, and waved his Elephantine Colossus hat at her as if saying good-bye. He then jumped, pulling the canvas with him as he landed in the wagon.

Mary took off, descending the stairs as fast as she could. When she bolted out of the toboggan ride, she screamed to Arthur, "He's in a ragpicker's wagon heading for the beach!"

Arthur was confused, but that didn't stop him from following her, along with the two men who were guarding the exit. When they had gotten out onto the street, the wagon had already turned the corner by the beach, and they lit out in that direction.

Halfway there, they heard a huge explosion, which caused them to stop as they saw flames shooting into the sky. Unlike the others', Mary's hesitation was brief, and she continued running toward the explosion. When she turned the corner, she saw that the ragpicker's wagon had collided with what looked like a wagon that was carrying kerosene. Both of them had caught on fire. It was intense and all-consuming. The bells of fire wagons could be heard in the distance as Mary fought the flames, trying to get closer. She saw a man on the perch of the ragpicker's wagon and naturally assumed it was the ragpicker. He was burned beyond recognition. She continued battling the flames, which were much more severe in the back, where all the goods were. She saw a man stretched there, also burned beyond recognition. Mary dared to get closer. Even though all logic told her it was Leo, she wanted some concrete evidence that it was him. That's when she spotted the hat with ELEPHANTINE COLOSSUS emblazoned on it next to the man in the wagon just before it was consumed by the flames. She stood there staring, hypnotized by it, thinking about Ameer and Edgar and whether she'd just watched their last chance at freedom being destroyed.

Suddenly, Mary was yanked away from the fire. It was Arthur.

"You're not going to do Edgar any good if you're burned to a crisp."

Mary snapped out of her trance. "Thanks."

He gave Mary a minute to recover, then asked, "So, what's our next step?"

Mary realized she had no next step. "It's time to go home. Leo is dead."

"We have to do something."

Mary didn't reply. Depressed, she slowly started her walk to the train station.

34

Over the next few days, Mary tried to rest and to count the positives. Once the ether wore off, her father was fine. Ameer's doctor told her he would make a full recovery. Ivan Nowak returned to Brooklyn and, with Superintendent Campbell's permission, examined the scalpel that had been found in Edgar's hand. It turned out there was a second bloody thumbprint on it that also matched the one on Carrie Brown's room key. That was enough evidence to set Edgar free.

Andrew Carnegie had called Mary to his home and wanted to show his gratitude for her saving his life. Mary would never have asked for anything for herself, and that's why she, Harper, and Arthur were down at the New York docks to see Edgar off to London.

"I can't thank you enough, Mary. I—" Edgar stopped as emotion overtook him.

"Don't thank me. It's Andrew Carnegie's money. I have absolutely no problem spending his."

"You can make light of it as much as you want, but the

truth is you've made a dream come true for me." He hugged her.

"You're welcome."

"You realize the pressure is on, Edgar," said Harper. "Now you have to be the best Othello ever."

"What about Hamlet, King Lear, or Romeo?"

"As long as it's not the lead in Kill the Coon," said Arthur, "which I'm closing down."

"How come? Is business off?"

"Yeah, but that's not the reason. It's wrong, clear wrong."

Edgar smiled. "All of a sudden you've acquired scruples." He shook Arthur's hand. "I'm glad I know you."

"Don't get me wrong. I'll find some other scam to perpetuate on the American public. As P. T. Barnum used to say—"

They all joined in: "There's a sucker born every minute."

The four of them laughed. The ship's horn sounded, signaling passengers it was time to board. The three of them stayed to watch Edgar walk up the plank. After he waved to them from the deck, they left.

Outside on the street, Mary and Harper said their goodbyes to Arthur. They promised to see each other again, but they all knew that would never happen. It was not because they didn't like one another but rather that they lived very different lives.

When they were alone, Harper turned to Mary. "I'm proud of you. That was the single most generous and selfless act I've seen anyone do."

They kissed.

~

Harper went back to his apartment and Mary went to Lazlo's. They were going to meet that night at her parents' house for their traditional Friday night dinner. Jeffrey and Elizabeth had invited Harper to thank him for bringing Jeffrey home and also hoping he was Mary's new beau. That day, after seeing Edgar off, they finally admitted how much they cared for each other, and so at the dinner that night, Mary's parents would get what they wished for.

Lazlo's Books was crowded. He barely had time to tell Mary that she had a client waiting for her in her office before returning to a customer. It was Mrs. Norcross.

"So nice to see you again, Mrs. Norcross." Mrs. Norcross stood and they shook hands. "Please sit. How can I help you?" Mrs. Norcross sat facing Mary, who sat down behind her desk.

"This is difficult to do."

"Whatever it is, take your time."

"You have to understand. He was always a good boy, my Henry. Always considerate, respectful. I never heard a harsh word out of his mouth."

"Sounds like he was a wonderful son."

"He was. I saw in the newspapers how you helped thwart an anarchist bombing."

"The man was a confused human being but basically good. It's no excuse, but in a way, he was pushed into it by a failed system."

"I think that's what happened to my Henry." She took a letter out of her pocketbook and placed it on Mary's desk. "There was a second letter that James and I never told anyone about. I'd like you to read it."

Mary picked it up.

Dear Mother and Father, I am on my way to New York. I probably won't return, but please don't despair. I am sickened by what has happened to the country I love so dearly, and I am trying to accomplish something for the good of all. Millions of us live in abject poverty where we catch diseases and die too young because of the holy profit motive that benefits only a few. My brethren in Europe and Asia have been eliminating heads of state. Though they are certainly culpable, the real problems lie with the greedy capitalists. Maybe acts like mine will scare them into reason or inspire us to revolution.

Your loving son,
Henry

Mary put down the letter. She didn't know what to say.

"You see, Miss Handley? What he did, it wasn't for himself like they say. It was never for himself."

"He never expected to get the money."

Mrs. Norcross shook her head no. "He was there to sacrifice himself." Fighting back tears, she was barely audible. "Henry always had a way with words. James and I thought he'd make a wonderful writer. Maybe if he had, he could have used his talent to vent that anger and he wouldn't have—" She couldn't go on.

"Mrs. Norcross, you and your husband have experienced an unspeakable tragedy. How can I help? What would you like me to do?"

"I wish I knew. I'm returning to Massachusetts tomorrow. Ever since our meeting a few days ago, I've had this urge to tell you. I don't know why. I just thought you'd understand."

"Rest assured I do. I assume you don't want me to make this public."

"Certainly not."

"I would like to discreetly show it to one person and one person only. Then I will mail it back to you. It certainly won't cure all the ills at once but it might give us a start."

"Who is that person?"

~

Teddy Roosevelt and his family were checking out of the Waldorf Hotel and heading back to Washington, D.C. They had mounds of luggage and the bellmen were busy strapping it onto two carriages that would take them to Grand Central Depot. Edith and her nanny were corralling the children, and he was instructing the bellmen on how to properly secure their bags.

"That's it," said Roosevelt. "Now tie it in a knot. Tight."

Mary approached. "Mr. Roosevelt."

"Wait one second. That's it. Good job." He turned to Mary.

"I'm sorry to interrupt you, sir, but I know you're leaving today—"

"We've met. The other night with Henry and Jacob—"

"Yes, I'm—"

"I remember, Miss Handley. What can I do for you?"

"It's about our conversation the other night. I remember you mentioning that there was no evidence of Henry L.

Norcross being an anarchist. His mother just visited me and gave me a letter he had written to her and his father. She doesn't want to make it public, but she's given me permission to show it to you." She gave the letter to him. "Now, keep in mind, this is from a man who was born here, as were his parents. He had a normal American upbringing; he was not a recent immigrant or foreign agitator, according to the popular notion of people who commit these acts."

After he read it, he handed it back. "This is astounding, but what do you want me to do?"

"Change has to start somewhere. If you come to New York and show them you can't be bought and you're willing to throw out all the rotten apples, it might give some people hope. Who knows? Maybe honesty and fairness will catch on and push aside the greed and violence that have gripped our country."

"Why, Miss Handley, you're an idealist."

"As much as I try to deny it, I guess I am."

He whispered, "Don't tell anyone, but so am I."

Edith approached. "Sorry to interrupt, darling, but if we don't leave now, we'll miss our train."

He looked at his pocket watch. "By golly, you're right, dear. Okay, Alice, Ted, and Kermit with me in the second carriage and everyone else with Mother in the first."

They all scurried for their respective carriages. As Roosevelt was about to enter his, Mary spoke up again. "Please tell me you'll consider it, sir."

"I will. To be honest though, the only way I know how to do a job is to go full throttle, and as you can see"—he waved his hand, indicating his large family—"I'm carrying quite a load." He opened the door to the carriage. Before stepping in, he added, "I meant what I said the other night. I would very much like to see women get more opportunities. Hopefully, that, too, will change someday."

They said good-bye and the Roosevelts drove off, leaving Mary with an empty feeling. He was perfect for the job. The way things were going, someone like Byrnes might be offered it.

~

Before dinner, Mary stopped at Walter and Sarah's house. Their mood was significantly different than it had been the last time she was there. Russell Sage had fulfilled his promise to Mary, and Walter now had all his clients back. Mary always marveled at the power of the rich. They could accomplish feats in a single phone call that others failed to accomplish in a lifetime. She understood the power hierarchy and had nothing against it as long as everyone had an equal opportunity to attain that status. But she wasn't there to dwell on the inequities of the world. She was there to correct one.

"Why do you want me to take this man's case?" Walter asked.

"Ameer Ben Ali and his family have suffered greatly from the dark part of our judicial system. He was falsely convicted of murder, then stabbed while incarcerated. His brother's family was wiped out in the Johnstown Flood. We need to show him, other immigrants, and anyone who doesn't have a leg up in the power structure that America is fair and his brother Basem's choice of violence was wrong."

"What does Inspector Byrnes say?"

"In spite of my new evidence, he won't budge and views

it as a personal affront that someone might question one of his arrests. He could make things easier, but there's little hope of that."

"Sounds like a man who is hiding something."

"There's no question that he is, but I have to think of Ameer first. You'll have to go through the courts, and I know how long and arduous that is."

"And you want Walter to do this all for free?" said Sarah.

"Yes. Ameer has no money, and I know this is a big favor to ask—"

"Nonsense, Mary. Walter would be proud to take on Ameer's case. Won't you, dear?"

"Actually," Walter replied, "that's exactly what I was thinking. This past week has given me a taste of what it's like to be the little guy. I didn't enjoy being stepped on. No one should be bullied like that."

Proud of her husband, Sarah hugged Walter. Mary thanked her good friends, and Sarah invited her and Harper over for dinner the next weekend. Mary had another dinner to attend very shortly and she had to prepare Harper for the bizarre behavior that was typical of a Handley Friday dinner.

35

Since Harper was officially her boyfriend and this was his first dinner with Mary's family, she expected Elizabeth to be oozing Irish female charm. That would seem better than the usual Handley free-for-all, except that Mary always cringed at her mother's phony performances at these events. To her, it was akin to squeaking chalk on a blackboard.

"So, Mr. Lloyd, I understand you're a fine writer. In which publications can I read your work?"

Harper ran down an earnest list, from the *Brooklyn Daily Eagle* to the *New York Times* to the *World*, the *Sun*, and many magazines. He stopped short of everything, fearing he was being too braggadocious. "There are more," he said, "but I don't want to bore you."

"To the contrary, I find your work fascinating."

Mary turned to Harper with an impish smile. "Yes, very fascinating."

Harper had to turn away from Mary to keep from laughing. "Thank you, Mrs. Handley, I do, too, or I wouldn't be doing it."

That exchange was followed by silence as the four Handleys and Harper resumed eating. Elizabeth couldn't stand silence when she was entertaining. She felt it reflected on her as a hostess. She was about to continue the conversation when Sean beat her to it. Knowing what it was like to be in Elizabeth's hot seat, he mercifully tried to divert attention away from Harper. "Dad, when do you start working for Mr. Carnegie?"

Mary had asked two favors of Andrew Carnegie. One was sending Edgar to London, and the other was procuring a job for her father. With Leo gone, no one knew what would happen to his stores.

"I'm supposed to meet with one of his executives on Monday," said Jeffrey, feeling insecure. "I don't know what kind of work I can do for them. I've only known meats."

"You're a bright man, Dad," Mary interjected. "It may take time to learn the specifics, but I'm confident you can handle any job they throw at you."

He sighed. "I don't know. Maybe."

"Jeffrey," Elizabeth said, "what kind of way is this to act in front of our guest, Mr. Lloyd? Surely he doesn't want to hear about your shortcomings." She turned to Harper. "Is the roast to your liking, Mr. Lloyd?"

"Please call me Harper, and quite frankly, I see no harm in discussing this with Mr. Handley. Writers often brainstorm with each other to come up with ideas. Maybe we can join together and do the same thing with Mr. Handley. Come up with a good approach for his meeting on Monday."

Mary patted Harper's arm. "Harper is a very supportive person."

"Are you saying I'm not?"

Mary looked straight at Elizabeth. "Let's not do this now, Mother."

"I'm just asking for the truth."

"I only meant to compliment Harper. I can't help it if you decided to take it personally."

"I know you too well, Mary."

"You don't believe me?"

Elizabeth turned to Harper. "I apologize for my daughter, Mr. Lloyd. She—"

"Since you insist on pursuing the truth, Mother, you are one hundred percent right. The truth is you're not, nor have you ever been, supportive of any of us."

Sean and Jeffrey both winced, well aware that the fireworks had been lit and were ready to explode. Desperately trying to change the subject, Sean asked, "Would anyone like more of anything?"

"That's my job, Sean, unless you'd like to start cooking. I'll gladly hand it over to you."

"No thank you, Mother."

"Exactly what I thought." Elizabeth turned back to Mary. "Have you no pride? Don't you know not to air the family's dirty laundry in public?"

"First of all, you're the one who dragged the dirty laundry out, and Harper is not the public. He's my boyfriend and hopefully someday, my lover." Harper flinched and she immediately whispered in his ear, "Don't get too excited. I just said that to annoy her."

Elizabeth put her hands to her face. "Worse and worse. I am mortified by your behavior."

Mary was about to answer when Jeffrey banged the table and stood up. "Everyone, stop it. Whatever the job is, I'll take it, no questions asked, and I'll do well. I felt vulnerable, but I don't anymore. I can't in this family, so I'll just be angry like everybody else."

Everyone turned toward Jeffrey, surprised at his outburst. Sean was the first to speak, also banging the table. "I'm behind you a thousand percent. I'm angry, too."

They all began to laugh and one by one everyone banged the table and agreed with Jeffrey and Sean. The argument was officially over. Mary turned to Harper. "Welcome to the Handleys. Are you having second thoughts?"

"This is child's play compared to a Lloyd dinner. I'm used to gunfire."

Elizabeth looked at Harper. "So Lloyd really is your last name?"

Harper shook his head. They laughed some more, enjoying themselves, and almost didn't hear the knock on the door. Almost. Sean answered it. Standing before him was a man of about sixty who had sparse gray hair and was about twenty pounds heavier than his small frame should have carried. Though he wasn't presently smoking, the smell of a cigar followed him wherever he went.

"Mr. Flanagan," said Sean. "What a nice surprise. Please come in."

"Thank ya, Sean," he said in his Irish accent. "Yer lookin' good, son."

"I take no credit for it. It's the Handley genes."

The others had heard Flanagan's name and were surprised at his visit. In the thirty-two years that Jeffrey had worked for Mr. Flanagan, he had been to their house once, maybe twice. He entered the dining room and Jeffrey rose.

"Mr. Flanagan, good to see you, sir."

"Same here. Sit, Jeffrey. I'm in your home."

Always the perfect hostess, Elizabeth said, "Please join us. We'd love to have your company."

"Thank ya, but I won't be long. Mrs. Flanagan has dinner on the table waitin' for me." He glanced at everyone in the room. "I'm glad to see the Handley Friday night tradition is still goin' strong."

"It will never die," said Mary with a tinge of sarcasm.

"Jeffrey, I've gotta say what I gotta say and then I'll be goin'. I just came from an auction where I bought back Flanagan's Butcher Shop."

"Congratulations, Mr. Flanagan. What made you change your mind about retiring?"

"Oh, I'm still retirin'. If I didn't, Mrs. Flanagan would have my . . . well, it would be trouble. What I'm tryin' to say is, I want ya to have it."

Jeffrey wasn't sure he had heard Flanagan correctly. "Have it? I don't—"

"It means it's yers."

Jeffrey was stunned. "What? But your retirement—"

"I'll be fine. I bought it for a fraction of what I was paid for it."

"Still, I don't know if I can—"

"Sure ya can." Flanagan took an envelope out of his pocket and gave it to Jeffrey. "I shoulda done this in the first place. Yer as much a reason why Flanagan's was a success as I was. Thirty-two years of service should account for somethin'."

Jeffrey jumped out of his seat and started pumping Flanagan's hand. "This is incredible. I don't know what to do to thank you."

"Ya can start by lettin' go of my hand. I'd like ta use it again." Embarrassed, Jeffrey dropped his hand and stepped back.

Elizabeth also stood and shook his hand. "Mr. Flanagan, your generosity is greatly appreciated. We'll never forget it."

"I'm countin' on that, 'cause when I stop by from time to time, I'm expectin' Jeffrey here'll throw me a coupla pork chops."

"You've got it, Mr. Flanagan."

After a round of thank-yous and good-byes, Mr. Flanagan left. The envelope still in his hand, Jeffrey was taking in the enormity of what had just happened.

"I own a business," he said with a good amount of wonder in his voice. "I'm a business owner." He sat down as if it were all too much for him to take standing.

Elizabeth, Mary, and Sean were ecstatic and gathered around him, hugging and congratulating him. Harper shook his hand. Elizabeth kissed him.

"I knew you would do it. I just knew it!" Elizabeth got out a bottle of Irish whiskey they had saved for special occasions. They drank to Jeffrey, to the butcher shop, and to the Handleys until the bottle was empty. It was the happiest time Mary could ever remember experiencing in that house.

After everyone had left, Jeffrey and Elizabeth couldn't stop celebrating. They danced for only the third time since their wedding night. No music was necessary.

When Jeffrey went to bed, he was still bursting with joy. He had come to this country, worked hard, and now he owned a business. His dream was now a reality.

He had a smile on his face when he died in his sleep that night.

In March of 1895, Superintendent Campbell retired. He was never thrilled with his superintendent job and finally decided to take it easy. Mary was in shock.

"You can't quit, Chief. You're the only one I know with enough clout to help me fight the corruption that we both know—hell, everyone knows—exists in this city."

"Mary, if I've learned anything in my many years on the force, it's this: no one's indispensible. When I leave, someone else will come along. You'll see."

His words turned out to be prophetic.

Two months later, on the night of May 17, 1895, Clubber Williams stepped out of one of the many restaurants/gambling houses in the Tenderloin District, stuffing his weekly bribe into his pocket. He had just begun twirling his infamous club when he heard a voice call to him from a carriage.

"Captain Williams." Williams ignored it. He figured whoever it was would catch up to him and get out of the carriage if he wanted to speak to him badly enough. After all, Williams was king in this part of New York.

"Captain, or do you prefer Clubber?" The voice now sounded familiar to him, and he figured he had better turn around. He was right. As he stood there and the carriage caught up to him, he could see who was inside. It was Theodore Roosevelt.

"Sorry, Mr. Roosevelt, I didn't know it was you."

Two weeks before Roosevelt had finally accepted the job as president of New York's police commission. He wasn't one to sit idly in an office. Roosevelt had taken to the streets every night to check on his officers. He had found a lot that he didn't like, and Williams was about to find out how much. He got out of his carriage and approached.

"You straighten them out in there, Captain Williams, making sure there was no illegal gambling going on?"

"Yes, sir. I believe in showing a strong police presence just in case they get any ideas." He twirled his club as if defining what that presence was.

"So you weren't in there just to get your weekly handout?"

The big guy had been caught off guard and stammered for a few seconds before he responded. "Handout? I don't know what you mean."

"Handout. It's when a policeman is given a bribe to look the other way. Maybe you know it better as extortion."

"Mr. Roosevelt, I take great offense—"

"Be offended all you like . . . as a civilian. You're fired."

"You can't—"

"But I can. Turn your badge and uniform in tomorrow." Roosevelt headed back to his carriage.

"You won't get away with it. I'm gonna fight this."

Roosevelt had entered his carriage and now leaned out

the window. "Please do. You'll find you don't have a leg to stand on. Or should I say a club?" He signaled and the carriage took off.

For the first time in years the bombastic Williams was left with nothing to say.

The next morning Roosevelt had a visitor in his outer office waiting for him when he came in. He was expecting this visitor and was slightly surprised he hadn't gotten a phone call from him the night before.

Upon seeing Roosevelt, Byrnes marched right up to him. "We need ta speak."

"Indeed we do, Inspector Byrnes. Please step into my office." He gestured for Byrnes to go first. At the door, Roosevelt offered, "Open or closed? Your choice."

"Close it."

"As you wish." He then took a seat behind his big mahogany desk. Byrnes was too excited to sit. He paced.

"How could ya fire Clubber? Give me one good reason."

"He's a crook. Is that good enough or do you want more?"

"That's never been proven. The Lexow Committee tried several times and nothin'. Nothin' at all."

"The beauty of my situation is I'm not the Lexow Committee. I don't have to prove how he made hundreds of thousands of dollars on a meager policeman's salary. If I smell crooked, he's gone."

"Yer makin' a huge mistake. He's one of our finest."

"It depends on your definition of 'finest.' If it means being your partner in cover-ups and crimes, then you're right."

"What are ya implyin'?

"I don't imply. Maybe you haven't heard. I'm a straight talker."

"Ya callin' me a crook?"

"It took time, but you're finally catching on."

"I'm gonna sue ya for slander."

"You can. Of course, then you'd have to explain the three hundred and five thousand dollars you have in the bank. Even if a jury believes you acquired it from, as you have said in the past, stock tips from your friends Andrew Carnegie, Jay Gould, and Russell Sage, they're going to wonder what you did to make them so friendly."

"I did nothin' wrong!"

"That would be your contention. But before entering such a suit, you should know it will look much worse if you win and they only award you a dollar for damages to your precious reputation."

"Yer gonna regret this." Byrnes headed for the door.

"I don't think so. And by the way, if I haven't said it yet, you're fired, Inspector Byrnes."

Byrnes stomped out. Roosevelt sat back in his chair. Two weeks on the job and he was already having a fine time of it. He was glad that Henry had been so insistent and Edith so accommodating. And he had to thank Jacob for bringing Mary Handley to that meeting. She was a very bright lady and very convincing.

~

May 18 was Jeffrey's birthday, and Mary couldn't think of a better way to honor her father than to get married on his day. In a way, she had found out how much she cared about Harper because of Jeffrey. When he died, she was devastated, and the only one she could think of seeing was Harper. She ran to his apartment and collapsed into his arms. He was incredibly gentle. He held and soothed her and made her feel secure and loved. Besides the sadness, there was something special about the weeks after her father died. Harper was always there for her, always considerate, and always patient when her mood turned dark and she felt the need to strike out at someone. He took it, sometimes deflecting her upset with humor and sometimes just remaining silent. She got to meet Harper's large and boisterous family and really enjoyed them. Harper's father was the opposite of him: a working-class man of few words who was inarticulate but who also adored his son. It was evident Harper loved him, too.

Mary decided he definitely was a keeper. That was why she stood alone in the vestibule of their local church in the bridal dress that her mother had worn, waiting to marry Harper Lloyd.

Elizabeth entered. "What's going on, Mary? We're already an hour late."

"I'm waiting for Sean. He's giving me away."

"If he doesn't get here soon, I'm going to or the meat is going to be overcooked and I'll kick myself for using prime instead of chuck."

After Jeffrey died, Mary and Sean had tried to convince Elizabeth to sell the butcher shop to give her a cushion until she could find a job. Elizabeth refused.

"No, it was your father's dream, and I'm going to run it."

"What do you know about running a butcher shop?" they both asked.

"I know meats. I've been cooking all my life, and really, what is there to know? All I have to do is hire a hard worker who's desperate and loyal to a fault like your poor father was and I'll be fine."

Elizabeth was right, and even more surprising to her children, she turned out to be a very good businesswoman. Her special skill was haggling with the meat sellers over price. No one took advantage of her. She was hardworking and demanding of her employees but also fair. One unexpected perk of her work was that it changed her obsession from her children to the butcher shop, for which they were forever grateful. It had been eight months since Jeffrey's death, and she was already successful enough to be contemplating a second Handley Meats store.

Sean entered, a bit out of breath. "I'm finally here. Sorry."

"It's about time," said Elizabeth. "Let's get this wedding started." She left.

"I couldn't help it, Mary. Just as I was about to leave the station I got called into the captain's office." He paused, then a smile engulfed his face. "He promoted me, gave me my own office. A nice one, too."

"That's wonderful, Sean! Congratulations!" She hugged him.

"A pretty good day for the Handleys—you get married and I get promoted, all on Dad's birthday."

"Yes, and speaking of getting married—"

"Right. Let's get to it." He held out his arm and she took it.

It didn't take long for Elizabeth to burst into tears. The first sight of Sean escorting Mary coupled with the beginning chords of the "Wedding March" was more than enough. Her sobs grew as they walked down the aisle together, passing Lazlo, Gerta, Superintendent Campbell and his wife, Jacob Riis, Ivan Nowak, Sarah, Walter, and their children. Harper's huge family cheered and burst into applause.

As Sean was about to deliver Mary to Harper, they exchanged impish glances, happy for their mother and in a way relishing sweet revenge after the many years of aggravation she had given Mary about this.

Irrespective of that, it was clear that Mary and Harper were very much in love as they stared into each other's eyes and took their vows.

~

A woman with long brunette hair and a sensible church dress sat in the back row by herself. As the wedding ceremony began, she rose and left. She had plans for that day and she didn't want to put them off. While walking down the street, she saw two German tourists who were lost. She very politely interrupted and gave them the directions they needed in flawless German, then continued on her way. Crossing the street, she reached under the neckline of her dress, revealing a burn scar on her hand. She pulled out a necklace that had been tucked inside. It was a gold chain with a beautiful diamond and gold heart locket. Reacquiring it had been a bit of a bother but worth it. She picked up her pace, feeling emboldened and sure that opportunities were awaiting her.

EPILOGUE

Roosevelt's nighttime patrols to check on officers became a regular habit. He shook up the New York City Police Department, ridding it of all the rotten apples he could find. After two years, the politicians got nervous that their own "favored" positions would be threatened. They got together and abolished the position of president of the police commission, giving all members an equal vote, thus ending the Roosevelt purge. Motivated to get Roosevelt out of New York City, the Republicans secured another post for him as assistant secretary of the navy. Not too long afterward the Spanish-American War broke out and his Rough Riders became legendary. He returned to New York, ran for governor, and won. Again, the politicians were worried about how much he might usurp their power and they offered him a place on the presidential ticket as vice president because it was well-known the vice president had no power at all. Needless to say, that strategy backfired. The presidential candidate was William McKinley and shortly after being elected he was assassinated. The assassin was an anarchist.

The wheels of justice sometimes grind slowly, as Ameer Ben Ali found out. Even though it was clearly shown that his conviction was a sham, overturning a guilty verdict takes time. Eleven years after his conviction, on April 16, 1902, Ameer was finally set free and the Algerian government paid for his transport back to Algeria.

William Laidlaw was not as lucky. Russell Sage kept appealing his case until 1899 when Laidlaw, exhausted and broke, finally gave up. True to his proclamation, Sage spent a fortune in legal fees but never had to pay Laidlaw a penny. Bitter and in pain, Laidlaw spent the rest of his life in the Home for the Incurables.

Russell Sage died in 1906 and left all his money to his wife, Margaret Olivia Slocum Sage. She wasted no time immersing herself in something he had forbidden throughout their marriage: using their money to help others. She donated liberally to many educational, charitable, and social causes, establishing the Russell Sage Foundation in 1907 and Russell Sage College in 1916. Both are still around today, and the name of the skinflint who never wanted to part with a dollar is now hugely associated with philanthropy and education.

Mary told Harper about the letter that Mrs. Norcross had shown her. He respected her wishes and didn't put it in his piece about the Russell Sage bombing. In the long run, it didn't matter. Since the Sage/Laidlaw case dragged on for years and Harper had promised not to publish until it was over, people soon lost interest. They had moved on to other news cycles.

Mary and Harper's marriage started off well. They seemed to have the mutual respect for each other that is necessary in such unions. After all her joking, it turned out Mary didn't mind having two first names after all, as long as the second one was Lloyd.

AUTHOR'S NOTE

This is a work of historical fiction, and though fiction looms large in the storytelling, there are many real people involved and real facts of actual events that happened. Let's start with the most obvious and easily researched.

Theodore Roosevelt was president of the police commission in New York City for two years starting in May of 1895. He did try to clean up the department and fired Inspector Thomas Byrnes and Captain Alexander "Clubber" Williams. His job was eliminated after two years because the politicians were afraid he would eventually get to them. Williams did make that infamous statement about the Tenderloin District and Byrnes did make that statement about arresting Jack the Ripper within thirty-six hours if he ever dared to come to New York City.

Carrie Brown, or "Old Shakespeare," was murdered at the East River Hotel very much in the style of Jack the Ripper. Ameer Ben Ali became an easy target of Inspector Byrnes and was arrested within his time frame and eventually convicted of the crime on flimsy and trumped-up evidence. He was freed in the early 1900s and went back to Algeria.

Henry L. Norcross did bomb Russell Sage's Wall Street office and every detail of that bombing, down to the unfortunate Benjamin Norton, who wound up in the street with his typewriter on his face, is true. Inspector Byrnes did bring Norcross's head to Russell Sage's house for identification purposes. Norcross did leave two different letters for his parents. It is considered to be the first suicide bombing in the United States.

William Laidlaw sued Russell Sage and won several judgments against him but in the long run gave up as Sage kept appealing. Joseph Hodges Choate was Laidlaw's lawyer until he had to leave to argue a case before the Supreme Court.

Coney Island actually had a booth called Kill the Coon along with segregated bathhouses for blacks and whites. There was an area called the Gut filled with prostitutes, gambling, and honky-tonks. Austin Corbin was the owner of the Oriental and Manhattan Beach Hotels and also the owner of the Long Island Rail Road. A bigot and rabid anti-Semite, he really did ask the question, "If America is a free country, why can't we be free of the Jews?" Along those lines, the Immigration Restriction League was a real organization established by three Harvard grads.

The Elephantine Colossus, better known as the Elephant Hotel, was designed by James Lafferty and burned down in 1896. If I had invented it, people wouldn't believe it.

The Johnstown Flood was a real event and Andrew Carnegie was a prominent member of the South Fork Fishing and Hunting Club, which did alter the dam that caused the flood. George Rutter was a real person who was shot by Pinkertons during the Homestead Steel Strike.

From the day of the Norcross bombing until a year later when he died, Jay Gould lived in fear of being the next victim. He rarely went out and when he did, he wore disguises.

Possibly more important, though, signs like HIRING. DOGS AND IRISH NEED NOT APPLY were sadly commonplace, as was also the prejudice against Italians, Jews, Arabs, and African-Americans. The new immigrants were blamed for the country's problems when the reasons for those problems ran much deeper.

As the famous saying goes, "If we don't learn from history, we're bound to repeat it."

ACKNOWLEDGMENTS

My editor, Nate Roberson, has been extremely helpful with his notes and positive attitude. It's very important to have an editorial champion who believes in you and your work. Nate more than fits that bill, and I'm forever grateful for him.

I'd like to thank my publicist, Christine Johnson, and my marketing managers, Alaina Wagner and Kathleen Quinlan. It's one thing to write a book, and it's another to make people aware of it. I thank them for their monumental efforts on my behalf.

My wonderful agent, Paul Fedorko, has been with me since I first started writing novels, and he is a dream agent in every aspect of that job. Paul's assistant, Chloe Rabinowitz, has also been very helpful.

I have written before about the incredible support I get from my wife, Fran, my son, Joshua, and my daughter, Erin. They mean the world to me, and they show it every day.

My good friend David Garber has once again provided a great sounding board for my ideas, and his input is greatly appreciated.

I'd be remiss if I didn't thank Michael and Helen Levy, Bob and Randy Myer, Stan Finkelberg, Charley and Nikki Garrett, and Lois Feller. All of them read an early version of this book and were extremely encouraging with their responses.

ABOUT THE AUTHOR

LAWRENCE H. LEVY is a highly regarded film and TV writer who is a Writers Guild Award winner and a two-time Emmy nominee. He has written for various hit TV shows, such as *Family Ties, Saved by the Bell, Seventh Heaven, Roseanne,* and *Seinfield. Last Stop in Brooklyn* is his third novel in the Mary Handley Mystery series.

More in Lawrence H. Levy's Mary Handley Mystery Series

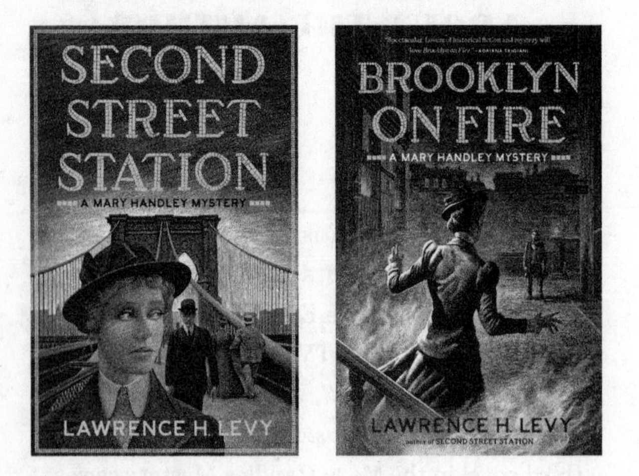

"Following Mary Handley through this Victorian adventure makes you feel like you've found some lost Sherlock Holmes story. It's impressive that the characters, many based on actual historical figures, are always funny, but the greatest delight is the mystery itself."

—Matthew Weiner, creator of *Mad Men*

B \ D \ W \ Y

AVAILABLE EVERYWHERE BOOKS ARE SOLD